Six Strange Souls In Search Of Salvation!

HOAG
Why would dirty fingernails drive a man half-mad with fear?

WATTS
There was this traveling salesman, get it? What was his line? Why—elephants, of course . . .

JANE
She was too much—or rather, too many . . .

HAYWARD
The psychiatrist who was something else . . .

KITTEN
It's a good wind that blows no ill . . .

TEAL
He built a house that wasn't there, but then again —what was there?

Six striking stories of logical fantasy, fantastic science, and uncommon imagination by America's most powerful science fiction writer, Robert Heinlein.

For twenty-odd years

ROBERT A. HEINLEIN

has been blazing science-fiction trails—
perhaps most notably with his "future
history" series. At the same time, he has
been producing masterful stories of the
fantastic. Both of these soaring fortes are
represented in this collection.

Mr. Heinlein turned to writing after ill-
health forced his retirement from a
military career, and has drawn on his
background for convincing detail and
atmosphere in many of his stories,
including the controversial, and award-
winning "Starship Trooper."

6 x H

SIX STORIES
by
Robert A. Heinlein

★ ★ ★ ★

(original title:
**THE UNPLEASANT PROFESSION
OF JONATHAN HOAG)**

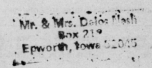
 PYRAMID BOOKS • NEW YORK

To Eugene R. Guild

6 x H
(Original title: THE UNPLEASANT PROFESSION OF JONATHAN HOAG)

A PYRAMID BOOK

Published by arrangement with Gnome Press

Pyramid edition published August 1961

Ninth printing, February 1975

ACKNOWLEDGMENTS
The Unpleasant Profession of Jonathan Hoag, Street &
Smith Publications, Inc., 1942; The Man Who Traveled
in Elephants, Candar Publishing Co., Inc., 1957; They,
Street & Smith Publications, Inc., Our Fair City, Weird
Tales, 1948; "All You Zombies," Mercury Press, Inc.,
1959; "And He Built a Crooked House," Street & Smith
Publications, Inc., 1940.

ISBN 0-515-02822-3

Printed in the United States of America

Pyramid Books are published by Pyramid Communications, Inc.
Its trademarks, consisting of the word "Pyramid" and the portrayal
of a pyramid, are registered in the United States Patent Office.

Pyramid Communications, Inc.,
919 Third Avenue, New York, N.Y. 10022

TABLE OF CONTENTS

THE UNPLEASANT PROFESSION
OF JONATHAN HOAG

> —the end it is not well.
> From too much love of living,
> From hope and fear set free,
> We thank with brief thanksgiving
> Whatever gods may be
> That no life lives forever;
> That dead men rise up never;
> That even the weariest river
> Winds somewhere safe to sea.
> —SWINBURNE

"Is it blood, doctor?" Jonathan Hoag moistened his lips with his tongue and leaned forward in the chair, trying to see what was written on the slip of paper the medico held.

Dr. Potbury brought the slip of paper closer to his vest and looked at Hoag over his spectacles. "Any particular reason," he asked, "why you should find blood under your fingernails?"

"No. That is to say— Well, no—there isn't. But it *is* blood—isn't it?"

"No," Potbury said heavily. "No, it isn't blood."

Hoag knew that he should have felt relieved. But he was not. He knew in that moment that he had clung to the notion that the brown grime under his fingernails was dry blood rather than let himself dwell on other, less tolerable, ideas.

He felt sick at his stomach. But he had to know—

"What is it, doctor? Tell me."

Potbury looked him up and down. "You asked me a

specific question. I've answered it. You did not ask me
what the substance was; you asked me to find out
whether or not it was blood. It is not."

"But— You are playing with me. Show me the analysis." Hoag half rose from his chair and reached for
the slip of paper.

The doctor held it away from him, then tore it carefully in two. Placing the two pieces together he tore
them again, and again.

"Why, you!"

"Take your practice elsewhere," Potbury answered.
"Never mind the fee. Get out. And don't come back."

Hoag found himself on the street, walking toward
the elevated station. He was still much shaken by the
doctor's rudeness. He was afraid of rudeness as some
persons are of snakes, or great heights, or small rooms.
Bad manners, even when not directed at him personally
but simply displayed to others in his presence, left him
sick and helpless and overcome with shame.

If he himself were the butt of boorishness he had no
defense save flight.

He set one foot on the bottom step of the stairs
leading up to the elevated station and hesitated. A trip
by elevated was a trying thing at best, what with the
pushing and the jostling and the grimy dirt and the
ever-present chance of uncouth behavior; he knew that
he was not up to it at the moment. If he had to listen
to the cars screaming around the curve as they turned
north toward the Loop, he suspected that he would
scream, too.

He turned away suddenly and was forced to check
himself abruptly, for he was chest to chest with a man
who himself was entering the stairway. He shied away.
"Watch your step, buddy," the man said, and brushed
on past him.

"Sorry," Hoag muttered, but the man was already
on by.

The man's tone had been brisk rather than unkind;
the incident should not have troubled Hoag, but it did.
The man's dress and appearance, his very odor, upset
Hoag. Hoag knew that there was no harm in well-
worn dungarees and leather windbreaker, no lack of

virtue in a face made a trifle greasy by sweat dried in place in the course of labor. Pinned to the bill of the man's cap was an oval badge, with a serial number and some lettering. Hoag guessed that he was a truck driver, a mechanic, a rigger, any of the competent, muscular crafts which keep the wheels turning over. Probably a family man as well, a fond father and a good provider, whose greatest lapse from virtue might be an extra glass of beer and a tendency to up it a nickel on two pairs.

It was sheer childishness for Hoag to permit himself to be put off by such appearance and to prefer a white shirt, a decent topcoat, and gloves. Yet if the man had smelled of shaving lotion rather than sweat the encounter would not have been distasteful.

He told himself so and told himself that he was silly and weak. Still—could such a coarse and brutal face really be the outward mark of warmth and sensitivity? That shapeless blob of nose, those piggish eyes?

Never mind, he would go home in a taxi, not looking at anyone. There was a stand just ahead, in front of the delicatessen.

"Where to?" The door of the cab was open; the hackman's voice was impersonally insistent.

Hoag caught his eye, hesitated and changed his mind. That brutishness again—eyes with no depth to them and a skin marred by blackheads and enlarged pores.

"Unnh . . . excuse me. I forgot something." He turned away quickly and stopped abruptly, as something caught him around the waist. It was a small boy on skates who had bumped into him. Hoag steadied himself and assumed the look of paternal kindliness which he used to deal with children. "Whoa, there, young fellow!" He took the boy by the shoulder and gently dislodged him.

"*Maurice!*" The voice screamed near his ear, shrill and senseless. It came from a large woman, smugly fat, who had projected herself out of the door of the delicatessen. She grabbed the boy's other arm, jerking him away and aiming a swipe at his ear with her free hand as she did so. Hoag started to plead on the boy's behalf when he saw that the woman was glaring at him. The youngster, seeing or sensing his mother's attitude, kicked at Hoag.

The skate clipped him in the shin. It hurt. He hurried away with no other purpose than to get out of sight. He turned down the first side street, his shin causing him to limp a little, and his ears and the back of his neck burning quite as if he had indeed been caught mistreating the brat. The side street was not much better than the street he had left. It was not lined with shops nor dominated by the harsh steel tunnel of the elevated's tracks, but it was solid with apartment houses, four stories high and crowded, little better than tenements.

Poets have sung of the beauty and innocence of childhood. But it could not have been this street, seen through Hoag's eyes, that they had in mind. The small boys seemed rat-faced to him, sharp beyond their years, sharp and shallow and snide. The little girls were no better in his eyes. Those of eight or nine, the shapeless stringy age, seemed to him to have tattletale written in their pinched faces—mean souls, born for trouble-making and cruel gossip. Their slightly older sisters, gutter-wise too young, seemed entirely concerned with advertising their arrogant new sex—not for Hoag's benefit, but for their pimply counterparts loafing around the drugstore.

Even the brats in baby carriages—Hoag fancied that he liked babies, enjoyed himself in the role of honorary uncle. Not these. Snotty-nosed and sour-smelling, squalid and squalling—

The little hotel was like a thousand others, definitely third rate without pretension, a single bit of neon reading: "Hotel Manchester, Transient & Permanent," a lobby only a half lot wide, long and narrow and a little dark. They are stopped at by drummers careful of their expense accounts and are lived in by bachelors who can't afford better. The single elevator is an iron-grille cage, somewhat disguised with bronze paint. The lobby floor is tile, the cuspidors are brass. In addition to the clerk's desk there are two discouraged potted palms and eight leather armchairs. Unattached old men, who seem never to have had a past, sit in these chairs, live in the rooms above, and every now and then one is found hanging in his room, necktie to light fixture.

Hoag backed into the door of the Manchester to avoid being caught in a surge of children charging along the sidewalk. Some sort of game, apparently—he caught the tail end of a shrill chant, "—give him a slap to shut his trap; the last one home's a dirty Jap!"

"Looking for someone, sir? Or did you wish a room?"

He turned quickly around, a little surprised. A room? What he wanted was his own snug apartment but at the moment a room, any room at all, in which he could be alone with a locked door between himself and the world seemed the most desirable thing possible. "Yes, I do want a room."

The clerk turned the register around. "With or without? Five fifty with, three and a half without."

"With."

The clerk watched him sign, but did not reach for the key until Hoag counted out five ones and a half. "Glad to have you with us. Bill! Show Mr. Hoag up to 412."

The lone bellman ushered him into the cage, looked him up and down with one eye, noting the expensive cut of his topcoat and the absence of baggage. Once in 412 he raised the window a trifle, switched on the bathroom light, and stood by the door.

"Looking for something?" he suggested. "Need any help?"

Hoag tipped him. "Get out," he said hoarsely.

The bellman wiped off the smirk. "Suit yourself," he shrugged.

The room contained one double bed, one chest of drawers with mirror, one straight chair and one armchair. Over the bed was a framed print titled "The Colosseum by Moonlight." But the door was lockable and equipped with a bolt as well and the window faced the alley, away from the street. Hoag sat down in the armchair. It had a broken spring, but he did not mind.

He took off his gloves and stared at his nails. They were quite clean. Could the whole thing have been hallucination? Had he ever gone to consult Dr. Potbury? A man who has had amnesia may have it again, he supposed, and hallucinations as well.

Even so, it could not all be hallucinations; he remembered the incident too vividly. Or could it be? He strained to recall exactly what had happened.

Today was Wednesday, his customary day off. Yesterday he had returned home from work as usual. He had been getting ready to dress for dinner—somewhat absent-mindedly, he recalled, as he had actually been thinking about where he would dine, whether to try a new Italian place recommended by his friends, the Robertsons, or whether it would be more pleasing to return again for the undoubtedly sound goulash prepared by the chef at the Buda-Pesth.

He had about decided in favor of the safer course when the telephone had rung. He had almost missed it, as the tap was running in the washbasin. He had thought that he heard something and had turned off the tap. Surely enough, the phone rang again.

It was Mrs. Pomeroy Jameson, one of his favorite hostesses—not only a charming woman for herself but possessed of a cook who could make clear soups that were not dishwater. And sauces. She had offered a solution to his problem. "I've been suddenly left in the lurch at the last moment and I've just got to have another man for dinner. Are you free? Could you help me? Dear Mr. Hoag!"

It had been a very pleasant thought and he had not in the least resented being asked to fill in at the last minute. After all, one can't expect to be invited to every small dinner. He had been delighted to oblige Edith Pomeroy. She served an unpretentious but sound dry white wine with fish and she never committed the vulgarism of serving champagne at any time. A good hostess and he was glad she felt free to ask him for help. It was a tribute to him that she felt he would fit in, unplanned.

He had had such thoughts on his mind, he remembered, as he dressed. Probably, in his preoccupation, what with the interruption of the phone call breaking his routine, he had neglected to scrub his nails.

It must have been that. Certainly there had been no opportunity to dirty his nails so atrociously on the way to the Pomeroys'. After all, one wore gloves.

It had been Mrs. Pomeroy's sister-in-law—a woman he preferred to avoid!—who had called his attention to his nails. She had been insisting with the positiveness called "modern" that every man's occupation was written on his person. "Take my husband—what could he be but a lawyer? Look at him. And you, Dr. Fitts —the bedside manner!"

"Not at dinner, I hope."

"You can't shake it."

"But you haven't proved your point. You *knew* what we are."

Whereupon that impossible woman had looked around the table and nailed him with her eye. "Mr. Hoag can test me. I don't know what he does. No one does."

"Really, Julia." Mrs. Pomeroy had tried hopelessly to intervene, then had turned to the man on her left with a smile. "Julia has been studying psychology this season."

The man on her left, Sudkins, or Snuggins—Stubbins, that was his name. Stubbins had said, "What does Mr. Hoag do?"

"It's a minor mystery. He never talks shop."

"It's not that," Hoag had offered. "I do not consider—"

"Don't tell me!" that woman had commanded. "I'll have it in a moment. Some profession. I can see you with a brief case." He had not intended to tell her. Some subjects were dinner conversation; some were not. But she had gone on.

"You might be in finance. You might be an art dealer or a book fancier. Or you might be a writer. Let me see your hands."

He was mildly put off by the demand, but he had placed his hands on the table without trepidation. That woman had pounced on him. "Got you! You are a chemist."

Everyone looked where she pointed. Everyone saw the dark mourning under his nails. Her husband had broken the brief silence by saying, "Nonsense, Julia. There are dozens of things that will stain nails. Hoag may dabble in photography, or do a spot of engraving. Your inference wouldn't stand up in court."

"That's a lawyer for you! I know I'm right. Aren't I, Mr. Hoag?"

He himself had been staring unbrokenly at his hands. To be caught at a dinner party with untidy manicure would have been distressing enough—*if* he had been able to understand it.

But he had no slightest idea how his nails had become dirtied. At his work? Obviously—but what did he *do* in the daytime?

He did not know.

"Tell us, Mr. Hoag. I was right, was I not?"

He pulled his eyes away from those horrid fingernails and said faintly, "I must ask to be excused." With that he had fled from the table. He had found his way to the lavatory where, conquering an irrational revulsion, he had cleaned out the gummy reddish-brown filth with the blade of his penknife. The stuff stuck to the blade; he wiped it on cleansing tissue, wadded it up, and stuck it into a pocket of his waistcoat. Then he had scrubbed his nails, over and over again.

He could not recall when he had become convinced that the stuff was blood, was human blood.

He had managed to find his bowler, his coat, gloves, and stick without recourse to the maid. He let himself out and got away from there as fast as he could.

Thinking it over in the quiet of the dingy hotel room he was convinced that his first fear had been instinctive revulsion at the sight of the dark-red under his nails. It was only on second thought that he had realized that he did not remember where he had dirtied his nails because he had no recollection of where he had been that day, nor the day before, nor any of the days before that. He did not know what his profession was.

It was preposterous, but it was terribly frightening.

He skipped dinner entirely rather than leave the dingy quiet of the hotel room; about ten o'clock he drew a tub of water just as hot as he could get it and let himself soak. It relaxed him somewhat and his twisted thoughts quieted down. In any case, he consoled himself, if he could not remember his occupation, then he certainly could not return to it. No chance again of finding that grisly horror under his fingernails.

He dried himself off and crawled under the covers. In spite of the strange bed he managed to get to sleep.

A nightmare jerked him awake, although he did not realize it at first, as the tawdry surroundings seemed to fit the nightmare. When he did recall where he was and why he was there the nightmare seemed preferable, but by that time it was gone, washed out of his mind. His watch told him that it was his usual getting-up time; he rang for the bellman and arranged for a breakfast tray to be fetched from around the corner.

By the time it arrived he was dressed in the only clothes he had with him and was becoming anxious to get home. He drank two cups of indifferent coffee standing up, fiddled with the food, then left the hotel.

After letting himself into his apartment he hung up his coat and hat, took off his gloves, and went as usual straight to his dressing room. He had carefully scrubbed the nails of his left hand and was just commencing on his right when he noticed what he was doing.

The nails of his left hand were white and clean; those of the right were dark and dirty. Carefully holding himself in check he straightened up, stepped over and examined his watch where he had laid it on his dresser, then compared the time with that shown by the electric clock in his bedroom. It was ten minutes past six P.M.—his usual time for returning home in the *evening*.

He might not recall his profession; his profession had certainly not forgotten him.

II

The firm of Randall & Craig, Confidential Investigation, maintained its night phone in a double apartment. This was convenient, as Randall had married Craig early in their association. The junior partner had just put the supper dishes to soak and was trying to find out whether or not she wanted to keep the book-of-the-month when the telephone rang. She reached out, took the receiver, and said, "Yes?" in noncommittal tones.

To this she added, "Yes."

The senior partner stopped what he was doing—he was engaged in a ticklish piece of scientific research, involving deadly weapons, ballistics and some esoteric aspects of aero-dynamics; specifically he was trying to perfect his overhand throw with darts, using a roto-gravure likeness of café society's latest glamour girl thumbtacked to the bread board as a target. One dart had nailed her left eye; he was trying to match it in the right.

"Yes," his wife said again.

"Try saying 'No,' " he suggested.

She cupped the mouthpiece. "Shut up and hand me a pencil." She made a long arm across the breakfast-nook table and obtained a stenographer's pad from a hook there. "Yes. Go ahead." Accepting the pencil she made several lines of the hooks and scrawls that stenographers use in place of writing. "It seems most likely," she said at last. "Mr. Randall is not usually in at this hour. He much prefers to see clients during office hours. Mr. Craig? No, I'm sure Mr. Craig couldn't help you. Positive. So? Hold the line and I'll find out."

Randall made one more try at the lovely lady; the dart stuck in the leg of the radio-record player. "Well?"

"There is a character on the other end of this who wants to see you very badly tonight. Name of Hoag, Jonathan Hoag. Claims that it is a physical impossibility for him to come to see you in the daytime. Didn't want to state his business and got all mixed up when he tried to."

"Gentleman or lug?"

"Gentleman."

"Money?"

"Sounds like it. Didn't seem worried about it. Better take it, Teddy. April 15th is coming up."

"O.K. Pass it over."

She waved him back and spoke again into the phone. "I've managed to locate Mr. Randall. I think he will be able to speak with you in a moment or two. Will you hold the line, please?" Still holding the phone away from her husband she consulted her watch, carefully counted off thirty seconds, then said, "Ready with Mr. Randall. Go ahead, Mr. Hoag," and slipped the instrument to her husband.

"Edward Randall speaking. What it it, Mr. Hoag?

"Oh, really now, Mr. Hoag, I think you had better come in in the morning. We are all human and we like our rest—I do, anyhow.

"I must warn you, Mr. Hoag, my prices go up when the sun goes down.

"Well, now, let me see—I was just leaving for home. Matter of fact, I just talked with my wife so she's expecting me. You know how women are. But if you could stop by my home in twenty minutes, at . . . uh . . . seventeen minutes past eight, we could talk for a few minutes. All right—got a pencil handy? Here is the address—" He cradled the phone.

"What am I this time? Wife, partner, or secretary?"

"What do you think? You talked to him."

" 'Wife,' I'd guess. His voice sounded prissy."

"O.K."

"I'll change to a dinner gown. And you had better get your toys up off the floor, Brain."

"Oh, I don't know. It gives a nice touch of eccentricity."

"Maybe you'd like some shag tobacco in a carpet slipper. Or some Regie cigarettes." She moved around the room, switching off the overhead lights and arranging table and floor lamps so that the chair a visitor would naturally sit in would be well lighted.

Without answering he gathered up his darts and the bread board, stopping as he did so to moisten his finger and rub the spot where he had marred the radio, then dumped the whole collection into the kitchen and closed the door. In the subdued light, with the kitchen and breakfast nook no longer visible, the room looked serenely opulent.

"How do you do, sir? Mr. Hoag, my dear. Mr. Hoag . . . Mrs. Randall."

"How do you do, madame."

Randall helped him off with his coat, assuring himself in the process that Mr. Hoag was not armed, or— if he was—he had found somewhere other than shoulder or hip to carry a gun. Randall was not suspicious, but he was pragmatically pessimistic.

"Sit down, Mr. Hoag. Cigarette?"

"No. No, thank you."

Randall said nothing in reply. He sat and stared, not rudely but mildly, nevertheless thoroughly. The suit might be English or it might be Brooks Brothers. It was certainly not Hart, Schaffner & Marx. A tie of that quality had to be termed a cravat, although it was modest as a nun. He upped his fee mentally. The little man was nervous—he wouldn't relax in his chair. Woman's presence, probably. Good—let him come to a slow simmer, then move him off the fire.

"You need not mind the presence of Mrs. Randall," he said presently. "Anything that I may hear, she may hear also."

"Oh . . . oh, yes. Yes, indeed." He bowed from the waist without getting up. "I am very happy to have Mrs. Randall present." But he did not go on to say what his business was.

"Well, Mr. Hoag," Randall added presently, "you wished to consult me about something, did you not?"

"Uh, yes."

"Then perhaps you had better tell me about it."

"Yes, surely. It— That is to say— Mr. Randall, the whole business is preposterous."

"Most businesses are. But go ahead. Woman trouble? Or has someone been sending you threatening letters?"

"Oh, no! Nothing as simple as that. But I'm afraid."

"Of what?"

"I don't know," Hoag answered quickly with a little intake of breath. "I want you to find out."

"Wait a minute, Mr. Hoag," Randall said. "This seems to be getting more confused rather than less. You say you are afraid and you want me to find out what you are afraid of. Now I'm not a psychoanalyst; I'm a detective. What is there about this business that a detective can do?"

Hoag looked unhappy, then blurted out, "I want you to find out what I do in the daytime."

Randall looked him over, then said slowly, "You want *me* to find out what *you* do in the daytime?"

"Yes. Yes, that's it."

"Mm-m-m. Wouldn't it be easier for you to *tell* me what you do?"

"Oh, I couldn't tell you!"

"Why not?"

"I don't know."

Randall was becoming somewhat annoyed. "Mr. Hoag," he said, "I usually charge double for playing guessing games. If you won't tell me what you do in the daytime, it seems to me to indicate a lack of confidence in me which will make it very difficult indeed to assist you. Now come clean with me—what is it you do in the daytime and what has it to do with the case? What *is* the case?"

Mr. Hoag stood up. "I might have known I couldn't explain it," he said unhappily, more to himself than to Randall. "I'm sorry I disturbed you. I—"

"Just a minute, Mr. Hoag." Cynthia Craig Randall spoke for the first time. "I think perhaps you two have misunderstood each other. You mean, do you not, that you really and literally do not *know* what you do in the daytime?"

"Yes," he said gratefully. "Yes, that is exactly it."

"And you want us to find out what you do? Shadow you, find out where you go, and tell you what you have been doing?"

Hoag nodded emphatically. "That is what I have been trying to say."

Randall glanced from Hoag to his wife and back to Hoag. "Let's get this straight," he said slowly. "You really don't know what you do in the daytime and you want me to find out. How long has this been going on?"

"I . . . I don't know."

"Well— what *do* you know?"

Hoag managed to tell his story, with prompting. His recollection of any sort ran back about five years, to the St. George Rest Home in Dubuque. Incurable amnesia —it no longer worried him and he had regarded himself as completely rehabilitated. They—the hospital authorities—had found a job for him when he was discharged.

"What sort of a job?"

He did not know that. Presumably it was the same job he now held, his present occupation. He had been strongly advised, when he left the rest home, never to worry about his work, never to take his work home with him, even in his thoughts. "You see," Hoag explained, "they work on the theory that amnesia is brought on by overwork and worry. I remember Dr. Rennault telling me emphatically that I must never talk shop, never let my mind dwell on the day's work. When I got home at night I was to forget such things and occupy myself with pleasant subjects. So I tried to do that."

"Hm-m-m. You certainly seem to have been successful, almost too successful for belief. See here—did they use hypnosis on you in treating you?"

"Why, I really don't know."

"Must have. How about it, Cyn? Does it fit?"

His wife nodded, "It fits. Posthypnosis. After five years of it he couldn't possibly think about his work after hours no matter how he tried. Seems like a very odd therapy, however."

Randall was satisfied. She handled matters psychological. Whether she got her answers from her rather extensive formal study, or straight out of her subconscious, he neither knew nor gave a hang. They seemed to work. "Something still bothers me," he added. "You go along for five years, apparently never knowing where or how you work. Why this sudden yearning to know?"

He told them the story of the dinner-table discussion, the strange substance under his nails, and the non-co-operative doctor. "I'm frightened," he said miserably. "I thought it was blood. And now I know it's something—worse."

Randall looked at him. "Why?"

Hoag moistened his lips. "Because—" He paused and looked helpless. "You'll help me, won't you?"

Randall straightened up. "This isn't in my line," he said. "You need help all right, but you need help from a psychiatrist. Amnesia isn't in my line. I'm a detective."

"But I *want* a detective. I want you to watch me and find out what I do."

Randall started to refuse; his wife interrupted. "I'm sure we can help you, Mr. Hoag. Perhaps you should see a psychiatrist—"

"Oh, no!"

"—but if you wish to be shadowed, it will be done."

"I don't like it," said Randall. "He doesn't need us."

Hoag laid his gloves on the side table and reached into his breast pocket. "I'll make it worth your while." He started counting out bills. "I brought only five hundred," he said anxiously. "Is it enough?"

"It will do," she told him.

"As a retainer," Randall added. He accepted the money and stuffed it into his side pocket. "By the way," he added, "if you don't know what you do during business hours and you have no more background than a hospital, where do you get the money?" He made his voice casual.

"Oh, I get paid every Sunday. Two hundred dollars, in bills."

When he had gone Randall handed the cash over to his wife. "Pretty little tickets," she said, smoothing them out and folding them neatly. "Teddy, why did you try to queer the pitch?"

"Me? I didn't—I was just running up the price. The old 'get-away-closer.' "

"That's what I thought. But you almost overdid it."

"Not at all. I knew I could depend on you. *You* wouldn't let him out of the house with a nickel left on him."

She smiled happily. "You're a nice man, Teddy. And we have so much in common. We both like money. How much of his story did you believe?"

"Not a damned word of it."

"Neither did I. He's rather a horrid little beast— I wonder what he's up to."

"I don't know, but I mean to find out."

"You aren't going to shadow him yourself, are you?"

"Why not? Why pay ten dollars a day to some ex-flattie to muff it?"

"Teddy, I don't like the set-up. Why should he be willing to pay this much"—she gestured with the bills —"to lead you around by the nose?"

"That is what I'm going to find out."

"You be careful. You remember 'The Red-headed League.'"

"The 'Red-headed—' Oh, Sherlock Holmes again. Be your age, Cyn."

"I am. You be yours. That little man is *evil*."

She left the room and cached the money. When she returned he was down on his knees by the chair in which Hoag had sat, busy with an insufflator. He looked around as she came in.

"Cyn—"

"Yes, Brain."

"You haven't touched this chair?"

"Of course not. I polished the arms as usual before he showed up."

"That's not what I mean. I meant since he left. Did he ever take off his gloves?"

"Wait a minute. Yes, I'm sure he did. I looked at his nails when he told his yarn about them."

"So did I, but I wanted to make sure I wasn't nuts. Take a look at that surface."

She examined the polished chair arms, now covered with a thin film of gray dust. The surface was unbroken —no fingerprints. "He must never have touched them —But he did. I saw him. When he said, 'I'm frightened,' he gripped both arms. I remember noticing how blue his knuckles looked."

"Collodion, maybe?"

"Don't be silly. There isn't even a smear. You shook hands with him. Did he have collodion on his hands?"

"I don't think so. I think I would have noticed it. The Man with No Fingerprints. Let's call him a ghost and forget it."

"Ghosts don't pay out hard cash to be watched."

"No, they don't. Not that I ever heard of." He stood up and marched out into the breakfast nook, grabbed the phone and dialed long distance. "I want the Medical Exchange in Dubuque, uh—" He cupped the phone and called to his wife. "Say, honey, what the hell state *is* Dubuque in?"

Forty-five minutes and several calls later he slammed the instrument back into its cradle. "That tears it," he announced. "There is no St. George Rest Home in Dubuque. There never was and probably never will be. And no Dr. Rennault."

III

"There he is!" Cynthia Craig Randall nudged her husband.

He continued to hold the *Tribune* in front of his face as if reading it. "I see him," he said quietly. "Control yourself. Yuh'd think you had never tailed a man before. Easy does it."

"Teddy, do be careful."

"I will be." He glanced over the top of the paper and watched Jonathan Hoag come down the steps of the swank Gotham Apartments in which he made his home. When he left the shelter of the canopy he turned to the left. The time was exactly seven minutes before nine in the morning.

Randall stood up, folded his paper with care, and laid it down on the bus-station bench on which he had been waiting. He then turned toward the drugstore behind him, dropped a penny in the slot of a gum-vending machine in the shop's recessed doorway. In the mirror on the face of the machine he watched Hoag's unhurried progress down tho far side of the street. With equal lack of rush he started after him, without crossing the street.

Cynthia waited on the bench until Randall had had time enough to get a half block ahead of her, then got up and followed him.

Hoag climbed on a bus at the second corner. Randall took advantage of a traffic-light change which held the bus at the corner, crossed against the lights, and managed to reach the bus just as it was pulling out. Hoag had gone up to the open deck; Randall seated himself down below.

Cynthia was too late to catch the bus, but not too late to note its number. She yoohooed at the first cruising taxi that came by, told the driver the number of the bus, and set out. They covered twelve blocks before the bus came in sight; three blocks later a red light enabled the driver to pull up alongside the bus. She spotted her husband inside; it was all she needed to know. She occupied the time for the rest of the ride in keeping the exact amount shown by the meter plus a quarter tip counted out in her hand.

When she saw them get out of the bus she told the driver to pull up. He did so, a few yards beyond the bus stop. Unfortunately they were headed in her direction; she did not wish to get out at once. She paid the driver the exact amount of the tariff while keeping one eye—the one in the back of her head—on the two men. The driver looked at her curiously.

"Do you chase after women?" she said suddenly.

"No, lady. I gotta family."

"*My* husband does," she said bitterly and untruthfully. "Here." She handed him the quarter.

Hoag and Randall were some yards past by now. She got out, headed for the shop just across the walk, and waited. To her surprise she saw Hoag turn and speak to her husband. She was too far away to hear what was said.

She hesitated to join them. The picture was wrong; it made her apprehensive—yet her husband seemed unconcerned. He listened quietly to what Hoag had to say, then the two of them entered the office building in front of which they had been standing.

She closed in at once. The lobby of the office building was as crowded as one might expect at such an hour in the morning. Six elevators, in bank, were doing rushing business. No. 2 had just slammed its doors. No. 3 had just started to load. They were not in No. 3; she posted herself near the cigar stand and quickly cased the place.

They were not in the lobby. Nor were they, she quickly made sure, in the barber shop which opened off the lobby. They had probably been the last passengers to catch Elevator No. 2 on its last trip. She had been watching the indicator for No. 2 without learning anything useful from it; the car had stopped at nearly every floor.

No. 2 was back down by now; she made herself one of its passengers, not the first nor the last, but one of the crowd. She did not name a floor, but waited until the last of the others had gotten off.

The elevator boy raised his eyebrows at her. "Floor, please!" he commanded.

She displayed a dollar bill. "I want to talk to you."

He closed the gates, accomplishing an intimate privacy. "Make it snappy," he said, glancing at the signals on his board.

"Two men got on together your last trip." She described them quickly and vividly. "I want to know what floor they got off at."

He shook his head. "I wouldn't know. This is the rush hour."

She added another bill. "Think. They were probably the last two to get aboard. Maybe they had to step out to let others off. The shorter one probably called out the floor."

He shook his head again. "Even if you made it a fin I couldn't tell you. During the rush Lady Godiva *and* her horse could ride this cage and I wouldn't know it. Now—do you want to get out or go down?"

"Down." She handed him one of the bills. "Thanks for trying."

He looked at it, shrugged, and pocketed it.

There was nothing to do but to take up her post in the lobby. She did so, fuming. Done in, she thought, done in by the oldest trick known for shaking a tail. Call yourself a dick and get taken in by the office-building trick! They were probably out of the building and gone by now, with Teddy wondering where she was and maybe needing her to back up his play.

She ought to take up tatting! Damn!

She bought a bottle of Pepsi-Cola at the cigar stand and drank it slowly, standing up. She was just wondering whether or not she could stand another, in the interest of protective coloration, when Randall appeared.

It took the flood of relief that swept over her to make her realize how much she had been afraid. Nevertheless, she did not break character. She turned her head away, knowing that her husband would see her and recognize the back of her neck quite as well as her face.

He did not come up and speak to her, therefore she took position on him again. Hoag she could not see anywhere; had she missed him herself, or what?

Randall walked down to the corner, glanced speculatively at a stand of taxis, then swung aboard a bus which had just drawn up to its stop. She followed him, allowing several others to mount it before her. The bus pulled away. Hoag had certainly not gotten aboard; she concluded that it was safe to break the routine.

He looked up as she sat down beside him. "Cyn! I thought we had lost you."

"You darn near did," she admitted. "Tell me—what's cookin'?"

"Wait till we get to the office."

She did not wish to wait, but she subsided. The bus they had entered took them directly to their office, a mere half-dozen blocks away. When they were there he unlocked the door of the tiny suite and went at once to the telephone. Their listed office phone was connected through the PBX of a secretarial service.

"Any calls?" he asked, then listened for a moment. "O.K. Send up the slips. No hurry."

He put the phone down and turned to his wife.

"Well, babe, that's just about the easiest five hundred we ever promoted."

"You found out what he does with himself?"

"Of course."

"What does he do?"

"Guess."

She eyed him. "How would you like a paste in the snoot?"

"Keep your pants on. You wouldn't guess it, though it's simple enough. He works for a commercial jeweler —polishes gems. You know that stuff he found under his fingernails, that got him so upset?"

"Yes?"

"Nothing to it. Jeweler's rouge. With the aid of a diseased imagination he jumps to the conclusion it's dried blood. So we make half a grand."

"Mm-m-m. And that seems to be that. This place he works is somewhere in the Acme Building, I suppose."

"Room 1310. Or rather Suite 1310. Why didn't you tag along?"

She hesitated a little in replying. She did not want to admit how clumsy she had been, but the habit of complete honesty with each other was strong upon her. "I let myself get misled when Hoag spoke to you outside the Acme Building. I missed you at the elevator."

"I see. Well, I— Say! What did you say? Did you say Hoag *spoke* to me?"

"Yes, certainly."

"But he didn't speak to me. He never laid eyes on me. What are you talking about?"

"What am *I* talking about? What are *you* talking about! Just before the two of you went into the Acme Building, Hoag stopped, turned around and spoke to you. The two of you stood there chinning, which threw me off stride. Then you went into the lobby together, practically arm in arm."

He sat there, saying nothing, looking at her for a long moment. At last she said, "Don't sit there staring like a goon! That's what happened."

He said, "Cyn, listen to my story. I got off the bus after he did and followed him into the lobby. I used the old heel-and-toe getting into the elevator and swung behind him when he faced the front of the car. When he got out, I hung back, then fiddled around, half in and half out, asking the operator simpleton questions, and giving him long enough to get clear. When I turned the corner he was just disappearing into 1310. He never spoke to me. He never saw my face. I'm sure of that."

She was looking white, but all she said was, "Go on."

"When you go in this place there is a long glass partition on your right, with benches built up against it. You can look through the glass and see the jewelers, or jewelsmiths, or whatever you call 'em at work. Clever—good salesmanship. Hoag ducked right on in and by the time I passed down the aisle he was already on the other side, his coat off and a smock on, and one of those magnifying dinguses screwed into his eye. I went on past him to the desk—he never looked up— and asked for the manager. Presently a little birdlike guy shows up and I ask him if they have a man named Jonathan Hoag in their employ. He says yes and asks if I want to speak to him. I told him no, that I was an investigator for an insurance company. He wants· to know if there is anything wrong and I told him that it was simply a routine investigation of what he had said on his application for a life policy, and how long had he worked there? Five years, he told me. He said that Hoag was one of the most reliable and skillful employees. I said fine, and asked if he thought Mr. Hoag could afford to carry as much as ten thousand. He says certainly and that they were always glad to see their employees invest in life insurance. Which was what I figured when I gave him the stall.

"As I went out I stopped in front of Hoag's bench and looked at him 'through the glass. Presently he looked up and stared at me, then looked down again. I'm sure I would have spotted it if he had recognized me. A case of complete skeezo, sheezo . . . how do you pronounce it?"

"Schizophrenia. Completely split personalities. But look, Teddy—"

"Yeah?"

"You *did* talk with him. I saw you."

"Now slow down, puss. You may think you did, but you must have been looking at two other guys. How far away were you?"

"Not *that* far. I was standing in front of Beecham's Bootery. Then comes *Chez Louis,* and then the entrance to the Acme Building. You had your back to the newspaper stand at the curb and were practically facing me. Hoag had his back to me, but I couldn't have been mistaken, as I had him in full profile when the two of you turned and went into the building together."

Randall looked exasperated. "I didn't speak with him. And I didn't go in with him; I followed him in."

"Edward Randall, don't give me that! I admit I lost the two of you, but that's no reason to rub it in by trying to make a fool of me."

Randall had been married too long and too comfortably not to respect danger signals. He got up, went to her, and put an arm around her. "Look, kid," he said, seriously and gently, "I'm not pulling your leg. We've got our wires crossed somehow, but I'm giving it to you just as straight as I can, the way I remember it."

She searched his eyes, then kissed him suddenly, and pulled away. "All right. We're both right and it's impossible. Come on."

" 'Come on' where?"

"To the scene of the crime. If I don't get this straightened out I'll never sleep again."

The Acme Building was just where they had left it. The Bootery was where it belonged, likewise *Chez Louis,* and the newsstand. He stood where she had stood and agreed that she could not have been mistaken in her identification unless blind drunk. But he was equally positive as to what he had done.

"You didn't pick up a snifter or two on the way, did you?" he suggested hopefully.

"Certainly not."

"What do we do now?"

"I don't know. Yes, I do, too! We're finished with Hoag, aren't we? You've traced him down and that's that."

"Yes . . . why?"

"Take me up to where he works. I want to ask his daytime personality whether or not he spoke to you getting off the bus."

He shrugged. "O.K., kid. It's your party."

They went inside and entered the first free elevator. The starter clicked his castanets, the operator slammed his doors and said, "Floors, please."

Six, three, and nine. Randall waited until all those had been served before announcing, "Thirteen."

The operator looked around. "I can give you twelve and fourteen, buddy, and you can split 'em."

"Huh?"

"There ain't no thirteenth floor. If there was, nobody would rent on it."

"You must be mistaken. I was on it this morning."

The operator gave him a look of marked restraint. "See for yourself." He shot the car upward and halted it. "Twelve." He raised the car slowly, the figure 12 slid out of sight and was quickly replaced by another. "Fourteen. Which way will you have it?"

"I'm sorry," Randall admitted. "I've made a silly mistake. I really was in here this morning and I thought I had noted the floor."

"Might ha' been eighteen," suggested the operator. "Sometimes an eight will look like a three. Who you lookin' for?"

"Detheridge & Co. They're manufacturing jewelers."

The operator shook his head. "Not in this building. No jewelers, and no Detheridge."

"You're sure?"

Instead of answering, the operator dropped his car back to the tenth floor. "Try 1001. It's the office of the building."

No, they had no Detheridge. No, no jewelers, manufacturing or otherwise. Could it be the Apex Building the gentleman wanted, rather than the Acme? Randall thanked them and left, considerably shaken.

Cynthia had maintained complete silence during the proceedings. Now she said, "Darling—"

"Yeah. What is it?"

"We could go up to the top floor, and work down."

"Why bother? If they were here, the building office would know about it."

"So they would, but they might not be telling. There is something fishy about this whole business. Come to think about it, you could hide a whole floor of an office building by making its door look like a blank wall."

"No, that's silly. I'm just losing my mind, that's all. You better take me to a doctor."

"It's not silly and you're not losing your grip. How do you count height in an elevator? By floors. If you didn't see a floor, you would never realize an extra one was tucked in. We may be on the trail of something big." She did not really believe her own arguments, but she knew that he needed something to do.

He started to agree, then checked himself. "How about the stairways? You're bound to notice a floor from a staircase."

"Maybe there is some hanky-panky with the staircases, too. If so, we'll be looking for it. Come on."

But there was not. There were exactly the same number of steps—eighteen—between floors twelve and fourteen as there were between any other pair of adjacent floors. They worked down from the top floor and examined the lettering on each frosted-glass door. This took them rather long, as Cynthia would not listen to Randall's suggestion that they split up and take half a floor apiece. She wanted him in her sight.

No thirteenth floor and nowhere a door which announced the tenancy of a firm of manufacturing jewelers, neither Detheridge & Co. nor any other name. There was no time to do more than read the firm names on the doors; to have entered each office, on one pretext or another, would have taken much more than a day.

Randall stared thoughtfully at a door labeled: "Pride, Greenway, Hamilton, Steinbolt, Carter & Greenway, Attorneys at Law." "By this time," he mused, "they could have changed the lettering on the door."

"Not on *that* one," she pointed out. "Anyhow, if it was a set-up, they could have cleaned out the whole

joint, too. Changed it so you wouldn't recognize it."
Nevertheless she stared at the innocent-seeming letters
thoughtfully. An office building was a terribly remote
and secret place. Soundproof walls, Venetian blinds—
and a meaningless firm name. Anything could go in
such a place—anything. Nobody would know. Nobody
would care. No one would ever notice. No policeman
on his beat, neighbors as remote as the moon, not even
scrub service if the tenant did not wish it. As long as
the rent was paid on time, the management would leave
a tenant alone. Any crime you fancied and park the
bodies in the closet.

She shivered. "Come on, Teddy. Let's hurry."

They covered the remaining floors as quickly as possible and came out at last in the lobby. Cynthia felt
warmed by the sight of faces and sunlight, even though
they had not found the missing firm. Randall stopped
on the steps and looked around. "Do you suppose we
could have been in a different building?" he said
doubtfully.

"Not a chance. See that cigar stand? I practically
lived there. I know every flyspeck on the counter."

"Then what's the answer?"

"Lunch is the answer. Come on."

"O.K. But I'm going to drink mine."

She managed to persuade him to encompass a plate
of corned-beef hash after the third whiskey sour. That
and two cups of coffee left him entirely sober, but unhappy. "Cyn—"

"Yes, Teddy."

"What happened to me?"

She answered slowly. "I think you were made the
victim of an amazing piece of hypnosis."

"So do I—now. Either that, or I've finally cracked
up. So call it hypnosis. I want to know why."

She made doodles with her fork. "I'm not sure that
I want to know. You know what I would like to do,
Teddy?"

"What?"

"I would like to send Mr. Hoag's five hundred dollars
back to him with a message that we can't help him, so
we are returning his money."

He stared at her. "Send the money back? Good heavens!"

Her face looked as if she had been caught making an indecent suggestion, but she went on stubbornly. "I know. Just the same, that's what I would like to do. We can make enough on divorce cases and skip-tracing to eat on. We don't have to monkey with a thing like this."

"You talk like five hundred was something you'd use to tip a waiter."

"No, I don't. I just don't think it's enough to risk your neck—or your sanity—for. Look, Teddy, somebody is trying to get us in the nine hole; before we go any further, I want to know *why*."

"And I want to know why, too. Which is why I'm not willing to drop the matter. Damn it, I don't like having shenanigans put over on me."

"What are you going to tell Mr. Hoag?"

He ran a hand through his hair, which did not matter as it was already mussed. "I don't know. Suppose you talk to him. Give him a stall."

"That's a *fine* idea. That's a *swell* idea. I'll tell him you've broken your leg but you'll be all right tomorrow."

"Don't be like that, Cyn. You know you can handle him."

"All right. But you've got to promise me this, Teddy."

"Promise what?"

"As long as we're on this case we do everything together."

"Don't we always?"

"I mean really together. I don't want you out of my sight *any* of the time."

"But see here, Cyn, that may not be practical."

"Promise."

"O.K., O.K. I promise."

"That's better." She relaxed and looked almost happy. "Hadn't we better get back to the office?"

"The hell with it. Let's go out and take in a triple feature."

"O.K., Brain." She gathered up her gloves and purse.

The movies failed to amuse him, although they had
selected an all-Western bill, a fare of which he was
inordinately fond. But the hero seemed as villainous
as the foreman, and the mysterious masked riders, for
once, appeared really sinister. And he kept seeing the
thirteenth floor of the Acme Building, the long glass
partition behind which the craftsmen labored, and the
little dried-up manager of Detheridge & Co. Damn it
—could a man be hypnotized into believing that he
had seen anything as detailed as that?

Cynthia hardly noticed the pictures. She was preoccupied with the people around them. She found herself studying their faces guardedly whenever the lights
went up. If they looked like this when they were amusing themselves, what were they like when they were
unhappy? With rare exceptions the faces looked, at the
best, stolidly uncomplaining. Discontent, the grim
marks of physical pain, lonely unhappiness, frustration,
and stupid meanness, she found in numbers, but rarely
a merry face. Even Teddy, whose habitual debonair
gaiety was one of his chief virtues, was looking dour—
with reason, she conceded. She wondered what were
the reasons for those other unhappy masks.

She recalled having seen a painting entitled "Sub-
way." It showed a crowd pouring out the door of an
underground train while another crowd attempted to
force its way in. Getting on or getting off, they were
plainly in a hurry, yet it seemed to give them no
pleasure. The picture had no beauty in itself; it was
plain that the artist's single purpose had been to make
a bitter criticism of a way of living.

She was glad when the show was over and they
could escape to the comparative freedom of the street.
Randall flagged a taxi and they started home.

"Teddy—"

"Uh?"

"Did you notice the faces of the people in the
theater?"

"No, not especially. Why?"

"Not a one of them looked as if they got any fun
out of life."

"Maybe they don't."

"But why don't they? Look—we have fun, don't we?"

"You bet."

"We always have fun. Even when we were broke and trying to get the business started we had fun. We went to bed smiling and got up happy. We still do. What's the answer?"

He smiled for the first time since the search for the thirteenth floor and pinched her. "It's fun living with you, kid."

"Thanks. And right back at you. You know, when I was a little girl, I had a funny idea."

"Spill it."

"I was happy myself, but as I grew up I could see that my mother wasn't. And my father wasn't. My teachers weren't—most of the adults around me weren't happy. I got an idea in my head that when you grew up you found out something that kept you from ever being happy again. You know how a kid is treated: 'You're not old enough to understand, dear,' and 'Wait till you grow up, darling, and then you'll understand.' I used to wonder what the secret was they were keeping from me and I'd listen behind doors to try and see if I couldn't find out."

"Born to be a detective!"

"*Shush.* But I could see that, whatever it was, it didn't make the grown-ups happy; it made 'em sad. Then I used to pray never to find out." She gave a little shrug. "I guess I never did."

He chuckled. "Me neither. A professional Peter Pan, that's me. Just as happy as if I had good sense."

She placed a small gloved hand on his arm. "Don't laugh, Teddy. That's what scares me about this Hoag case. I'm afraid that if we go ahead with it we really will find out what it is the grown-ups know. And then we'll never laugh again."

He started to laugh, then looked at her hard. "Why, you're really serious, aren't you?" He chucked her under the chin. "Be your age, kid. What you need is dinner—and a drink."

IV

After dinner, Cynthia was just composing in her mind what she would say to Mr. Hoag on telephoning him when the house buzzer rang. She went to the entrance of their apartment and took up the house phone. "Yes?"

Almost immediately she turned to her husband and voicelessly shaped the words, "It's Mr. Hoag." He raised his brows, put a cautioning finger to his lips, and with an exaggerated tiptoe started for the bedroom. She nodded.

"Just a moment, please. There—that's better. We seem to have had a bad connection. Now who is it, please?

"Oh . . . Mr. Hoag. Come up, Mr. Hoag." She punched the button controlling the electrical outer lock.

He came in bobbing nervously. "I trust this is not an intrusion, but I have been so upset that I felt I couldn't wait for a report."

She did not invite him to sit down. "I am sorry," she said sweetly, "to have to disappoint you. Mr. Randall has not yet come home."

"Oh." He seemed pathetically disappointed, so much so that she felt a sudden sympathy. Then she remembered what her husband had been put through that morning and froze up again.

"Do you know," he continued, "when he will be home?"

"That I couldn't say. Wives of detectives, Mr. Hoag, learn not to wait up."

"Yes, I suppose so. Well, I presume I should not impose on you further. But I *am* anxious to speak with him."

"I'll tell him so. Was there anything in particular you had to say to him? Some new data, perhaps?"

"No—" he said slowly. "No, I suppose . . . it all seems so silly!"

"What does, Mr. Hoag?"

He searched her face. "I wonder— Mrs. Randall, do you believe in possession?"

"Possession?"

"Possession of human souls—by devils."

"I can't say that I've thought much about it," she answered cautiously. She wondered if Teddy were listening, if he could reach her quickly if she screamed.

Hoag was fumbling strangely at his shirt front; he got a button opened; she whiffed an acrid, unclean smell, then he was holding out something in his hand, something fastened by a string around his neck under his shirt.

She forced herself to look at it and with intense relief recognized it for what it was—a cluster of fresh cloves of garlic, worn as a necklace. "Why do you wear it?" she asked.

"It does seem silly, doesn't it?" he admitted. "Giving way to superstition like that—but it comforts me. I've had the most frightening feeling of being watched—"

"Naturally. We've been— Mr. Randall has been watching you, by your instructions."

"Not that. A man in a mirror—" He hesitated.

"A man in a mirror?"

"Your reflection in a mirror watches you, but you expect it; it doesn't worry you. This is something new, as if someone were trying to get at me, waiting for a chance. Do you think I'm crazy?" he concluded suddenly.

Her attention was only half on his words, for she had noticed something when he held out the garlic which had held her attention. His fingertips were ridged and grooved in whorls and loops and arches like anyone else's—and they were certainly not coated with collodion tonight. She decided to get a set of prints for Teddy. "No, I don't think you're crazy," she said soothingly, "but I think you've let yourself worry too much. You should relax. Wouldn't you like a drink?"

"I would be grateful for a glass of water."

Water or liquor, it was the glass she was interested in. She excused herself and went out to the kitchen where she selected a tall glass with smooth, undecorated sides. She polished it carefully, added ice and water with equal care not to wet the sides. She carried it in, holding it near the bottom.

Intentionally or unintentionally, he had outmaneuvered her. He was standing in front of the mirror near the door, where he had evidently been straightening his tie and tidying himself and returning the garlic to its hide-away. When he turned around at her approach she saw that he had put his gloves back on.

She invited him to sit down, thinking that if he did so he would remove his gloves. But he said, "I've imposed on you too long as it is." He drank half the glass of water, thanked her, and left silently.

Randall came in. "He's gone?"

She turned quickly. "Yes, he's gone. Teddy, I wish you would do your own dirty work. He makes me nervous. I wanted to scream for you to come in."

"Steady, old girl."

"That's all very well, but I wish we had never laid eyes on him." She went to a window and opened it wide.

"Too late for Herpicide. We're in it now." His eye rested on the glass. "Say—did you get his prints?"

"No such luck. I think he read my mind."

"Too bad."

"Teddy, what do you intend to do about him now?"

"I've got an idea, but let me work it out first. What was this song and dance he was giving you about devils and a man in a mirror watching him?"

"That wasn't what he said."

"Maybe I was the man in the mirror. I watched him in one this morning."

"Huh-uh. He was just using a metaphor. He's got the jumps." She turned suddenly, thinking that she had seen something move over her shoulder. But there was nothing there but the furniture and the wall. Probably just a reflection in the glass, she decided, and said nothing about it. "I've got 'em, too," she added. "As for devils, he's all the devil I want. You know what I'd like?"

"What?"

"A big stiff drink and early to bed."

"Good idea." He wandered out into the kitchen and started mixing the prescription. "Want a sandwich, too?"

Randall found himself standing in his pajamas in the living room of their apartment, facing the mirror that hung near the outer door. His reflection—no, not his reflection, for the image was properly dressed in conservative clothes appropriate to a solid man of business —the image spoke to him.

"Edward Randall."

"Huh?"

"Edward Randall, you are summoned. Here—take my hand. Pull up a chair and you will find you can climb through easily."

It seemed a perfectly natural thing to do, in fact the only reasonable thing to do. He placed a straight chair under the mirror, took the hand offered him, and scrambled through. There was a washstand under the mirror on the far side, which gave him a leg down. He and his companion were standing in a small, white-tiled washroom such as one finds in office suites.

"Hurry," said his companion. "The others are all assembled."

"Who are you?"

"The name is Phipps," the other said, with a slight bow. "This way, please."

He opened the door of the washroom and gave Randall a gentle shove. He found himself in a room that was obviously a board room—with a meeting in session, for the long table was surrounded by about a dozen men. They all had their eyes on him.

"Up you go, Mr. Randall."

Another shove, not quite so gentle and he was sitting in the middle of the polished table. Its hard top felt cold through the thin cotton of his pajama trousers.

He drew the jacket around him tightly and shivered. "Cut it out," he said. "Let me down from here. I'm not dressed." He tried to get up, but he seemed unable to accomplish that simple movement.

Somebody behind him chuckled. A voice said, "He's

not very fat." Someone answered, "That doesn't matter, for this job."

He was beginning to recognize the situation—the last time it had been Michigan Boulevard without his trousers. More than once it had found him back in school again, not only undressed, but lessons unprepared, and late in the bargain. Well, he knew how to beat it—close your eyes and reach down for the covers, then wake up safe in bed.

He closed his eyes.

"No use to hide, Mr. Randall. We can see you and you are simply wasting time."

He opened his eyes. "What's the idea?" he said savagely. "Where am I? Why'dju bring me here? What's going on?"

Facing him at the head of the table was a large man. Standing, he must have measured six feet two at least, and he was broad-shouldered and heavy-boned in proportion. Fat was laid over his huge frame liberally. But his hands were slender and well shaped and beautifully manicured; his features were not large and seemed smaller, being framed in fat jowls and extra chins. His eyes were small and merry; his mouth smiled a good deal and he had a trick of compressing his lips and shoving them out.

"One thing at a time, Mr. Randall," he answered jovially. "As to where you are, this is the thirteenth floor of the Acme Building—you remember." He chuckled, as if they shared a private joke. "As to what goes on, this is a meeting of the board of Detheridge & Co. I"—he managed to bow sitting down, over the broad expanse of his belly—"am R. Jefferson Stoles, chairman of the board, at your service, sir."

"But—"

"Please, Mr. Randall—introductions first. On my right. Mr. Townsend."

"How do you do, Mr. Randall."

"How do you do," Randall answered mechanically. "Look here, this has gone far—"

"Then Mr. Gravesby, Mr. Wells, Mr. Yoakum, Mr. Printemps, Mr. Jones. Mr. Phipps you have met. He is our secretary. Beyond him is seated Mr. Reifsnider and Mr. Snyder—no relation. And finally Mr. Parker and Mr. Crewes. Mr. Potiphar, I am sorry to say, could not attend, but we have a quorum."

Randall tried to get up again, but the table top seemed unbelievably slippery. "I don't care," he said bitterly, "whether you have a quorum or a gang fight. Let me out of here."

"*Tut*, Mr. Randall. *Tut*. Don't you want your questions answered?"

"Not that bad. Damn it, let me—"

"But they really must be answered. This is a business session and you are the business at hand."

"Me?"

"Yes, you. You are, shall we say, a minor item on the agenda, but one which must be cleared up. We do not like your activity, Mr. Randall. You really must cease it."

Before Randall could answer, Stoles shoved a palm in his direction. "Don't be hasty, Mr. Randall. Let me explain. Not all of your activities. We do not care how many blondes you plant in hotel rooms to act as complacent correspondents in divorce cases, nor how many wires you tap, nor letters you open. There is only one activity of yours we are concerned with. I refer to Mr. Hoag." He spat out the last word.

Randall could feel a stir of uneasiness run through the room.

"What about Mr. Hoag?" he demanded. There was the stir again. Stoles' face no longer even pretended to smile.

"Let us refer to him hereafter," he said, "as 'your client.' It comes to this, Mr. Randall. We have other plans for Mr. . . . for your client. You must leave him alone. You must forget him, you must never see him again."

Randall stared back, uncowed. "I've never welshed on a client yet. I'll see you in hell first."

"That," admitted Stoles, shoving out his lips, "is a distinct possibility, I grant you, but one that neither you nor I would care to contemplate, save as a bombastic metaphor. Let us be reasonable. You *are* a rea-

sonable man, I know, and my confreres and I, we are
reasonable creatures, too. Instead of trying to coerce
or cajole you I want to tell you a story, so that you
may understand why."

"I don't care to listen to any stories. I'm leaving."

"Are you really? I think not. And you will listen!"

He pointed a finger at Randall; Randall attempted
to reply, found that he could not. "This," he thought,
"is the damnedest no-pants dream I ever had. Shouldn't
eat before going to bed—knew better."

"In the Beginning," Stoles stated, "there was the
Bird." He suddenly covered his face with his hands; all
the others gathered around the table did likewise.

The Bird—Randall felt a sudden vision of what
those two simple words meant when mouthed by this
repulsive fat man; no soft and downy chick, but a bird
of prey, strong-winged and rapacious—unwinking eyes,
whey-colored and staring—purple wattles—but most
especially he saw its feet, bird feet, covered with yellow
scales, fleshless and taloned and foul from use. Obscene
and terrible—

Stoles uncovered his face. "The Bird was alone. Its
great wings beat the empty depths of space where there
was none to see. But deep within It was the Power and
the Power was Life. It looked to the north when there
was no north; It looked to the south when there was
no south; east and west It looked, and up and down.
Then out of the nothingness and out of Its Will It wove
the nest.

"The nest was broad and deep and strong. In the
nest It laid one hundred eggs. It stayed on the nest
and brooded the eggs, thinking Its thoughts, for ten
thousand thousand years. When the time was ripe It
left the nest and hung it about with lights that the
fledglings might see. It watched and waited.

"From each of the hundred eggs a hundred Sons of
the Bird were hatched—ten thousand strong. Yet so
wide and deep was the nest there was room and to
spare for each of them—a kingdom apiece and each
was a king—king over the things that creep and crawl
and swim and fly and go on all fours, things that had

been born from the crevices of the nest, out of the warmth and the waiting.

"Wise and cruel was the Bird, and wise and cruel were the Sons of the Bird. For twice ten thousand thousand years they fought and ruled and the Bird was pleased. Then there were some who decided that they were as wise and strong as the Bird Itself. Out of the stuff of the nest they created creatures like unto themselves and breathed in their nostrils, that they might have sons to serve them and fight for them. But the sons of the Sons were not wise and strong and cruel, but weak and soft and stupid. The Bird was not pleased.

"Down It cast Its Own Sons and let them be chained by the softly stupid— Stop fidgeting, Mr. Randall! I know this is difficult for your little mind, but for once you really must think about something longer than your nose and wider than your mouth, believe me!

"The stupid and the weak could not hold the Sons of the Bird; therefore, the Bird placed among them, here and there, others more powerful, more cruel, and more shrewd, who by craft and cruelty and deceit could circumvent the attempts of the Sons to break free. Then the Bird sat back, well content, and waited for the game to play itself out.

"The game is being played. Therefore, we cannot permit you to interfere with your client, nor to assist him in any way. You see that, don't you?"

"I don't see," shouted Randall, suddenly able to speak, "a damn thing! To hell with the bunch of you! This joke has gone far enough."

"Silly and weak and stupid," Stoles sighed. "Show him, Mr. Phipps."

Phipps got up, placed a brief case on the table, opened it, and drew something from it, which he shoved under Randall's nose—a mirror.

"Please look this way, Mr. Randall," he said politely.

Randall looked at himself in the mirror.

"What are you thinking of, Mr. Randall?"

The image faded, he found himself staring into his own bedroom, as if from a slight height. The room was dark, but he could plainly see his wife's head on her pillow. His own pillow was vacant.

She stirred, and half turned over, sighing softly. Her lips were parted a trifle and smiling faintly, as if what she dreamed were pleasant.

"See, Mr. Randall?" said Stoles. "You wouldn't want anything to happen to her, now, would you?"

"Why, you dirty, low-down—"

"Softly, Mr. Randall, softly. And that will be enough from you. Remember your own interests—and *hers*." Stoles turned away from him. "Remove him, Mr. Phipps."

"Come, Mr. Randall." He felt again that undignified shove from behind, then he was flying through the air with the scene tumbling to pieces around him.

He was wide-awake in his own bed, flat on his back and covered with cold sweat.

Cynthia sat up. "What's the matter, Teddy?" she said sleepily. "I heard you cry out."

"Nothing. Bad dream, I guess. Sorry I woke you."

" 'S all right. Stomach upset?"

"A little, maybe."

"Take some bicarb."

"I will." He got up, went to the kitchen and fixed himself a small dose. His mouth was a little sour, he realized, now that he was awake; the soda helped matters.

Cynthia was already asleep when he got back; he slid into bed quietly. She snuggled up to him without waking, her body warming his. Quickly he was asleep, too.

" 'Never mind trouble! Fiddle-de-dee!' " He broke off singing suddenly, turned the shower down sufficiently to permit ordinary conversation, and said, "Good morning, beautiful!"

Cynthia was standing in the door of the bathroom, rubbing one eye and looking blearily at him with the other. "People who sing before breakfast—good morning."

"Why shouldn't I sing? It's a beautiful day and I've

had a beautiful sleep. I've got a new shower song. Listen."

"Don't bother."

"This is a song," he continued, unperturbed, "dedicated to a Young Man Who Has Announced His Intention of Going Out into the Garden to Eat Worms."

"Teddy, you're nasty."

"No, I'm not. Listen." He turned the shower on more fully. "You have to have the water running to get the full effect," he explained. "First verse:

> *"I don't think I'll go out in the garden;*
> *I'll make the worms come in to me!*
> *If I have to be miser'ble,*
> *I might as well be so comfort'bly!"*

He paused for effect. "Chorus," he announced.

> *"Never mind trouble! Fiddle-de-dee!*
> *Eat your worms with Vitamin B!*
> *Follow this rule and you will be*
> *Still eating worms at a hundred 'n' three!"*

He paused again. "Second verse," he stated. "Only I haven't thought up a second verse yet. Shall I repeat the first verse?"

"No, thanks. Just duck out of that shower and give me a chance at it."

"You don't like it," he accused her.

"I didn't say I didn't."

"Art is rarely appreciated," he mourned. But he got out.

He had the coffee and the orange juice waiting by the time she appeared in the kitchen. He handed her a glass of the fruit juice. "Teddy, you're a darling. What do you want in exchange for all this coddling?"

"You. But not now. I'm not only sweet, I'm brainy."

"So?"

"Uh-huh. Look— I've figured out what to do with friend Hoag."

"Hoag? Oh, dear!"

"Look out—you'll spill it!" He took the glass from

her and set it down. "Don't be silly, babe. What's gotten into you?"

"I don't know, Teddy. I just feel as if we were tackling the kingpin of Cicero with a pea shooter."

"I shouldn't have talked business before breakfast. Have your coffee—you'll feel better."

"All right. No toast for me, Teddy. What's your brilliant idea?"

"It's this," he explained, while crunching toast. "Yesterday we tried to keep out of his sight in order not to shake him back into his nighttime personality. Right?"

"Uh-huh."

"Well, today we don't have to. We can stick to him like a leech, both of us, practically arm in arm. If it interferes with the daytime half of his personality, it doesn't matter, because we can lead him to the Acme Building. Once there, habit will take him where he usually goes. Am I right?"

"I don't know, Teddy. Maybe. Amnesia personalities are funny things. He might just drift into a confused state."

"You don't think it will work?"

"Maybe it will, maybe it won't. But as long as you plan for us to stay close together, I'm willing to try it —if you won't give up the whole matter."

He ignored the condition she placed on it. "Fine. I'll give the old buzzard a ring and tell him to wait for us at his apartment." He reached across the breakfast table and grabbed the phone, dialed it and talked with Hoag. "He's certainly a June bug, that one," he said as he put the phone down. "At first he couldn't place me at all. Then all of a sudden he seemed to click and everything was all right. Ready to go, Cyn?"

"Half a sec."

"O. K." He got up and went into the living room, whistling softly.

The whistling broke off; he came quickly back into the kitchen. "Cyn—"

"What's the matter, Teddy?"

"Come into the living room—please!"

She hurried to do so, suddenly apprehensive at the

sight of his face. He pointed to a straight chair which
had been pulled over to a point directly under the
mirror near the outer door. "Cyn—how did that get
where it is?"

"That chair? Why, I pulled a chair over there to
straighten the mirror just before I went to bed. I must
have left it there."

"Mm-m-m— I suppose you must have. Funny I
didn't notice it when I turned out the light."

"Why does it worry you? Think somebody might
have gotten into the apartment last night?"

"Yeah. Yeah, sure—that's what I was thinking." But
his brow was still wrinkled.

Cynthia looked at him, then went back into the bedroom. There she gathered up her purse, went through
it rapidly, then opened a small, concealed drawer in
her dressing table. "If anyone *did* manage to get in,
they didn't get much. Got your wallet? Everything in
it? How about your watch?"

He made a quick check and reported, "They're all
right. You must have left the chair there and I just
didn't notice it. Ready to go?"

"Be right with you."

He said no more about it. Privately he was thinking
what an involved mess a few subconscious memories
and a club sandwich just before turning in could make.
He must have noticed the chair just before turning out
the light—hence its appearance in the nightmare. He
dismissed the matter.

V

Hoag was waiting for them. "Come in," he said. "Come
in. Welcome, madame, to my little hide-away. Will you
sit down? Have we time for a cup of tea? I'm afraid,"
he added apologetically, "that I haven't coffee in the
house."

"I guess we have," agreed Randall. "Yesterday you
left the house at eight fifty-three and it's only eight

thirty-five now. I think we ought to leave at the same time."

"Good." Hoag bustled away, to return at once with a tea service on a tray, which he placed on a table at Cynthia's knees. "Will you pour, Mrs. Randall? It's Chinese tea," he added. "My own blend."

"I'd be pleased." He did not look at all sinister this morning, she was forced to admit. He was just a fussy little bachelor with worry lines around his eyes—and a most exquisite apartment. His pictures were good, just how good she had not the training to tell, but they looked like originals. There were not too many of them, either, she noticed with approval. Arty little bachelors were usually worse than old maids for crowding a room full of too much.

Not Mr. Hoag's flat. It had an airy perfection to it as pleasing, in its way, as a Brahms waltz. She wanted to ask him where he had gotten his drapes.

He accepted a cup of tea from her, cradled it in his hand and sniffed the aroma before sipping from it. He then turned to Randall. "I'm afraid, sir, that we are off on a wild-goose chase this morning."

"Perhaps. Why do you think so?"

"Well, you see, I really am at a loss as to what to do next. Your telephone call— I was preparing my morning tea—I don't keep a servant—as usual, when you called. I suppose I am more or less in a brown fog in the early mornings—absent-minded, you know, just doing the things one does when one gets up, making one's toilet and all that with one's thoughts elsewhere. When you telephoned I was quite bemused and it took me a moment to recall who you were and what business we had with each other. In a way the conversation cleared my head, made me consciously aware of myself, that is to say, but now—" He shrugged helplessly. "Now I haven't the slightest idea of what I am to do next."

Randall nodded. "I had that possibility in mind when I phoned you. I don't claim to be a psychologist but it seemed possible that your transition from your nighttime self to your daytime self took place as you left your apartment and that any interruption in your routine might throw you off."

"Then why—"

"It won't matter. You see, we shadowed you yesterday; we know where you go."

"You *do?* Tell me, sir! Tell me."

"Not so fast. We lost track of you at the last minute. What I had in mind is this: We could guide you along the same track, right up to the point where we lost track of you yesterday. At that point I am hoping that your habitual routine will carry you on through—and we will be in right at your heels.

"You say 'we.' Does Mrs. Randall assist you in this?"

Randall hesitated, realizing that he had been caught out in a slight prevarication. Cynthia moved in and took over the ball.

"Not ordinarily, Mr. Hoag, but this seemed like an exceptional case. We felt that you would not enjoy having your private affairs looked into by the ordinary run of hired operator, so Mr. Randall has undertaken to attend to your case personally, with my help when necessary."

"Oh, I say, that's awfully kind of you!"

"Not at all."

"But it is—it is. But, uh, in that case—I wonder if I have paid you enough. Do not the services of the head of the firm come a little higher?"

Hoag was looking at Cynthia; Randall signaled to her an emphatic "Yes"—which she chose to ignore. "What you have already paid, Mr. Hoag, seems sufficient. If additional involvements come up later, we can discuss them then."

"I suppose so." He paused and pulled at his lower lip. "I do appreciate your thoughtfulness in keeping my affairs to yourselves. I shouldn't like—" He turned suddenly to Randall. "Tell me—what would your attitude be if it should develop that my daytime life is—scandalous?" The word seemed to hurt him.

"I can keep scandal to myself."

"Suppose it were worse than that. Suppose it were —criminal. Beastly."

Randall stopped to choose his words. "I am licensed by the State of Illinois. Under that license I am obliged to regard myself as a special police officer in a limited sense. I certainly could not cover up any major felony. But it's not my business to turn clients in for any ordinary peccadillo. I can assure you that it would have to be something pretty serious for me to be willing to turn over a client to the police."

"But you can't assure me that you would *not* do so?"

"No," he said flatly.

Hoag sighed. "I suppose I'll just have to trust to your good judgment." He held up his right hand and looked at his nails. "No. No, I can't risk it. Mr. Randall, suppose you did find something you did not approve of —couldn't you just call me up and tell me that you were dropping the case?"

"No."

He covered his eyes and did not answer at once. When he did his voice was barely audible. "You've found nothing—yet?" Randall shook his head. "Then perhaps it is wiser to drop the matter now. Some things are better never known."

His evident distress and helplessness, combined with the favorable impression his apartment had made on her, aroused in Cynthia a sympathy which she would have thought impossible the evening before. She leaned toward him. "Why should you be so distressed, Mr. Hoag? You have no reason to think that you have done anything to be afraid of—have you?"

"No. No, nothing really. Nothing but an overpowering apprehension."

"But why?"

"Mrs. Randall, have you ever heard a noise behind you and been afraid to look around? Have you ever awakened in the night and kept your eyes tightly shut rather than find out what it was that had startled you? Some evils reach their full effect only when acknowledged and faced.

"I don't dare face this one," he added. "I thought that I did, but I was mistaken."

"Come now," she said kindly, "facts are never as bad as our fears—"

"Why do you say so? Why shouldn't they be much worse?"

"Why, because they just aren't." She stopped, suddenly conscious that her Pollyanna saying had no truth in it, that it was the sort of thing adults use to pacify children. She thought of her own mother, who had gone to the hospital, fearing an appendectomy—which her friends and loving family privately diagnosed as hypochondria—there to *die,* of cancer.

No, the facts were frequently worse than our most nervous fears.

Still, she could not agree with him. "Suppose we look at it in the worst possible light," she suggested. "Suppose you *have* been doing something criminal, while in your memory lapses. No court in the State would hold you legally responsible for your actions."

He looked at her wildly. "No. No, perhaps they would not. But you know what they would do? You do, don't you? Have you any idea what they do with the criminally insane?"

"I certainly do," she answered positively. "They receive the same treatment as any other psycho patient. They aren't discriminated against. I know; I've done field work at the State Hospital."

"Suppose you have—you looked at it from the *outside.* Have you any idea what it feels like from the inside? Have you ever been placed in a wet pack? Have you ever had a guard put you to bed? Or force you to eat? Do you know what it's like to have a key turned in a lock every time you make a move? Never to have *any* privacy no matter how much you need it?"

He got up and began to pace. "But that isn't the worst of it. It's the other patients. Do you imagine that a man, simply because his own mind is playing him tricks, doesn't recognize insanity in others? Some of them drool and some of them have habits too beastly to tell of. And they talk, they talk, they *talk.* Can you imagine lying in a bed, with the sheet bound down, and a *thing* in the next bed that keeps repeating, 'The little bird flew up and then flew away; the little bird flew up and then flew away; the little bird flew up, and then flew away—' "

"Mr. Hoag!" Randall stood up and took him by the arm. "Mr. Hoag—control yourself! That's no way to behave."

Hoag stopped, looking bewildered. He looked from one face to the other and an expression of shame came over him. "I . . . I'm sorry, Mrs. Randall," he said. "I quite forgot myself. I'm not myself today. All this worry—"

"It's all right, Mr. Hoag," she said stiffly. But her earlier revulsion had returned.

"It's not entirely all right," Randall amended. "I think the time has come to get a number of things cleared up. There has been entirely too much going on that I don't understand and I think it is up to you, Mr. Hoag, to give me a few plain answers."

The little man seemed honestly at a loss. "I surely will, Mr. Randall, if there is anything I can answer. Do you feel that I have not been frank with you?"

"I certainly do. First—when were you in a hospital for the criminally insane?"

"Why, I never was. At least, I don't *think* I ever was. I don't remember being in one."

"Then why all this hysterical balderdash you have been spouting the past five minutes? Were you just making it up?"

"Oh, no! That . . . that was . . . that referred to St. George Rest Home. It had nothing to do with a . . . with such a hospital."

"St. George Rest Home, eh? We'll come back to that. Mr. Hoag, tell me what happened yesterday."

"Yesterday? During the day? But Mr. Randall, you *know* I can't tell you what happened during the day."

"*I* think you can. There has been some damnable skulduggery going on and you're the center of it. When you stopped me in front of the Acme Building—*what did you say to me?*"

"The Acme Building? I know nothing of the Acme Building. Was I there?"

"You're damned right you were there and you pulled

some sort of a shenanigan on me, drugged me or doped me, or something. *Why?"*

Hoag looked from Randall's implacable face to that of his wife. But her face was impassive; she was having none of it. He turned hopelessly back to Randall. "Mr. Randall, believe me—I don't know what you are talking about. I may have been at the Acme Building. If I were and if I did anything to you, I know nothing of it."

His words were so grave, so solemnly sincere in their sound that Randall was unsettled in his own conviction. And yet—damn it, *somebody* had led him up an alley. He shifted his approach. "Mr. Hoag, if you have been as sincere with me as you claim to be, you won't mind what I'm going to do next." He drew from the inner pocket of his coat a silver cigarette case, opened it, and polished the mirrorlike inner surface of the cover with his handkerchief. "Now, Mr. Hoag, if you please."

"What do you want?"

"I want your fingerprints."

Hoag looked startled, swallowed a couple of times, and said in a low voice, "Why should you want my fingerprints?"

"Why not? If you haven't done anything, it can't do any harm, can it?"

"You're going to turn me over to the police!"

"I haven't any reason to. I haven't anything on you. Let's have your prints."

"No!"

Randall got up, stepped toward Hoag and stood over him. "How would you like both your arms broken?" he said savagely.

Hoag looked at him and cringed, but he did not offer his hands for prints. He huddled himself together, face averted and his hands drawn in tight to his chest.

Randall felt a touch on his arm. "That's enough, Teddy. Let's get out of here."

Hoag looked up. "Yes," he said huskily. "Get out. Don't come back."

"Come on, Teddy."

"I will in a moment. I'm not quite through. Mr. Hoag!"

Hoag met his eye as if it were a major effort.

"Mr. Hoag, you've mentioned St. George Rest Home twice as being your old *alma mater*. I just wanted you to know that *I* know that there is no such place!"

Again Hoag looked genuinely startled. "But there is," he insisted. "Wasn't I there for— At least they told me that was its name," he added doubtfully.

"Humph!" Randall turned toward the door. "Come on, Cynthia."

Once they were alone in the elevator she turned to him. "How did you happen to play it that way, Teddy?"

"Because," he said bitterly, "while I don't mind opposition, it makes me sore when my own client crosses me up. He dished us a bunch of lies, and obstructed us, and pulled some kind of sleight of hand on me in that Acme Building deal. I don't like for a client to pull stunts like that; I don't need their money that bad."

"Well," she sighed, "I, for one, will be very happy to give it back to him. I'm glad it's over."

"What do you mean, 'give it back to him'? I'm not going to give it back to him; I'm going to earn it."

The car had arrived at the ground floor by now, but she did not touch the gate. "Teddy! What do you mean?"

"He hired me to find out what he does. Well, damn it, I'm going to *find* out—with or without his co-operation."

He waited for her to answer, but she did not. "Well," he said defensively, "you don't have to have anything to do with it."

"If you are going on with it, I certainly am. Remember what you promised me?"

"What did I promise?" he asked, with a manner of complete innocence.

"*You* know."

"But look here, Cyn—all I'm going to do is to hang

around until he comes out, and then tail him. It may take all day. He may decide not to come out."

"All right. I'll wait with you."

"Somebody has to look out for the office."

"You look out for the office," she suggested. "I'll shadow Hoag."

"Now that's ridiculous. You——" The car started to move upward. "Woops! Somebody wants to use it." He jabbed the button marked "Stop," then pushed the one which returned the car to the ground floor. This time they did not wait inside; he immediately opened the gate and the door.

Adjacent to the entrance of the apartment house was a little lounge or waiting room. He guided her into it. "Now let's get this settled," he commenced.

"It *is* settled."

"O.K., you win. Let's get ourselves staked out."

"How about right here? We can sit down and he can't possibly get out without us seeing him."

"O.K."

The elevator had gone up immediately after they had quitted it; soon they heard the typical clanging grunt which announced its return to the ground floor. "On your toes, kid."

She nodded and drew back into the shadows of the lounge. He placed himself so that he could see the elevator door by reflection in an ornamental mirror hanging in the lounge. "Is it Hoag?" she whispered.

"No," he answered in a low voice, "it's a bigger man. It looks like——" He shut up suddenly and grabbed her wrist.

Past the open door of the lounge she saw the hurrying form of Jonathan Hoag go by. The figure did not turn its eyes in their direction but went directly through the outer door. When it swung closed Randall relaxed the hold on her wrist. "I darn near muffed that one," he admitted.

"What happened?"

"Don' know. Bum glass in the mirror. Distortion. Tallyho, kid."

They reached the door as their quarry got to the sidewalk and, as on the day before, turned to the left.

Randall paused uncertainly. "I think we'll take a chance on him seeing us. I don't want to lose him."

"Couldn't we follow him just as effectively in a cab? If he gets on a bus where he did before, we'll be better off than we would be trying to get on it with him." She did not admit, even to herself, that she was trying to keep them away from Hoag.

"No, he might not take a bus. Come on."

They had no difficulty in following him; he was heading down the street at a brisk, but not a difficult, pace. When he came to the bus stop where he had gotten on the day before, he purchased a paper and sat down on the bench. Randall and Cynthia passed behind him and took shelter in a shop entrance.

When the bus came he went up to the second deck as before; they got on and remained on the lower level. "Looks like he was going right where he went yesterday," Randall commented. "We'll get him today, kid."

She did not answer.

When the bus approached the stop near the Acme Building they were ready and waiting—but Hoag failed to come down the steps. The bus started up again with a jerk; they sat back down. "What do you suppose he is up to?" Randall fretted. "Do you suppose he saw us?"

"Maybe he gave us the slip," Cynthia suggested hopefully.

"How? By jumping off the top of the bus? Hm-m-m!"

"Not quite, but you're close. If another bus pulled alongside us at a stop light, he could have done it by stepping across, over the railing. I saw a man do that once. If you do it toward the rear, you stand a good chance of getting away with it entirely."

He considered the matter. "I'm pretty sure no bus has pulled up by us. Still, he could do it to the top of a truck, too, though Lord knows how he would get off again." He fidgeted. "Tell you what—I'm going back to the stairs and sneak a look."

"And meet him coming down? Be your age, Brain."

He subsided; the bus went on a few blocks. "Coming to our own corner," he remarked.

She nodded, naturally having noticed as soon as he did that they were approaching the corner nearest the building in which their own office was located. She took out her compact and powdered her nose, a routine she had followed eight times since getting on the bus. The little mirror made a handy periscope whereby to watch the passengers getting off the rear of the bus. "There he is, Teddy!"

Randall was up out of his seat at once and hurrying down the aisle, waving at the conductor. The conductor looked annoyed but signaled the driver not to start. "Why don't you watch the streets?" he asked.

"Sorry, buddy. I'm a stranger here myself. Come on, Cyn."

Their man was just turning into the door of the building housing their own office. Randall stopped. "Something screwy about this, kid."

"What do we do?"

"Follow him," he decided.

They hurried on; he was not in the lobby. The Midway-Copton is not a large building, nor swank—else they could not have rented there. It has but two elevators. One was down and empty; the other, by the indicator, had just started up.

Randall stepped up to the open car, but did not enter. "Jimmie," he said, "how many passengers in that other car?"

"Two," the elevator pilot answered.

"Sure?"

"Yeah. I was breezin' with Bert when he closed the door. Mr. Harrison and another bird. Why?"

Randall passed him a quarter. "Never mind," he said, his eyes on the slowly turning arrow of the indicator. "What floor does Mr. Harrison go to?"

"Seven." The arrow had just stopped at seven.

"Swell." The arrow started up again, moved slowly past eight and nine, stopped at ten. Randall hustled Cynthia into the car. "Our floor, Jimmie," he snapped, "and step on it!"

An "up" signal flashed from the fourth floor; Jimmie

reached for his controls; Randall grabbed his arm. "Skip it this time, Jim."

The operator shrugged and complied with the request.

The corridor facing the elevators on the tenth floor was empty. Randall saw this at once and turned to Cynthia. "Give a quick gander down the other wing, Cyn," he said, and headed to the right, in the direction of their office.

Cynthia did so, with no particular apprehension. She was sure in her own mind that, having come this far, Hoag was certainly heading for their office. But she was in the habit of taking direction from Teddy when they were actually doing something; if he wanted the other corridor looked at, she would obey, of course.

The floor plan was in the shape of a capital H, with the elevators located centrally on the cross bar. She turned to the left to reach the other wing, then glanced to the left—no one in that alley. She turned around and faced the other way—no one down there. It occurred to her that just possibly Hoag could have stepped out on the fire escape; as a matter of fact the fire escape was in the direction she had first looked, toward the rear of the building—but habit played a trick on her; she was used to the other wing in which their office was located, in which, naturally, everything was swapped right for left from the way in which it was laid out in this wing.

She had taken three or four steps toward the end of the corridor facing the street when she realized her mistake—the open window certainly had no fire escape beyond it. With a little exclamation of impatience at her own stupidity she turned back.

Hoag was standing just behind her.

She gave a most unprofessional squeak.

Hoag smiled with his lips. "Ah, Mrs. Randall!"

She said nothing—she could think of nothing to say. There was a .32 pistol in her handbag; she felt a wild desire to snatch it out and fire. On two occasions, at a time when she was working as a decoy for the narcotics squad, she had been commended officially for her calm courage in a dangerous pinch—she felt no such calm now.

He took a step toward her. "You wanted to see me, did you not?"

She gave way a step. "No," she said breathlessly. "No!"

"Ah, but you did. You expected to find me at your office, but I chose to meet you—here!"

The corridor was deserted; she could not even hear a sound of typing or conversation from any of the offices around them. The glazed doors stared sightlessly; the only sounds, other than their own sparse words, were the street noises ten stories below, muted, remote and unhelpful.

He came closer. "You wanted to take my fingerprints, didn't you? You wanted to check them—find out things about me. You and your meddlesome husband."

"Get away from me!"

He continued to smile. "Come, now. You wanted my fingerprints—you shall have them." He raised his arms toward her and spread his fingers, reaching. She backed away from the clutching hands. He no longer seemed small; he seemed taller, and broader—bigger than Teddy. His eyes stared down at her.

Her heel struck something behind her; she knew that she had backed to the very end of the passage—dead end.

His hands came closer. "Teddy!" she screamed. "Oh, Teddy!"

Teddy was bending over her, slapping her face. "Stop that," she said indignantly. "It hurts!"

He gave a sigh of relief. "Gee, honey," he said tenderly. "You sure gave me a turn. You've been out for minutes."

"Unnnh!"

"Do you know where I found you? There!" He pointed to the spot just under the open window. "If you hadn't fallen just right, you would have been hamburger by now. What happened? Lean out and get dizzy?"

"Didn't you catch him?"

He looked at her admiringly. "Always the professional! No, but I damn near did. I saw him, from down the corridor. I watched a moment to see what he was up to. If you hadn't screamed, I would have had him."

"If I *hadn't* screamed?"

"Sure. He was in front of our office door, apparently trying to pick the lock, when—"

"*Who* was?"

He looked at her in surprise. "Why, Hoag, of course —*Baby!* Snap out of it! You aren't going to faint again, are you?"

She took a deep breath. "I'm all right," she said grimly, "—now. Just as long as you're here. Take me to the office."

"Shall I carry you?"

"No, just give me your hand." He helped her up and brushed at her dress. "Never mind that now." But she did stop to moisten, ineffectively, a long run in what had been until that moment brand-new stockings.

He let them into the office and sat her carefully in an armchair, then fetched a wet towel with which he bathed her face. "Feel better?"

"I'm all right—physically. But I want to get something straight. You say you saw Hoag trying to get into this office?"

"Yeah. Damned good thing we've special locks."

"This was going on when I screamed?"

"Yeah, sure."

She drummed on the arms of the chair.

" 'S matter, Cyn?"

"Nothing. Nothing at all—only this: The reason I screamed was because Hoag was trying to choke me!"

It took him some time even to say, "Hunh?"

She replied, "Yes, I know, darling. That's how it is and it's nuts. Somehow or other, he's done it to us again. But I swear to you that he was about to choke me. Or I thought he was." She rehearsed her experience, in detail. "What does it add up to?"

"I wish I knew," he told her, rubbing his face. "I wish I did. If it hadn't been for that business in the

Acme Building, I would say that you were sick and had fainted and when you came to you were still kinda lightheaded. But now I don't know which one of us is batty. I surely thought I saw him."

"Maybe we're both crazy. It might be a good idea if we both went to see a good psychiatrist."

"Both of us? Can two people go crazy the same way? Wouldn't it be one or the other of us?"

"Not necessarily. It's rare, but it does happen. *Folie à deux.*"

"Folee adooh?"

"Contagious insanity. Their weak points match up and they make each other crazier." She thought of the cases she had studied and recalled that usually one was dominant and the other subordinate, but she decided not to bring it up, as she had her own opinion as to who was dominant in their family, an opinion kept private for reasons of policy.

"Maybe," Randall said thoughtfully, "what we need is a nice, long rest. Down on the Gulf, maybe, where we could lie around in the sunshine."

"That," she said, "is a good idea in any case. Why in the world anyone chooses to live in a dismal, dirty, ugly spot like Chicago is beyond me."

"How much money have we?"

"About eight hundred dollars, after the bills and taxes are paid. And there's the five hundred from Hoag, if you want to count that."

"I think we've earned it," he said grimly. "Say! *Do* we have that money? Maybe that was a hoax, too."

"You mean maybe there never was any Mr. Hoag and pretty soon the nurse will be in to bring us our nice supper."

"Mm-m-m—that's the general idea. Have you got it?"

"I *think* I have. Wait a minute." She opened her purse, in turn opened a zippered compartment, and felt in it. "Yes, it's here. Pretty green bills. Let's take that vacation, Teddy. I don't know why we stay in Chicago, anyway."

"Because the business is here," he said practically.

"Coffee and cakes. Which reminds me, slaphappy or not, I'd better see what calls have come in." He reached across her desk for the phone; his eye fell on a sheet of paper in her typewriter. He was silent for a moment, then said in a strained voice, "Come here, Cyn. Take a look at this."

She got up at once, came around and looked over his shoulder. What she saw was one of their letter-heads, rolled into the typewriter; on it was a single line of typing:

CURIOSITY KILLED THE CAT.

She said nothing at all and tried to control the quivering at the pit of her stomach.

Randall asked, "Cyn, did you write that?"

"No."

"Positive?"

"Yes." She reached out to take it out of the machine; he checked her.

"Don't touch it. Fingerprints."

"All right. But I have a notion," she said, "that you won't find any fingerprints on *that*."

"Maybe not."

Nevertheless, he took his outfit out of the lower drawer of his desk and dusted the paper and the machine—with negative results on each. There were not even prints of Cynthia to confuse the matter; she had a business-college neatness in her office habits and made a practice of brushing and wiping her typewriter at the end of each day.

While watching him work she remarked, "Looks as if you saw him getting *out* rather than *in*."

"Huh? How?"

"Picked the lock, I suppose."

"Not that lock. You forget, baby, that that lock is one of Mr. Yale's proudest achievements. You could break it, maybe, but you couldn't pick it."

She made no answer—she could think of none. He stared moodily at the typewriter as if it should tell him what had happened, then straightened up, gathered up his gear, and returned it to its proper drawer. "The whole thing stinks," he said, and commenced to pace the room.

Cynthia took a rag from her own desk and wiped the print powder from the machine, then sat down and watched him. She held her tongue while he fretted with the matter. Her expression was troubled but she was not worried for herself—nor was it entirely maternal. Rather was she worried for them.

"Cyn," he said suddenly, "this has got to stop!"

"All right," she agreed. "Let's stop it."

"How?"

"Let's take that vacation."

He shook his head. "I can't run away from it. I've got to know."

She sighed. "I'd rather not know. What's wrong with running away from something too big for us to fight?"

He stopped and looked at her. "What's come over you, Cyn? You never went chicken before."

"No," she answered slowly, "I never did. But I never had reason to. Look at me, Teddy—you know I'm not a *female* female. I don't expect you to pick fights in restaurants when some lug tries to pick me up. I don't scream at the sight of blood and I don't expect you to clean up your language to fit my ladylike ears. As for the job, did I ever let you down on a case? Through timidity, I mean. Did I ever?"

"Hell, no. I didn't say you did."

"But this is a different case. I had a gun in my bag a few minutes ago, but I couldn't use it. Don't ask me why. I *couldn't*."

He swore, with emphasis and considerable detail. "I wish I had seen him then. I would have used mine!"

"Would you have, Teddy?" Seeing his expression, she jumped up and kissed him suddenly, on the end of his nose. "I don't mean you would have been afraid. You know I didn't mean that. You're brave and you're strong and *I* think you're brainy. But look, dear— yesterday he led you around by the nose and made you believe you were seeing things that weren't there. Why didn't you use your gun then?"

"I didn't see any occasion to use it."

"That's exactly what I mean. You saw what was intended for you to see. How can you fight when you can't believe your own eyes?"

"But, damn it, he can't do this to us—"

"*Can't* he? Here's what he *can* do." She ticked them off on her fingers. "He can be two places at once. He can make you see one thing and me another, at the same time—outside the Acme Building, remember? He can make you think you went to an office suite that doesn't exist on a floor that doesn't exist. He can pass through a locked door to use a typewriter on the other side. And he doesn't leave fingerprints. What does that add up to?"

He made an impatient gesture. "To nonsense. Or to magic. And I don't believe in magic."

"Neither do I."

"Then," he said, "we've both gone bats." He laughed, but it was not merry.

"Maybe. If it's magic, we had best see a priest—"

"I told you I don't believe in magic."

"Skip it. If it's the other, it won't do us any good to try to tail Mr. Hoag. A man with the D.T.'s can't catch the snakes he thinks he sees and take them to a zoo. He needs a doctor—and maybe we do, too."

Randall was suddenly alert. "Say!"

"Say what?"

"You've just reminded me of an angle that I had forgotten—Hoag's doctor. We never checked on *him*."

"Yes, you did, too. Don't you remember? There wasn't any such doctor."

"I don't mean Dr. Rennault; I mean Dr. Potbury —the one he went to see about the stuff under his fingernails."

"Do you think he really did that? I thought it was just part of the string of lies he told us."

"So do I. But we ought to check up on it."

"I'll bet you there isn't any such doctor."

"You're probably right, but we ought to *know*. Gimme the phone book." She handed it to him; he thumbed through it, searching for the P's. "Potbury— Potbury. There's half a column of them. But no M.D.'s, though," he announced presently. "Let's have the yellow section; sometimes doctors don't list their home addresses." She got it for him and he opened it. " 'Physical Culture Studios'—'Physicians & Surgeons." What a slog of 'em! More doctors than saloons—half the town must be sick most of the time. Here we are: 'Potbury, P.T., M.D.' "

"That *could* be the one," she admitted.

"What are we waiting for? Let's go find out."

"Teddy!"

"Why not?" he said defensively. "Potbury isn't Hoag—"

"I wonder."

"Huh? What do you mean? Do you mean that Potbury might be mixed up in this huggermugger, too?"

"I don't know. I'd just like to forget all about our Mr. Hoag."

"But there's no harm in this, bright eyes. I'll just pop into the car, slide down there, ask the worthy doctor a few pertinent questions, and be back for you in time for lunch."

"The car is laid up for a valve grind; you know that."

"O.K., I'll take the el. Quicker, anyway."

"If you insist on going, we'll both take the el. We stick together, Teddy."

He pulled at his lip. "Maybe you're right. We don't know where Hoag is. If you prefer it—"

"I certainly do. I got separated from you for just three minutes a little while ago and look what happened."

"Yeah, I guess so. I sure wouldn't want anything to happen to you, kid."

She brushed it away. "It's not me; it's *us*. If anything happens to us, I want it to be the same thing."

"All right," he said seriously. "From now on, we stick together. I'll handcuff us together, if you'd rather."

"You won't need to. I'm going to hang on."

VI

Potbury's office was to the south, beyond the university. The tracks of the elevated ran between familiar miles

of apartment houses. There were sights which one ordinarily sees without any impression registering on the
brain; today she looked at them and saw them, through
her own brown mood.

Four- and five-story walk-up apartment houses, with
their backs to the tracks, at least ten families to a
building, more usually twenty or more, and the buildings crushed together almost wall to wall. Wood-con-
struction back porches which proclaimed the fire-trap
nature of the warrens despite the outer brick shells,
family wash hung out to dry on those porches, garbage
cans, and trash bins. Mile after mile of undignified and
unbeautiful squalor, seen from the rear.

And over everything a film of black grime, old and
inescapable, like the dirt on the window sill beside her.

She thought of that vacation, clean air and clear
sunshine. Why stay in Chicago? What did the town
have to justify its existence? One decent boulevard, one
decent suburb to the north, priced for the rich, two
universities and a lake. As for the rest, endless miles of
depressing, dirty streets. The town was one big stock-
yard.

The apartments gave way to elevated-train yards;
the train turned left and headed east. After a few
minutes they got off at Stoney Island station; she was
glad to be off it and free of that too-frank back view
of everyday life, even though she exchanged it for the
noise and seedy commercialism of Sixty-third Street.

Potbury's office faced on the street, with an excellent
view of the elevated and the trains. It was the sort of
location in which a G. P. could be sure of a busy
practice and equally sure of never being bothered by
riches or fame. The stuffy little waiting room was
crowded but the turnover was fast; they did not have
long to wait.

Potbury looked them over as they came in. "Which
one of you is the patient?" he asked. His manner was
slightly testy.

They had planned to lead up to the subject of Hoag
by using Cynthia's fainting spell as an excuse for consultation; Potbury's next remark queered the scheme,
from Cynthia's viewpoint. "Whichever one it is, the

other can wait outside. I don't like holding conventions."

"My wife——" Randall began. She clutched his arm.

"My wife and I," he went on smoothly, "want to ask you a couple of questions, doctor."

"Well? Speak up."

"You have a patient——a Mr. Hoag."

Potbury got up hastily, went to the reception-room door, and assured himself that it was closed tightly. He then stood and faced them, his back to the only exit. "What about——Hoag?" he said forebodingly.

Randall produced his credentials. "You can see for yourself that I am a proper inquiry agent," he said. "My wife is licensed, too."

"What do you have to do with——the man you mentioned?"

"We are conducting an investigation for him. Being a professional man yourself, you can appreciate that I prefer to be frank——"

"You *work* for him?"

"Yes and no. Specifically, we are trying to find out certain things about him, but he is aware that we are doing so; we aren't going around behind his back. If you like, you can phone him and find out for yourself." Randall made the suggestion because it seemed necessary to make it; he hoped that Potbury would disregard it.

Potbury did so, but not in any reassuring manner. "Talk with *him?* Not if I can help it! What did you want to know about him?"

"A few days ago," Randall said carefully, "Hoag brought to you a substance to be analyzed. I want to find out what that substance was."

"Hrrumph! You reminded me a moment ago that we were both professional men; I am surprised that you should make such a request."

"I appreciate your viewpoint, doctor, and I know that a doctor's knowledge of his patients is privileged. But in this case there is——"

"You wouldn't want to know!"

Randall considered this. "I've seen a good deal of the seamy side of life, doctor, and I don't think there is anything that can shock me any more. Do you hesitate to tell me in Mrs. Randall's presence?"

Potbury looked him over quizzically, then surveyed Mrs. Randall. "You look like decent enough people," he conceded. "I suppose you do think you are beyond being shocked. But let me give you some advice. Apparently you are connected in some way with this man. *Stay away from him!* Don't have anything to do with him. And don't ask me what he had under his finger-nails."

Cynthia suppressed a start. She had been keeping out of the conversation but following it carefully. As she remembered it, Teddy had made no mention of fingernails.

"Why, doctor?" Randall continued insistently.

Potbury was beginning to be annoyed. "You are a rather stupid young man, sir. Let me tell you this: If you know no more of this person than you appear to know, then you have no conception of the depths of beastliness possible in this world. In that you are lucky. It is much, much better never to know."

Randall hesitated, aware that the debate was going against him. Then he said, "Supposing you are right, doctor—how is it, if he is so vicious, you have not turned Hoag over to the police?"

"How do you know I haven't? But I will answer that one, sir. No, I have not turned him over to the police, for the simple reason that it would do no good. The authorities have not had the wit nor the imagination to conceive of the possibility of the peculiar evil involved. No law can touch him—not in this day and age."

"What do you mean, 'not in this day and age'?"

"Nothing. Disregard it. The subject is closed. You said something about your wife when you came in; did she wish to consult me about something?"

"It was nothing," Cynthia said hastily. "Nothing of importance."

"Just a pretext, eh?" He smiled almost jovially. "What was it?"

"Nothing. I fainted earlier today. But I'm all right now."

"Hm-m-m. You're not expecting, are you? Your eyes don't look like it. You look sound enough. A little anemic, perhaps. Fresh air and sunshine wouldn't do any harm." He moved away from them and opened a white cabinet on the far wall; he busied himself with bottles for a moment. Presently he returned with a medicine glass filled with amber-brown liquid. "Here —drink this."

"What is it?"

"A tonic. It contains just enough of What Made the Preacher Dance to make you enjoy it."

Still she hesitated, looking to her husband. Potbury noticed it and remarked, "Don't like to drink alone, eh? Well, one wouldn't do us any harm, either." He returned to the cabinet and came back with two more medicine glasses, one of which he handed to Randall. "Here's to forgetting all unpleasant matters," he said. "Drink up!" He lifted his own glass to his lips and tossed it off.

Randall drank, Cynthia followed suit. It was not bad stuff, she thought. Something a little bitter in it, but the whiskey—it *was* whiskey, she concluded—covered up the taste. A bottle of that tonic might not do you any real good but it would make you feel better.

Potbury ushered them out. "If you have another fainting spell, Mrs. Randall, come back and see me and we'll give you a thorough going over. In the meantime, don't worry about matters you can't help."

They took the last car of the train in returning and were able to pick a seat far away enough from other passengers for them to talk freely. "Whatja make of it?" he asked, as soon as they were seated.

She wrinkled her brow. "I don't know, quite. He certainly doesn't like Mr. Hoag, but he never said why."

"Um-m-m."

"What do you make of it, Teddy?"

"First, Potbury knows Hoag. Second, Potbury is very anxious that we know nothing about Hoag. Third, Potbury hates Hoag—and is afraid of him!"

"Huh? How do you figure that out?"

He smiled maddeningly. "Use the little gray cells, my sweet. I think I'm on to friend Potbury—and if he thinks he can scare me out of looking into what Hoag does with his spare time he's got another think coming!"

Wisely, she decided not to argue it with him just then—they had been married quite some time.

At her request they went home instead of back to the office. "I don't feel up to it. Teddy. If *he* wants to play with my typewriter, let him!"

"Still feeling rocky from the Brodie you pulled?" he asked anxiously.

"Kinda."

She napped most of the afternoon. The tonic, she reflected, that Dr. Potbury had given her did not seem to have done her any good—left her dizzy, if anything, and with a furry taste in her mouth.

Randall let her sleep. He fiddled around the apartment for a few minutes, set up his dart board and tried to develop an underhand shot, then desisted when it occurred to him that it might wake Cynthia. He looked in on her and found that she was resting peacefully. He decided that she might like a can of beer when she woke up—it was a good excuse to go out; he wanted a beer himself. Bit of a headache, nothing much, but he hadn't felt really chipper since he left the doctor's office. A couple of beers would fix it up.

There was a taproom just this side of the nearest delicatessen. Randall decided to stop for one on draught before returning. Presently he found himself explaining to the proprietor just *why* the reform amalgamation would never turn out the city machine.

He recalled, as he left the place, his original intention. When he got back to their apartment, laden with beer and assorted cold cuts, Cynthia was up and making domestic noises in the kitchen. "Hi, babe!"

"Teddy!"

He kissed her before he put down the packages. "Were you scared when you woke up and found me gone?"

"Not really. But I would rather you had left a note. What have you got there?"

"Suds and cold cuts. Like?"

"Swell. I didn't want to go out for dinner and I was trying to see what I could stir up. But I hadn't any meat in the house." She took them from him.

"Anybody call?"

"Huh-uh. I called the exchange when I woke up. Nothing of interest. But the mirror came."

"Mirror?"

"Don't play innocent. It was a nice surprise, Teddy. Come see how it dresses up the bedroom."

"Let's get this straight," he said. "I don't know anything about a mirror."

She paused, puzzled. "I thought you bought it for me for a surprise. It came prepaid."

"Whom was it addressed to; you or me?"

"I didn't pay much attention; I was half asleep. I just signed something and they unpacked it and hung it for me."

It was a very handsome piece of glass, beveled plate, without a frame, and quite large. Randall conceded that it did things for her dressing table. "If you want a glass like that, honey, I'll get one for you. But this isn't ours. I suppose I'd better call up somebody and tell 'em to take it back. Where's the tag?"

"They took it off, I think. Anyhow it's after six o'clock."

He grinned at her indulgently. "You like it, don't you? Well, it looks like it's yours for tonight—and tomorrow I'll see about getting you another."

It *was* a beautiful mirror; the silvering was well-nigh perfect and the glass was air-clear. She felt as if she could push her hand through it.

He went to sleep, when they turned in, a little more readily than she did—the nap, no doubt. She rested on one elbow and looked at him for a long time after his breathing had become regular. Sweet Teddy! He was a good boy—good to her certainly. Tomorrow she would tell him not to bother about the other mirror—she didn't need it. All she really wanted was to be with him, for nothing ever to separate them. *Things* did not matter; just being together was the only thing that really mattered.

She glanced at the mirror. It certainly was handsome. So beautifully clear—like an open window. She felt as if she could climb through it, like Alice Through the Looking Glass.

He awoke when his name was called. "Up out of there, Randall! You're late!"

It wasn't Cynthia; that was sure. He rubbed the sleep out of his eyes and managed to focus them. "Wha's up?"

"You," said Phipps, leaning out through the beveled glass. "Get a move on! Don't keep us waiting."

Instinctively he looked toward the other pillow. Cynthia was gone.

Gone! Then he was up out of bed at once, wide awake, and trying frantically to search everywhere at once. Not in the bathroom. "Cyn!" Not in the living room, not in the kitchen-breakfast room. "Cyn! Cynthia! Where are you?" He pawed frantically in each of the closets. "Cyn!"

He returned to the bedroom and stood there, not knowing where to look next—a tragic, barefooted figure in rumpled pajamas and tousled hair.

Phipps put one hand on the lower edge of the mirror and vaulted easily into the room. "This room should have had a place to install a full-length mirror," he remarked curtly as he settled his coat and straightened his tie. "Every room should have a full-length mirror. Presently we will require it—I shall see to it."

Randall focused his eyes on him as if seeing him for the first time. "Where is she?" he demanded. "What have you done with her?" He stepped toward Phipps menacingly.

"None of your business," retorted Phipps. He inclined his head toward the mirror. "Climb through it."

"*Where is she?*" he screamed and attempted to grab Phipps by the throat.

Randall was never clear as to just what happened next. Phipps raised one hand—and he found himself tumbled against the side of the bed. He tried to struggle up again—fruitlessly. His efforts had a helpless, nightmare quality. "Mr. Crewes!" Phipps called out. "Mr. Reifsnider—I need your help."

Two more faces, vaguely familiar, appeared in the mirror. "On this side, Mr. Crewes, if you please," Phipps directed. Mr. Crewes climbed through. "Fine! We'll put him through feet first, I think."

Randall had nothing to say about it; he tried to resist, but his muscles were water. Vague twitchings were all he could accomplish. He tried to bite a wrist that came his way and was rewarded with a faceful of hard knuckles—a stinging rap rather than a blow.

"I'll add to that later," Phipps promised him.

They poked him through and dumped him on a table—*the* table. It was the same room he had been in once before, the board room of Detheridge & Co. There were the same pleasant, icy faces around the table, the same jovial, pig-eyed fat man at the head. There was one minor difference; on the long wall was a large mirror which did not reflect the room, but showed their bedroom, his and Cynthia's, as if seen in a mirror, with everything in it swapped left for right.

But he was not interested in such minor phenomena. He tried to sit up, found that he could not, and was forced to make do with simply raising his head. "Where did you put her?" he demanded of the huge chairman.

Stoles smiled at him sympathetically. "Ah, Mr. Randall! So you've come to see us again. You do get around, don't you? Entirely too much, in fact."

"Damn you—tell me what you did with her!"

"Silly and weak and stupid," Stoles mused. "To think that my own brothers and I could create nothing better than you. Well, you shall pay for it. The Bird is cruel!"

At his last emphatic remark he covered his face briefly. The others present followed his motions; someone reached out and clapped a hand roughly over Randall's eyes, then took it away.

Stoles was speaking again; Randall tried to interrupt him—once again Stoles thrust a finger at him and said sternly, "Enough!" Randall found himself unable to talk; his throat choked up and nauseated him whenever he tried it.

"One would suppose," Stoles continued urbanely, "that even one of your poor sort would understand the warning you were given, and heed it." Stoles stopped for a moment and shoved out his lips, pressing them tightly together. "I sometimes think that my only weakness lies in not realizing the full depths of the weakness and stupidity of men. As a reasonable creature myself I seem to have an unfortunate tendency to expect others unlike myself to be reasonable."

He stopped and turned his attention away from Randall and toward one of his colleagues. "Don't raise up any false hopes, Mr. Parker," he said, smiling sweetly. "I do not underrate *you*. And if you should wish to wrestle for my right to sit where I sit, I shall oblige you—later. I wonder," he added thoughtfully, "what your blood tastes like."

Mr. Parker was equally courteous. "Much the same as yours, Mr. Chairman, I imagine. It's a pleasant idea, but I am satisfied with the present arrangements."

"I'm sorry to hear it. I like you, Mr. Parker; I had hoped you were ambitious."

"I am patient—like our Ancestor."

"So? Well—back to business. Mr. Randall, I tried before to impress you with the necessity of having nothing to do with—your client. You know the client I mean. What do *you* think would impress you with the fact that the Sons of the Bird will tolerate no interference with their plans? Speak up—tell me."

Randall had heard little of what had taken place and had understood none of it. His whole being was engrossed with a single terrible thought. When he found he could speak again, it spilled forth. "Where is she?" he demanded in a hoarse whisper. "What have you done with her?"

Stoles gestured impatiently. "Sometimes," he said pettishly, "it is almost impossible to get into communication with one of them—almost no mind at all. Mr. Phipps!"

"Yes, sir."

"Will you please see that the other one is fetched in?"

"Certainly, Mr. Stoles." Phipps gathered up an assistant with his eye; the two left the room to return shortly with a burden which they dumped casually on the table beside Randall. It was Cynthia.

The surge of relief was almost more than he could stand. It roared through him, choking him, deafening him, blinding him with tears, and leaving him nothing with which to weigh the present danger of their situation. But gradually the throbbing of his being slowed down enough for him to see that something was wrong; she was quiet. Even if she had been asleep when they carried her in, the rough handling she had received should have been enough to waken her.

His alarm was almost as devastating as his joy had been. "What have you done to her?" he begged. "Is she—"

"No," Stoles answered in disgusted tones, "she is not dead. Control yourself, Mr. Randall." With a wave of his hand he directed his colleagues, "Wake her up."

One of them poked her in the ribs with a forefinger. "Don't bother to wrap it," he remarked; "I'll eat it on the way."

Stoles smiled. "Very witty, Mr. Printemps—but I said to wake her up. Don't keep me waiting."

"Certainly, Mr. Chairman." He slapped her stingingly across the face; Randall felt it on his own face—in his helpless condition it almost unhinged his reason. "In the Name of the Bird—wake up!"

He saw her chest heave under the silk of her nightgown; her eyes fluttered and she said one word, "Teddy?"

"Cyn! Here, darling, here!"

She turned her head toward him and exclaimed, "Teddy!" then added, "I had such a bad dream—*Oh!*" She had caught sight of them staring greedily at her. She looked slowly around her, wide-eyed and serious, then turned back to Randall. "Teddy—is this still a dream?"

"I'm afraid not, darling. Chin up."

She looked once more at the company, then back

to him. "I'm not afraid," she said firmly. "Make your play, Teddy. I won't faint on you again." Thereafter she kept her eyes on his.

Randall stole a glance at the fat chairman; he was watching them, apparently amused by the sight, and showed no present disposition to interfere. "Cyn," Randall said in an urgent whisper, "they've done something to me so I can't move. I'm paralyzed. So don't count on me too much. If you get a chance to make a break for it, take it!"

"I can't move, either," she whispered back. "We'll have to wait." She saw his agonized expression and added, " 'Chin up,' you said. But I wish I could touch you." The fingers of her right hand trembled slightly, found some traction on the polished table top, and began a slow and painful progress across the inches that seperated them.

Randall found that he could move his own fingers a little; he started his left hand on its way to join hers, a half inch at a time, his arm a dead weight against the movement, At last they touched and her hand crept into his, pressing it faintly. She smiled.

Stoles rapped loudly on the table. "This little scene is very touching," he said in sympathetic tones, "but there is business to attend to. We must decide the best thing to do with them."

"Hadn't we better eliminate them entirely?" suggested the one who had jabbed Cynthia in the ribs.

"That would be a pleasure," Stoles conceded, "but we must remember that these two are merely an incident in our plans for . . . for Mr. Randall's client. He is the one who must be destroyed!"

"I don't see—"

"Of course you don't see and that is why I am chairman. Our immediate purpose must be to immobilize these two in a fashion which will cause no suspicion on *his* part. The question is merely one of method and of the selection of the subject."

Mr. Parker spoke up. "It would be very amusing," he suggested, "to return them as they are. They would starve slowly, unable to answer the door, unable to answer the telephone, helpless."

"So it would be," Stoles said approvingly. "That is about the caliber of suggestion I expected from you. Suppose he attempted to see them, found them so. Do you think he would not understand their story? No, it must be something which seals their tongues. I intend to send them back with one of them—dead-alive!"

The whole business was so preposterous, so utterly unlikely, that Randall had been telling himself that it could not be real. He was in the clutches of a nightmare; if he could just manage to wake up, everything would be all right. The business of not being able to move—he had experienced that before in dreams. Presently you woke up from it and found that the covers had become wound around you, or you had been sleeping with both hands under your head. He tried biting his tongue so that the pain might wake him, but it did no good.

Stoles' last words brought his attention sharply to what was going on around him, not because he understood them—they meant very little to him, though they were fraught with horror—but because of the stir of approval and anticipation which went around the table.

The pressure of Cynthia's hand in his increased faintly. "What are they going to do, Teddy?" she whispered.

"I don't know, darling."

"The man, of course," Parker commented.

Stoles looked at him. Randall had a feeling that Stoles had intended the—whatever it was that was coming!—for the man, for him, until Parker had suggested it. But Stoles answered, "I'm always grateful for your advice. It makes it so easy to know just what one *should* do." Turning to the others he said, "Prepare the woman."

"*Now*," thought Randall. "It's got to be *now*." Summoning all the will he possessed he attempted to raise himself up from the table—rise up and fight!

He might just as well not have made the effort.

He let his head sink back, exhausted by the effort. "It's no use, kid," he said miserably.

Cynthia looked at him. If she felt any fear, it was masked by the concern she showed for him. "Chin up,

Brain," she answered with the mere suggestion of increased pressure of her hand in his.

Printemps stood up and leaned over her. "This is properly Potiphar's job," he objected.

"He left a prepared bottle," Stoles answered. "You have it, Mr. Phipps?"

Phipps answered by reaching into his brief case and producing it. At a nod from Stoles he passed it over; Printemps accepted it. "The wax?" he added.

"Here you are," Phipps acknowledged, dipping into his brief case again.

"Thank you, sir. Now, if someone will get *that* out of the way"—indicating Randall as he spoke—"we seem to be ready." Half a dozen savagely willing hands manhandled Randall to the extreme far edge of the table; Printemps bent over Cynthia, bottle in hand.

"One moment," Stoles interrupted. "I want them both to understand what is happening and why. Mrs. Randall," he continued, bowing gallantly, "in our short interview earlier I believe I made you understand that the Sons of the Bird will brook no interference from such as you two. You understood that, did you not?"

"I understood you," she answered. But her eyes were defiant.

"Good. Be it understood that it is our wish that your husband have nothing more to do with . . . a certain party. In order to insure that result we are about to split you into two parts. The part that keeps you going, that which you rather amusingly call the soul, we will squeeze into this bottle and keep. As for the rest, well, your husband may have that to keep with him, as a reminder that the Sons of the Birds have you in pawn. You understand me?"

She ignored the question. Randall tried to answer, found that his throat was misbehaving again.

"Listen to me, Mrs. Randall; if you are ever to see your husband again it is imperative that he obey us. He must not, on pain of your death, see his client again. Under the same penalty he must hold his tongue concerning us and all that has transpired. If he does not

—well, we will make your death very interesting, I assure you."

Randall tried to cry out that he would promise anything they wanted to spare her, but his voice was still silenced—apparently Stoles wanted to hear from Cynthia first. She shook her head. "He'll do as he thinks wise."

Stoles smiled. "Fine," he said. "That was the answer I wanted. You, Mr. Randall—do you promise?"

He wanted to agree, he was about to agree—but Cynthia was saying, "No!" with her eyes. From her expression he knew that *her* speech was now being blocked. Inside his head, clear as speech, he seemed to hear her say, "It's a trick, Brain. Don't promise!"

He kept quiet.

Phipps dug a thumb into his eye. "Answer when you are spoken to!"

He had to squint the injured eye in order to see Cynthia, but her expression still approved; he kept his mouth shut.

Presently Stoles said, "Never mind. Get on with it, gentlemen."

Printemps stuck the bottle under Cynthia's nose, held it against her left nostril. "Now!" he directed. Another of them pressed down on her short ribs vigorously, so that her breath was expelled suddenly. She grunted.

"Teddy," she said, "they're pulling me apar—*Ugh!*"

The process had been repeated with the bottle at the other nostril. Randall felt the soft warm hand in his suddenly relax. Printemps held up the bottle with his thumb over its top. "Let's have the wax," he said briskly. Having sealed it he passed it over to Phipps.

Stoles jerked a thumb toward the big mirror. "Put them back," he directed.

Phipps superintended the passing of Cynthia back through the glass, then turned to Stoles. "Couldn't we give him something to make him remember us?" he inquired.

"Help yourself," Stoles answered indifferently, as he stood up to go, "but try not to leave any permanent marks."

"Fine!" Phipps smiled, and hit Randall a backhanded swipe that loosened his teeth. "We'll be careful!"

He remained conscious through a considerable portion of it, though, naturally, he had no way of judging what proportion. He passed out once or twice, only to come to again under the stimulus of still greater pain. It was the novel way Phipps found of holding a man down without marking him which caused him to pass out for the last time.

He was in a small room, every side of which was a mirror—four walls, floor, and ceiling. Endlessly he was repeated in every direction and every image was himself—selves that hated him but from which there was no escape. "Hit him again!" they yelled—*he* yelled—and struck himself in the teeth with his closed fist. They—*he*—cackled.

They were closing in on him and he could not run fast enough. His muscles would not obey him, no matter how urgently he tried. It was because he was handcuffed—handcuffed to the treadmill they had put him on. He was blindfolded, too, and the handcuffs kept him from reaching his eyes. But he had to keep on—Cynthia was at the top of the climb; he had to reach her.

Only, of course, there is no top when you are on a treadmill.

He was terribly tired, but every time he slowed down the least little bit they hit him again. And he was required to count the steps, too, else he got no credit for it—ten thousand ninety-one, ten thousand ninety-two, ten thousand ninety-three, up and down, up and down—if he could only *see* where he was going.

He stumbled; they clipped him from behind and he fell forward on his face.

When he woke his face was pressed up against something hard and lumpy and cold. He shifted away from it and found that his whole body was stiff. His feet did not work as they should—he investigated by the uncertain light from the window and found that he had dragged the sheet half off the bed and had it tangled around his ankles.

The hard cold object was the steam radiator; he had been huddled in a heap against it. He was beginning to regain his orientation; he was in his own familiar bedroom. He must have walked in his sleep—he hadn't pulled that stunt since he was a kid! Walked in his sleep, tripped, and smashed his head into the radiator. Must 'a' knocked him silly, colder'n a coot—damn lucky he hadn't killed himself.

He was beginning to pull himself together, and to crawl painfully to his feet, when he noticed the one unfamiliar thing in the room—the new big mirror. It brought the rest of his dream back with a rush; he leaped toward the bed. "Cynthia!"

But she was there where she belonged, safe and unharmed. She had not awakened at his outcry, of which he was glad; he did not want to frighten her. He tiptoed away from the bed and let himself quietly into the bathroom, closing the door behind him before he turned on the light.

A pretty sight! he mused. His nose had been bloodied; it had long since stopped bleeding and the blood had congealed. It made a gory mess of the front of his pajama jacket. Beside that, he had apparently lain with the right side of his face in the stuff—it had dried on, messily, making him appear much more damaged than he was, as he discovered when he bathed his face.

Actually, he did not seem to be much damaged, except that—Wow!—the whole right side of his body was stiff and sore—probably banged it and wrenched it when he fell, then caught cold in it. He wondered how long he had been out.

He took off the jacket, decided that it would be too much effort to try to wash it out then, rolled it into a ball and chucked it behind the toilet seat. He didn't want Cyn to see it until he had had a chance to explain to her what had happened. "Why, Teddy, what in the world have you done to yourself?" "Nothing, kid, nothing at all—just ran into a radiator!"

That sounded worse than the old one about running into a door.

He was still groggy, groggier than he had thought—he had almost pitched on his head when he threw the jacket down, had been forced to steady himself by grabbing the top of the tank. And his head was pounding like a Salvation Army drum. He fiddled around in the medicine cabinet, located some aspirin and took three tablets, then looked thoughtfully at the prescription box of Amytal Cynthia had obtained some months before. He had never needed anything of the sort before; he slept soundly—but this was a special case. Nightmares two nights running and now sleepwalking and damn near breaking his silly neck.

He took one of the capsules, thinking as he did so that the kid had something when she thought they needed a vacation—he felt all shot.

Clean pajamas were too hard to find without turning on the bedroom light—he slipped into bed, waited a moment to see if Cyn would stir, then closed his eyes and tried to relax. Inside of a few minutes the drugs began to take hold, the throbbing in his head eased up, and soon he was sound asleep.

VII

Sunlight in his face woke him up; he focused one eye on the clock on the dressing table and saw that it was past nine o'clock, whereupon he got out of bed hastily. It was, he found, not quite a bright thing to do—his right side gave him fits. Then he saw the brown stain under the radiator and recalled his accident.

Cautiously he turned his head and took a look at his wife. She was still sleeping quietly, showing no disposition to stir. That suited him; it would be better, he thought, to tell her what had happened *after* he had dosed her with orange juice. No point in scaring the kid.

He groped on his slippers, then hung his bathrobe around him, as his bare shoulders felt cold and the muscles were sore. His mouth tasted better after he had brushed his teeth; breakfast began to seem like a good idea.

His mind dwelt absent-mindedly on the past night,

fingering his recollections rather than grasping them. These nightmares, he thought as he squeezed the oranges—not so good. Maybe not crazy, but definitely not so good, neurotic. Got to put a stop to 'em. Man couldn't work if he spent the night chasing butterflies, even if he didn't fall over his feet and break his neck. Man had to have sleep—definitely.

He drank his own glass of juice, then carried the other into the bedroom. "Come on, bright eyes—*reveille!*" When she did not stir at once he began to sing. "Up with the buttercup, come on, get up, get up! Here comes the sun!"

Still she did not budge. He set the glass down carefully on the bedside table, sat down on the edge of the bed, and took her by the shoulder. "Wake up, kid! They're movin' hell—two loads have gone by already!"

She did not move. Her shoulder was cold.

"Cyn!" he yelled. "Cyn! *Cyn!*" he shook her violently.

She flopped lifelessly. He shook her arm. "Cyn darling— Oh, God!"

Presently the shock itself steadied him; he blew his fuses, so to speak, and was ready, with a sort of ashy dead calmness to do whatever might be necessary. He was convinced without knowing why, nor yet fully appreciating it, that she was dead. He could not find her pulse—perhaps he was too clumsy, he told himself, or perhaps it was too weak; all the while a chorus in the back of his mind shouted, "She's dead . . . dead . . . dead—and you let her die!"

He placed an ear over her heart. It seemed that he could hear her heart beat, but he could not be sure; it might have been only the pounding of his own. He gave up presently and looked around for a small mirror.

He found what he wanted in Cynthia's handbag, a little make-up glass. He polished it carefully on the sleeve of his robe and held it to her half-opened mouth.

It fogged faintly.

He took it away in a bemused fashion, not letting himself hope, polished it again, and put it back to her mouth. Again it fogged, lightly but definitely.

She was alive—she was *alive!*

He wondered a moment later why he could not see her clearly and discovered that his face was wet. He wiped his eyes and went on with what he had to do. There was that needle business—if he could find a needle. He did find one in a pin-cushion on her dressing table. He brought it back to the bed, took a pinch of skin on her forearm, said, "Excuse me, kid," in a whisper, and jabbed it in.

The puncture showed a drop of blood, then closed at once—alive. He wished for a fever thermometer, but they had none—they were both too healthy. But he did remember something he had read somewhere, something about the invention of the stethoscope. You rolled up a piece of paper—

He found one of suitable size and rolled it into a one-inch tube which he pushed against the bare skin just over her heart. He put his ear to the other end and listened.

*Lubadup—lubadup—lubadup—lubadup—*Faint, but steady and strong. No doubt about it this time; she was alive; her heart was beating.

He had to sit down for a moment.

Randall forced himself to consider what to do next. Call a doctor, obviously. When people were sick, you called a doctor. He had not thought of it up to this time because Cyn and he just never did, never needed to. He could not recall that either one of them had had occasion to do so since they had been married.

Call the police and ask for an ambulance maybe? No, he'd get some police surgeon more used to crash cases and shootings than anything like this. He wanted the best.

But who? They didn't have a family physician. There was Smyles—a rum dum, no good. And Hartwick—hell, Hartwick specialized in very private operations for society people. He picked up the phone book.

Potbury! He didn't know anything about the old beezer, but he looked competent. He looked up the number, misdialed three times, then got the operator to call it for him.

"Yes, this is Potbury. What do you want? Speak up, man."

"I said this is Randall. Randall. R-A-N-D-A-double L. My wife and I came to see you yesterday, remember? About—"

"Yes, I remember. What is it?"

"My wife is sick."

"What's the trouble? Did she faint again?"

"No . . . yes. That is, she's unconscious. She woke up unconscious—I mean she never did wake up. She's unconscious now; she looks like she's dead."

"Is she?"

"I don't think so—but she's awful bad off, doctor. I'm scared. Can you come over right away?"

There was a short silence, then Potbury said gruffly, "I'll be over."

"Oh, good! Look—what should I do before you get here?"

"Don't do anything. Don't touch her. I'll be right over." He hung up.

Randall put the phone down and hurried back to the bedroom. Cynthia was just the same. He started to touch her, recalled the doctor's instructions, and straightened up with a jerk. But his eye fell on the piece of paper from which he had improvised a stethoscope and he could not resist the temptation to check up on his earlier results.

The tube gave back a cheering *lubadup;* he took it away at once and put it down.

Ten minutes of standing and looking at her with nothing more constructive to do than biting his nails left him too nervous to continue the occupation. He went out to the kitchen and removed a bottle of rye from the top shelf from which he poured a generous three fingers into a water glass. He looked at the amber stuff for a moment, then poured it down the sink, and went back into the bedroom.

She was still the same.

It suddenly occurred to him that he had not given Potbury the address. He dashed into the kitchen and snatched the phone. Controlling himself, he managed to dial the number correctly. A girl answered the phone. "No, the doctor isn't in the office. Any message?"

"My name is Randall. I—"

"Oh—Mr. Randall. The doctor left for your home about fifteen minutes ago. He should be there any minute now."

"But he doesn't have my address!"

"What? Oh, I'm sure he has—if he didn't have he would have telephoned me by now."

He put the phone down. It was damned funny—well, he would give Potbury three more minutes, then try another one.

The house phone buzzed; he was up out of his chair like a punch-drunk welterweight. "Yes?"

"Potbury. That you, Randall?"

"Yes, yes—come on up!" He punched the door release as he spoke.

Randall was waiting with the door open when Potbury arrived. "Come in, doctor! Come in, come in!" Potbury nodded and brushed on by him.

"Where's the patient?"

"In here." Randall conducted him with nervous haste into the bedroom and leaned over the other side of the bed while Potbury took his first look at the unconscious woman. "How is she? Will she be all right? Tell me, doctor—"

Potbury straightened up a little, grunting as he did so, and said, "If you will kindly stand away from the bed and quit crowding me, perhaps we will find out."

"Oh, sorry!" Randall retreated to the doorway. Potbury took his stethoscope from his bag, listened for a while with an inscrutable expression on his face which Randall tried vainly to read, shifted the instrument around, and listened again. Presently he put the stethoscope back in the bag, and Randall stepped forward eagerly.

But Potbury ignored him. He peeled up an eyelid with his thumb and examined her pupil, lifted an arm so that it swung free over the side of the bed and tapped it near the elbow, then straightened himself up and just looked at her for several minutes.

Randall wanted to scream.

Potbury performed several more of the strange, almost ritualistic things physicians do, some of which Randall thought he understood, others which he definitely did not. At last he said suddenly, "'What did she do yesterday—after you left my office?"

Randall told him; Potbury nodded sagely. "That's what I expected—it all dates back to the shock she had in the morning. All your fault, if I may say so!"

"My fault, doctor?"

"You were warned. Should never have let her get close to a man like that."

"But . . . but . . . you didn't warn me until *after* he had frightened her."

Potbury seemed a little vexed at this. "Perhaps not, perhaps not. Thought you told me someone had warned you before I did. Should know better, anyhow, with a creature like that."

Randall dropped the matter. "But how is she, doctor? Will she get well? She will, won't she?"

"You've got a very sick woman on your hands, Mr. Randall."

"Yes, I know she is—but what's the matter with her?"

"*Lethargica gravis,* brought on by psychic trauma."

"Is that—serious?"

"Quite serious enough. If you take proper care of her, I expect she will pull through."

"Anything, doctor, anything. Money's no object. What do we do now? Take her to a hospital?"

Potbury brushed the suggestion aside. "Worst thing in the world for her. If she wakes up in strange surroundings, she may go off again. Keep her here. Can you arrange your affairs so as to watch her yourself?"

"You bet I can."

"Then do so. Stay with her night and day. If she wakes up, the most favorable condition will be for her to find herself in her own bed with you awake and near her."

"Oughtn't she to have a nurse?"

"I wouldn't say so. There isn't much that can be done for her, except to keep her covered up warm.

You might keep her feet a little higher than her head. Put a couple of books under each of the lower feet of the bed."

"Right away."

"If this condition persists for more than a week or so, we'll have to see about glucose injections, or something of the sort." Potbury stooped over, closed his bag and picked it up. "Telephone me if there is any change in her condition."

"I will. I—" Randall stopped suddenly; the doctor's last remark reminded him of something he had forgotten. "Doctor—how did you find your way over here?"

Potbury looked startled. "What do you mean? This place isn't hard to find."

"But I didn't give you the address."

"Eh? Nonsense."

"But I didn't. I remembered the oversight just a few minutes later and called your office back, but you had already left."

"I didn't say you gave it to me today," Potbury said testily; "you gave it to me yesterday."

Randall thought it over. He *had* offered Potbury his credentials the day before, but they contained only his business address. True, his home telephone was listed, but it was listed simply as a night business number, without address, both in his credentials and in the phone book. Perhaps Cynthia—

But he could not ask Cynthia and the thought of her drove minor considerations out of his mind. "Are you sure there is nothing else I should do, doctor?" he asked anxiously.

"Nothing. Stay here and watch her."

"I will. But I surely wish I were twins for a while," he added emphatically.

"Why?" Potbury inquired, as he gathered up his gloves and turned toward the door.

"That guy Hoag. I've got a score to settle with him. Never mind—I'll put somebody else on his tail until I have a chance to settle his hash myself."

Potbury had wheeled around and was looking at

him ominously. "You'll do nothing of the sort. Your place is here."

"Sure, sure—but I want to keep him on ice. One of these days I'm going to take him apart to see what makes him tick!"

"Young man," Potbury said slowly, "I want you to promise me that you will have nothing to do *in any way* with . . . with this man you mentioned."

Randall glanced toward the bed. "In view of what has happened," he said savagely, "do you think I'm going to let him get away scot-free?"

"In the name of— Look. I'm older than you are and I've learned to expect silliness and stupidity. Still —how much does it take to teach you that some things are too dangerous to monkey with?" He gestured toward Cynthia. "How can you expect me to be responsible for her recovery if you insist on doing things that might bring on a catastrophe?"

"But—listen, Dr. Potbury, I told you that I intended to follow your instructions about *her*. But I'm not going to just forget what he has done. If she dies . . . if she dies, so help me, I'll take him apart with a rusty ax!"

Potbury did not answer at once. When he did all he said was, "And if she doesn't die?"

"If she doesn't die, my first business is here, taking care of her. But don't expect me to promise to forget Hoag. I won't—and that's final."

Potbury jammed his hat on his head. "We'll let it go at that—and trust she doesn't die. But let me tell you, young man, you're a fool." He stomped out of the apartment.

The lift he had gotten from tangling wills with Potbury wore off in a few minutes after the doctor had gone, and a black depression settled down on him. There was nothing to do, nothing to distract his mind from the aching apprehension he felt over Cynthia. He did make the arrangements to raise the foot of the bed a little as suggested by Potbury, but it takes only a few minutes to perform such a trifling chore; when it was done he had nothing to occupy him.

In raising the foot of the bed he had been very

cautious at first to avoid jarring the bed for fear of
waking her; then he realized that waking her was just
what he wanted most to do. Nevertheless he could not
bring himself to be rough and noisy about it—she
looked so helpless lying there.

He pulled a chair up close to the bed, where he
could touch one of her hands and watch her closely
for any change. By holding rigidly still he found that
he could just perceive the rise and fall of her breast. It
reassured him a little; he spent a long time watching
for it—the slow, unnoticeable intake, the much quicker
spilling of the breath.

Her face was pale and frighteningly deathlike, but
beautiful. It wrung his heart to look at her. So fragile
—she had trusted him so completely—and now there
was nothing he could do for her. If he had listened to
her, if he had only listened to what she had said, this
would not have happened to her. She had been afraid,
but she had done what he asked her to do.

Even the Sons of the Bird had not been able to
frighten her—

What was he saying? Get a grip on yourself, Ed—
that didn't happen; that was part of your nightmare.
Still, if anything like that had happened, that was just
what she would do—stick in there and back up his
play, no matter how badly things were going.

He got a certain melancholy satisfaction out of the
idea that, even in his dreams, he was sure of her, sure
of her courage and her devotion to him. Guts—more
than most men. There was the time she knocked the
acid bottle out of the hands of that crazy old biddy he
had caught out in the Midwell case. If she hadn't been
quick and courageous then, he would probably be
wearing smoked glasses now, with a dog to lead him
around.

He displaced the covers a little and looked at the
scar on her arm she had picked up that day. None of
the acid had touched him, but some had touched her
—it still showed, it always would show. But she didn't
seem to care.

"Cynthia! Oh, Cyn, my darling!"

There came a time when even he could not remain in one position any longer. Painfully—the cold he had caught in his muscles after the accident last night made his cramped legs ache like fury—he got himself up and prepared to cope with necessities. The thought of food was repugnant but he knew that he had to feed himself if he were to be strong enough to accomplish the watching and waiting that was going to be necessary.

Rummaging through the kitchen shelves and the ice-box turned up some oddments of food, breakfast things, a few canned goods, staples, some tired lettuce. He had no stomach for involved cooking; a can of soup seemed as good a bet as anything. He opened a can of Scotch broth, dumped it into a saucepan and added water. When it had simmered for a few minutes he took it off the fire and ate it from the pan, standing up. It tasted like stewed cardboard.

He went back to the bedroom and sat down again to resume the endless watching. But it soon developed that his feelings with respect to food were sounder than his logic; he bolted hastily for the bathroom and was very sick for a few minutes. Then he washed his face, rinsed out his mouth, and came back to his chair, weak and pale, but feeling sound enough physically.

It began to grow dusky outside; he switched on the dressing-table lamp, shaded it so that it would not shine directly in her eyes, and again sat down. She was unchanged.

The telephone rang.

It startled him almost out of rational response. He and his sorrow had been sitting there watching for so long that he was hardly aware that there could be anything else in the world. But he pulled himself together and answered it.

"Hello? Yes, this is Randall, speaking."

"Mr. Randall, I've had time to think it over and I feel that I owe you an apology—and an explanation."

"Owe me what? Who is this speaking?"

"Why, this is Jonathan Hoag, Mr. Randall. When you—"

"Hoag! Did you say *'Hoag'*?"

"Yes, Mr. Randall. I want to apologize for my peremptory manner yesterday morning and to beg your indulgence. I trust that Mrs. Randall was not upset by my—"

By this time Randall was sufficiently recovered from his first surprise to express himself. He did so, juicily, using words and figures of speech picked up during years of association with the sort of characters that a private detective inevitably runs into. When he had finished there was a gasp from the other end of the line and then a dead silence.

He was not satisfied. He wanted Hoag to speak so that he could interrupt him and continue the tirade. "Are you there, Hoag?"

"Uh, yes."

"I wanted to add this: Maybe you think that it is a joke to catch a woman alone in a hallway and scare the daylights out of her. I don't! But I'm not going to turn you over to the police—no, indeed! Just as soon as Mrs. Randall gets well, I'm going to look you up myself and then—God help you, Hoag. You'll need it."

There followed such a long silence that Randall was sure that his victim had hung up. But it seemed that Hoag was merely collecting his wits. "Mr. Randall, this is terrible—"

"You bet it is!"

"Do you mean to tell me that I accosted Mrs. Randall and frightened her?"

"You should know!"

"But I don't know, truly I don't." He paused, and then continued in an unsteady voice. "This is the sort of thing I have been afraid of, Mr. Randall, afraid that I might discover that during my lapses of memory I might have been doing terrible things. But to have harmed Mrs. Randall—she was so good to me, so kind to me. This is horrible."

"You're telling me!"

Hoag sighed as if he were tired beyond endurance. "Mr. Randall?" Randall did not answer. "Mr. Randall—there is no use in my deluding myself; there is only one thing to be done. You've got to turn me over to the police."

"Huh?"

"I've known it ever since our last conversation; I thought about it all day yesterday, but I did not have the courage. I had hoped that I was through with my . . . my *other* personality, but today it happened again. The whole day is a blank and I just came to myself this evening, on getting home. Then I knew that I *had* to do something about it, so I called you to ask you to resume your investigations. But I never suspected that I could possibly have done anything to Mrs. Randall." He seemed most convincingly overcome by shock at the idea. "When did . . . did *this* happen, Mr. Randall?"

Randall found himself in a most bewildered state of mind. He was torn between the desire to climb through the phone and wring the neck of the man he held responsible for his wife's desperate condition and the necessity for remaining where he was to care for her. In addition to that he was bothered by the fact that Hoag refused to talk like a villain. While speaking with him, listening to his mild answers and his worried tones, it was difficult to maintain the conception of him as a horrid monster of the Jack-the-Ripper type—although he knew consciously that villains were often mild in manner.

Therefore his answer was merely factual. "Nine thirty in the morning, about."

"Where was I at nine thirty this morning?"

"Not *this* morning, you so-and-so; yesterday morning."

"Yesterday morning? But that's not possible. Don't you remember? I was at home yesterday morning."

"Of course I remember, and I saw you leave. Maybe you didn't know *that*." He was not being very logical; the other events of the previous morning had convinced him that Hoag knew that they were shadowing him—but he was in no state of mind to be logical.

"But you couldn't have seen me. Yesterday morning was the only morning, aside from my usual Wednesdays, on which I can be sure where I was. I was at home, in my apartment. I didn't leave it until nearly one o'clock when I went to my club."

"Why, that's a—"

"Wait a minute, Mr. Randall, please! I'm just as

confused and upset about this as you are, but you've
got to listen to me. You broke my routine—remember?
And my other personality did not assert itself. After
you left I remained my . . . my *proper* self. That's why
I had had hopes that I was free at last."

"The hell you did. What makes you think you did?"

"I know my own testimony doesn't count for much,"
Hoag said meekly, "but I wasn't alone. The cleaning
woman arrived just after you left and was here all
morning."

"Damned funny I didn't see her go up."

"She works in the building," Hoag explained. "She's
the wife of the janitor—her name is Mrs. Jenkins.
Would you like to talk with her? I can probably locate
her and get her on the line."

"But—". Randall was getting more and more confused and was beginning to realize that he was at a dis-
advantage. He should never have discussed matters
with Hoag at all; he should have simply saved him up
until there was opportunity to take a crack at him.
Potbury was right; Hoag was a slick and insidious
character. Alibi indeed!

Furthermore he was becoming increasingly nervous
and fretful over having stayed away from the bedroom
as long as he had. Hoag must have had him on the
phone at least ten minutes; it was not possible to see
into the bedroom from where he sat at the breakfast
table. "No, I don't want to talk to her," he said roughly. "You lie in circles!" He slammed the phone back
into its cradle and hurried into the bedroom.

Cynthia was just as he had left her, looking merely
asleep and heartbreakingly lovely. She was breathing,
he quickly determined; her respiration was light but
regular. His homemade stethoscope rewarded him with
the sweet sound of her heartbeat.

He sat and watched her for a while, letting the
misery of his situation soak into him like a warm and
bitter wine. He did not want to forget his pain; he
hugged it to him, learning what countless others had
learned before him, that even the deepest pain concerning a beloved one is preferable to any surcease.

Later he stirred himself, realizing that he was indulging himself in a fashion that might work to her detriment. It was necessary to have food in the house for one thing, and to manage to eat some and keep it down. Tomorrow, he told himself, he would have to get busy on the telephone and see what he could do about keeping the business intact while he was away from it. The Night Watch Agency might do as a place to farm out any business that could not be put off; they were fairly reliable and he had done favors for them— but that could wait until tomorrow.

Just now—He called up the delicatessen on the street below and did some very desultory telephone shopping. He authorized the proprietor to throw in anything else that looked good and that would serve to keep a man going for a day or two. He then instructed him to find someone who would like to earn four bits by delivering the stuff to his apartment.

That done, he betook himself to the bathroom and shaved carefully, having a keen appreciation of the connection between a neat toilet and morale. He left the door open and kept one eye on the bed. He then took a rag, dampened it, and wiped up the stain under the radiator. The bloody pajama jacket he stuffed into the dirty-clothes hamper in the closet.

He sat down and waited for the order from the delicatessen to arrive. All the while he had been thinking over his conversation with Hoag. There was only one thing about Hoag that was clear, he concluded, and that was that everything about him was confusing. His original story had been wacky enough—imagine coming in and offering a high fee to have himself shadowed! But the events since made that incident seem downright reasonable. There was the matter of the thirteenth floor —damn it! He *had* seen that thirteenth floor, been on it, watched Hoag at work with a jeweler's glass screwed in his eye.

Yet he could not possibly have done so.

What did it add up to? Hypnotism, maybe? Randall was not naïve about such things; he knew that hypnotism existed, but he knew also that it was not nearly as potent as the Sunday-supplement feature writers would have one believe. As for hypnotizing a man in a

split second on a crowded street so that he believed in
and could recall clearly a sequence of events that had
never taken place—well, he just didn't believe in it. If
a thing like that were true, then the whole world might
be just a fraud and an illusion.

Maybe it was.

Maybe the whole world held together only when you
kept your attention centered on it and believed in it.
If you let discrepancies creep in, you began to doubt
and it began to go to pieces. Maybe this had happened
to Cynthia because he had doubted her reality. If he
just closed his eyes and *believed* in her alive and well,
then she would be—

He tried it. He shut out the rest of the world and
concentrated on Cynthia—Cynthia alive and well, with
that little quirk to her mouth she had when she was
laughing at something he had said—Cynthia, waking
up in the morning, sleepy-eyed and beautiful—Cynthia
in a tailored suit and a pert little hat, ready to start out
with him anywhere. Cynthia—

He opened his eyes and looked at the bed. There she
still lay, unchanged and deathly. He let himself go for
a while, then blew his nose and went in to put some
water on his face.

VIII

The house buzzer sounded. Randall went to the hall
door and jiggled the street-door release without using
the apartment phone—he did not want to speak to
anyone just then, certainly not to whoever it was that
Joe had found to deliver the groceries.

After a reasonable interval there was a soft knock
at the door. He opened it, saying, "Bring 'em in," then
stopped suddenly.

Hoag stood just outside the door.

Neither of them spoke at first. Randall was as-
tounded; Hoag seemed diffident and waiting for Randall
to commence matters. At last he said shyly, "I *had* to
come, Mr. Randall. May I . . . come in?"

Randall stared at him, really at a loss for words. The brass of the man—the sheer gall!

"I came because I had to prove to you that I would not willingly harm Mrs. Randall," he said simply. "If I have done so unknowingly, I want to do what I can to make restitution."

"It's too late for restitution!"

"But, Mr. Randall—why do you think that *I* have done anything to your wife? I don't see how I could have—not yesterday morning." He stopped and looked hopelessly at Randall's stony face. "You wouldn't shoot a dog without a fair trial—would you?"

Randall chewed his lip in an agony of indecision. Listening to him, the man seemed so damned decent— He threw the door open wide. "Come in," he said gruffly.

"Thank you, Mr. Randall." Hoag came in diffidently. Randall started to close the door.

"Your name Randall?" Another man, a stranger, stood in the door, loaded with bundles.

"Yes," Randall admitted, fishing in his pocket for change. "How did you get in?"

"Came in with *him,*" the man said, pointing at Hoag, "but I got off at the wrong floor. The beer is cold, chief," he added ingratiatingly. "Right off the ice."

"Thanks." Randall added a dime to the half dollar and closed the door on him. He picked the bundles up from the floor and started for the kitchen. He would have some of that beer now, he decided; there was never a time when he needed it more. After putting the packages down in the kitchen he took out one of the cans, fumbled in the drawer for an opener, and prepared to open it.

A movement caught his eye—Hoag, shifting restlessly from one foot to the other. Randall had not invited him to sit down; he was still standing. "Sit down!"

"Thank you." Hoag sat down.

Randall turned back to his beer. But the incident had reminded him of the other's presence; he found himself caught in the habit of good manners; it was almost impossible for him to pour himself a beer and offer none to a guest, no matter how unwelcome.

He hesitated just a moment, then thought, Shucks, it can't hurt either Cynthia or me to let him have a can of beer. "Do you drink beer?"

"Yes, thank you." As a matter of fact Hoag rarely drank beer, preferring to reserve his palate for the subtleties of wines, but at the moment he would probably have said yes to synthetic gin, or ditch water, if Randall had offered it.

Randall brought in the glasses, put them down, then went into the bedroom, opening the door for the purpose just enough to let him slip in. Cynthia was just as he had come to expect her to be. He shifted her position a trifle, in the belief that any position grows tiring even to a person unconscious, then smoothed the coverlet. He looked at her and thought about Hoag and Potbury's warnings against Hoag. Was Hoag as dangerous as the doctor seemed to think? Was he, Randall, even now playing into his hands?

No, Hoag could not hurt him now. When the worst has happened any change is an improvement. The death of both of them—or even Cyn's death alone, for then he would simply follow her. That he had decided earlier in the day—and he didn't give a damn who called it cowardly!

No—if Hoag were responsible for this, at least he had shot his bolt. He went back into the living room.

Hoag's beer was still untouched. "Drink up," Randall invited, sitting down and reaching for his own glass. Hoag complied, having the good sense not to offer a toast nor even to raise his glass in the gesture of one. Randall looked him over with tired curiosity. "I don't understand you, Hoag."

"I don't understand myself, Mr. Randall."

"Why did you come here?"

Hoag spread his hands helplessly. "To inquire about Mrs. Randall. To find out what it is that I have done to her. To make up for it, if I can."

"You admit you did it?"

"No, Mr. Randall. No. I don't see how I could possibly have done anything to Mrs. Randall *yesterday* morning—"

"You forget that I saw you."

"But— What did I do?"

"You cornered Mrs. Randall in a corridor of the Midway-Copton Building and tried to choke her."

"Oh, dear! But—you *saw* me do this?"

"No, not exactly. I was—" Randall stopped, realizing how it was going to sound to tell Hoag that he had not seen him in one part of the building because he was busy watching Hoag in another part of the building.

"Go on, Mr. Randall, please."

Randall got nervously to his feet. "It's no use," he snapped. "I don't know what you did. I don't know that you did anything! All I know is this: Since the first day you walked in that door, odd things have been happening to my wife and me—*evil* things—and now she's lying in there as if she were dead. She's—" He stopped and covered his face with his hands.

He felt a gentle touch on his shoulder. "Mr. Randall . . . please, Mr. Randall. I'm sorry and I would like to help."

"I don't know how anyone can help—unless you know some way of waking up my wife. Do you, Mr. Hoag?"

Hoag shook his head slowly. "I'm afraid I don't. Tell me—what is the matter with her? I don't know yet."

"There isn't much to tell. She didn't wake up this morning. She acts as if she never would wake up."

"You're sure she's not . . . , dead?"

"No, she's not dead."

"You had a doctor, of course. What did he say?"

"He told me not to move her and to watch her closely."

"Yes, but what did he say was the matter with her?"

"He called it *lethargica gravis*."

"*Lethargica gravis!* Was that all he called it?"

"Yes—why?"

"But didn't he attempt to diagnose it?"

"That was his diagnosis—*lethargica gravis*."

Hoag still seemed puzzled. "But, Mr. Randall, that isn't a diagnosis; it is just a pompous way of saying 'heavy sleep.' It really doesn't mean anything. It's like telling a man with skin trouble that he has *dermatitis*, or a man with stomach trouble that he has *gastritis*. What tests did he make?"

"Uh ... I don't know. I—"

"Did he take a sample with a stomach pump?"

"No."

"X ray?"

"No, there wasn't any way to."

"Do you mean to tell me, Mr. Randall, that a doctor just walked in, took a look at her, and walked out again, without doing anything for her, or applying any tests, or bringing in a consulting opinion? Was he your family doctor?"

"No," Randall said miserably. "I'm afraid I don't know much about doctors. We never need one. But you ought to know whether he's any good or not—it was Potbury."

"Potbury? You mean the Dr. Potbury I consulted? How did you happen to pick him?"

"Well, we didn't *know* any doctors—and we had been to see him, checking up on your story. What have you got against Potbury?"

"Nothing, really. He was rude to me—or so I thought."

"Well, then, what's he got against you?"

"I don't see how he could have anything against me," Hoag answered in puzzled tones. "I only saw him once. Except, of course, the matter of the analysis. Though why he should—" He shrugged helplessly.

"You mean about the stuff under your nails? I thought that was just a song and dance."

"No."

"Anyhow it couldn't be just that. After all the things he said about you."

"What did he say about me?"

"He said—" Randall stopped, realizing that Potbury had not said anything specific against Hoag; it had been entirely what he did not say. "It wasn't so much what he said; it was how he felt about you. He hates you, Hoag—and he is afraid of you."

"Afraid of me?" Hoag smiled feebly, as if he were sure Randall must be joking.

"He didn't *say* so, but it was plain as daylight."

Hoag shook his head. "I don't understand it. I'm more used to being afraid of people than of having them afraid of me. Wait—did he tell *you* the results of the analysis he made for me?"

"No. Say, that reminds me of the queerest thing of all about you, Hoag." He broke off, thinking of the impossible adventure of the thirteenth floor. "Are you a hypnotist?"

"Gracious, no! Why do you ask?"

Randall told him the story of their first attempt to shadow him. Hoag kept quiet through the recital, his face intent and bewildered. "And that's the size of it," Randall concluded emphatically. "No thirteenth floor, no Detheridge & Co., no nothing! And yet I remember every detail of it as plainly as I see your face."

"That's all?"

"Isn't that enough? Still, there is one more thing I might add. It can't be of real importance, except in showing the effect the experience had on me."

"What is it?"

"Wait a minute."

Randall got up and went again into the bedroom. He was not quite so careful this time to open the door the bare minimum, although he did close it behind him. It made him nervous, in one way, not to be constantly at Cynthia's side; yet had he been able to answer honestly he would have been forced to admit that even Hoag's presence was company and some relief to his anxiety. Consciously, he excused his conduct as an attempt to get to the bottom of their troubles.

He listened for her heartbeats again. Satisfied that she still was in this world, he plumped her pillow and brushed vagrant hair up from her face. He leaned over and kissed her forehead lightly, then went quickly out of the room.

Hoag was waiting. "Yes?" he inquired.

Randall sat down heavily and rested his head on his hands. "Still the same." Hoag refrained from making a useless answer; presently Randall commenced in a tired voice to tell him of the nightmares he had experienced the last two nights. "Mind you, I don't say they are significant," he added, when he had done. "I'm not superstitious."

"I wonder," Hoag mused.

"What do you mean?"

"I don't mean anything supernatural, but isn't it possible that the dreams were not entirely accidental ones, brought on by your experiences? I mean to say, if there is someone who can make you dream the things you dreamed in the Acme Building in broad daylight, why couldn't they force you to dream at night as well?"

"Huh?"

"Is there anyone who hates you, Mr. Randall?"

"Why, not that I know of. Of course, in my business, you sometimes do things that don't exactly make friends, but you do it for somebody else. There's a crook or two who doesn't like me any too well, but—well, they couldn't do anything like this. It doesn't make sense. Anybody hate you? Besides Potbury?"

"Not that I know of. And I don't know why he should. Speaking of him, you're going to get some other medical advice, aren't you?"

"Yes. I guess I don't think very fast. I don't know just what to do, except to pick up the phone book and try another number."

"There's a better way. Call one of the big hospitals and ask for an ambulance."

"I'll do that!" Randall said, standing up.

"You might wait until morning. You wouldn't get any useful results until morning, anyway. In the meantime she *might* wake up."

"Well . . . yes, I guess so. I think I'll take another look at her."

"Mr. Randall?"

"Eh?"

"Uh, do you mind if— May I see her?"

Randall looked at him. His suspicions had been lulled more than he had realized by Hoag's manner and words, but the suggestion brought him up short, making him recall Potbury's warnings vividly. "I'd rather you didn't," he said stiffly.

Hoag showed his disappointment but tried to cover it. "Certainly. I quite understand, sir."

When Randall returned he was standing near the door with his hat in his hand. "I think I had better go," he said. When Randall did not comment he added, "I would sit with you until morning if you wished it."

"No. Not necessary. Good night."

"Good night, Mr. Randall."

When Hoag had gone he wandered around aimlessly for several minutes, his beat ever returning him to the side of his wife. Hoag's comments about Potbury's methods had left him more uneasy than he cared to admit; in addition to that Hoag had, by partly allaying his suspicions of the man, taken from him his emotional whipping boy—which did him no good.

He ate a cold supper and washed it down with beer—and was pleased to find it remained in place. He then dragged a large chair into the bedroom, put a footstool in front of it, got a spare blanket, and prepared to spend the night. There was nothing to do and he did not feel like reading—he tried it and it didn't work. From time to time he got up and obtained a fresh can of beer from the icebox. When the beer was gone he took down the rye. The stuff seemed to quiet his nerves a little, but otherwise he could detect no effect from it. He did not want to become drunk.

He woke with a terrified start, convinced for the moment that Phipps was at the mirror and about to kidnap Cynthia. The room was dark; his heart felt as if it would burst his ribs before he could find the switch and assure himself that it was not so, that his beloved, waxy pale, still lay on the bed.

He had to examine the big mirror and assure himself that it did reflect the room and not act as a window to some other, awful place before he was willing to snap off the light. By the dim reflected light of the city he poured himself a bracer for his shaken nerves.

He thought that he caught a movement in the mirror, whirled around, and found that it was his own reflection. He sat down again and stretched himself out, resolving not to drop off to sleep again.

What was that?

He dashed into the kitchen in pursuit of it. Nothing

—nothing that he could find. Another surge of panic swept him back into the bedroom—it could have been a ruse to get him away from her side.

They were laughing at him, goading him, trying to get him to make a false move. He *knew* it—they had been plotting against him for days, trying to shake his nerve. They watched him out of every mirror in the house, ducking back when he tried to catch them at it. The Sons of the Bird—

"The Bird is Cruel!"

Had he said that? Had someone shouted it at him? The Bird is Cruel. Panting for breath, he went to the open window of the bedroom and looked out. It was still dark, pitch-dark. No one moved on the streets below. The direction of the lake was a lowering bank of mist. What time was it? Six o'clock in the morning by the clock on the table. Didn't it *ever* get light in this God-forsaken city?

The Sons of the Bird. He suddenly felt very sly; they thought they had him, but he would fool them—they couldn't do this to him and to Cynthia. He would smash every mirror in the place. He hurried out to the kitchen, where he kept a hammer in the catch-all drawer. He got it and came back to the bedroom. First, the big mirror—

He hesitated just as he was about to swing on it. Cynthia wouldn't like this—seven years' bad luck! He wasn't superstitious himself, but—Cynthia wouldn't like it! He turned to the bed with the idea of explaining it to her; it seemed so obvious—just break the mirrors and then they would be safe from the Sons of the Bird.

But he was stumped by her still face.

He thought of a way around it. They had to use a mirror. What was a mirror? A piece of glass that reflects. Very well—fix 'em so they wouldn't reflect! Furthermore he knew how he could do it; in the same drawer with the hammer were three or four dime-store cans of enamel, and a small brush, leftovers from a splurge of furniture refinishing Cynthia had once indulged in.

He dumped them all into a small mixing bowl; to-

gether they constituted perhaps a pint of heavy pigment
—enough, he thought, for his purpose. He attacked the
big beveled glass first, slapping enamel over it in quick
careless strokes. It ran down his wrists and dripped
onto the dressing table; he did not care. Then the
others—

There was enough, though barely enough, to finish
the living-room mirror. No matter—it was the last
mirror in the house—except, of course, the tiny mirrors
in Cynthia's bags and purses, and he had already decided that they did not count. Too small for a man to
crawl through and packed away out of sight, anyhow.

The enamel had been mixed from a small amount of
black and perhaps a can and a half, net, of red. It was
all over his hands now; he looked like the central figure
in an ax murder. No matter—he wiped it, or most of it,
off on a towel and went back to his chair and his bottle.

Let 'em try now! Let 'em try their dirty, filthy black
magic! He had them stymied.

He prepared to wait for the dawn.

The sound of the buzzer brought him up out of his
chair, much disorganized, but convinced that he had
not closed his eyes. Cynthia was all right—that is to
say, she was still asleep, which was the best he had expected. He rolled up his tube and reassured himself
with the sound of her heart.

The buzzing continued—or resumed; he did not
know which. Automatically he answered it.

"Potbury," came a voice. "What's the matter? You
asleep? How's the patient?"

"No change, doctor," he answered, striving to control his voice.

"That so? Well, let me in."

Potbury brushed on by him when he opened the door
and went directly to Cynthia. He leaned over her for a
moment or two, then straightened up. "Seems about the
same," he said. "Can't expect much change for a day
or so. Crisis about Wednesday, maybe." He looked
Randall over curiously. "What in the world have you
been doing? You look like a four-day bender."

"Nothing," said Randall. "Why didn't you have me send her to a hospital, doctor?"

"Worst thing you could do for her."

"What do you know about it? You haven't really examined her. You don't know what's wrong with her. *Do you?*"

"Are you crazy? I told you yesterday."

Randall shook his head. "Just double talk. You're trying to kid me about her. And I want to know why."

Potbury took a step toward him. "You *are* crazy— and drunk, too." He looked curiously at the big mirror. "*I* want to know what's been going on around here." He touched a finger to smeared enamel.

"Don't touch it!"

Potbury checked himself. "What's it for?"

Randall looked sly. "I foxed 'em."

"Who?"

"The Sons of the Bird. They come in through mirrors—but I stopped them."

Potbury stared at him. "I know them," Randall said. "They won't fool me again. The Bird is Cruel."

Potbury covered his face with his hands.

They both stood perfectly still for several seconds. It took that long for a new idea to percolate through Randall's abused and bemused mind. When it did he kicked Potbury in the crotch. The events of the next few seconds were rather confused. Potbury made no outcry, but fought back. Randall made no attempt to fight fair, but followed up his first panzer stroke with more dirty work.

When matters straightened out, Potbury was behind the bathroom door, whereas Randall was on the bedroom side with the key in his pocket. He was breathing hard but completely unaware of such minor damage as he had suffered.

Cynthia slept on.

"Mr. Randall—let me out of here!"

Randall had returned to his chair and was trying to think his way out of his predicament. He was fully sobered by now and made no attempt to consult the bottle. He was trying to get it through his head that there really were "Sons of the Bird" and that he had one of them locked up in there right now.

In that case Cynthia was unconscious because—God help them!—the Sons had stolen her soul. Devils—they had fallen afoul of devils.

Potbury pounded on the door. "What's the meaning of this, Mr. Randall? Have you lost your mind? Let me out of here!"

"What'll you do if I do? Will you bring Cynthia back to life?"

"I'll do what a physician can for her. Why did you do it?"

"You know why. Why did you cover your face?"

"What do you mean? I started to sneeze and you kicked me."

"Maybe I should have said, 'Gesundheit!' You're a devil, Potbury. You're a Son of the Bird!"

There was a short silence. "What nonsense is this?"

Randall thought about it. Maybe it was nonsense; maybe Potbury *had* been about to sneeze. No! This was the only explanation that made sense. Devils, devils and black magic. Stoles and Phipps and Potbury and the others.

Hoag? That would account for—wait a minute, now. Potbury hated Hoag. Stoles hated Hoag. All the Sons of the Bird hated Hoag. Very well, devil or whatever, he and Hoag were on the same side.

Potbury was pounding on the door again, no longer with his fists, but with a heavier, less frequent blow which meant the shoulder with the whole weight of the body behind it. The door was no stronger than interior house doors usually are; it was evident that it could take little of such treatment.

Randall pounded on his side. "Potbury! Potbury! Do you hear me?"

"Yes."

"Do you know what I'm going to do now? I'm going to call up Hoag and get him to come over here. Do you hear that, Potbury? He'll kill you, Potbury, he'll kill you!"

There was no answer, but presently the heavy pounding resumed. Randall got his gun. "Potbury!" No answer. "Potbury, cut that out or I'll shoot." The pounding did not even slacken.

Randall had a sudden inspiration. "Potbury—*in the Name of the Bird*—get away from that door!"

The noise stopped as if chopped off.

Randall listened and then pursued his advantage. "In the Name of the Bird, don't touch that door again. Hear me, Potbury?" There was no answer, but the quiet continued.

It was early; Hoag was still at his home. He quite evidently was confused by Randall's incoherent explanations, but he agreed to come over, at once, or a little quicker.

Randall went back into the bedroom and resumed his double vigil. He held his wife's still, cool hand with his left hand; in his right he carried his gun, ready in case the invocation failed to bind. But the pounding was not resumed; there was a deathly silence in both rooms for some minutes. Then Randall heard, or imagined he heard, a faint scraping sibilance from the bathroom—an unaccountable and ominous sound.

He could think of nothing to do about it, so he did nothing. It went on for several minutes and stopped. After that—nothing.

Hoag recoiled at the sight of the gun. "Mr. Randall!"

"Hoag," Randall demanded, "are you a devil?"

"I don't understand you."

" 'The Bird is Cruel!' "

Hoag did not cover his face; he simply looked confused and a bit more apprehensive.

"O.K.," decided Randall. "You pass. If you *are* a devil, you're my kind of a devil. Come on—I've got Potbury locked up, and I want you to confront him."

"Me? Why?"

"Because he *is* a devil—a Son of the Bird. And they're afraid of you. Come on!" He urged Hoag into the bedroom, continuing with, "The mistake I made was in not being willing to believe in something when it happened to me. *Those weren't dreams.*" He pounded on the door with the muzzle of the gun. "Potbury! Hoag is here. Do what I want and you *may* get out of it alive."

"What do you want of him?" Hoag said nervously.

"*Her*—of course."

"Oh—" Randall pounded again, then turned to Hoag and whispered, "If I open the door, will you confront him? I'll be right alongside you."

Hoag gulped, looked at Cynthia, and answered, "Of course."

The bath was empty; it had no window, nor any other reasonable exit, but the means by which Potbury had escaped were evident. The surface of the mirror had been scraped free of enamel, with a razor blade.

They risked the seven years of bad luck and broke the mirror. Had he known how to do so, Randall would have swarmed through and tackled them all; lacking the knowledge it seemed wiser to close the leak.

After that there was nothing to do. They discussed it, over the silent form of Randall's wife, but there was nothing to do. They were not magicians. Hoag went into the living room presently, unwilling to disturb the privacy of Randall's despair but also unwilling to desert him entirely. He looked in on him from time to time. It was on one such occasion that he noticed a small black bag half under the bed and recognized it for what it was—a doctor's kit. He went in and picked it up. "Ed," he asked, "have you looked at this?"

"At what?" Randall looked up with dull eyes, and read the inscription, embossed in well-worn gold letters on the flap:

POTIPHAR T. POTBURY, M.D.

"Huh?"

"He must have left it behind."

"He didn't have a chance to take it." Randall took it from Hoag and opened it—a stethoscope, head forceps, clamps, needles, an assortment of vials in a case, the usual props of a G.P.'s work. There was one prescription bottle as well; Randall took it out and read the prescription. "Hoag, look at this."

POISON!

This Prescription Can Not Be Refilled

MRS. RANDALL—TAKE AS PRESCRIBED

BONTON CUTRATE PHARMACY

"Was he trying to poison her?" Hoag suggested.

"I don't think so—that's the usual narcotic warning. But I want to see what it is." He shook it. It seemed empty. He started to break the seal.

"Careful!" Hoag warned.

"I will be." He held it well back from his face to open it, then sniffed it very cautiously. It gave up a fragrance, subtle and infinitely sweet.

"Teddy?" He whirled around, dropping the bottle. It was indeed Cynthia, eyelids fluttering. "Don't promise them anything, Teddy!" She sighed and her eyes closed again.

" 'The Bird is Cruel!' " she whispered.

IX

"Your memory lapses are the key to the whole thing," Randall was insisting. "If we knew what you do in the daytime, if we knew your profession, we would know why the Sons of the Bird are out to get you. More than that, we would know how to fight them—for they are obviously afraid of you."

Hoag turned to Cynthia. "What do you think, Mrs. Randall?"

"I think Teddy is right. If I knew enough about hypnotism, we would try that—but I don't, so scopolamine is the next best bet. Are you willing to try it?"

"If you say so, yes."

"Get the kit, Teddy." She jumped down from where she had been perched, on the edge of his desk. He put out a hand to catch her.

"You ought to take it easy, baby," he complained.

"Nonsense, I'm all right—now."

They had adjourned to their business office almost as soon as Cynthia woke up. To put it plainly, they were scared—scared stiff, but not scared silly. The apartment seemed an unhealthy place to be. The office did not seem much better. Randall and Cynthia had decided to *get out of town*—the stop at the office was a penultimate stop, for a conference of war.

Hoag did not know what to do.

"Just forget you ever saw this kit," Randall warned him, as he prepared the hypodermic. "Not being a doctor, nor an anaesthetist, I shouldn't have it. But it's convenient, sometimes." He scrubbed a spot of Hoag's forearm with an alcohol swab. "Steady now—there!" He shoved the needle.

They waited for the drug to take hold. "What do you expect to get," Randall whispered to Cynthia.

"I don't know. If we're lucky, his two personalities will knit. Then we may find out a lot of things."

A little later Hoag's head sagged forward; he breathed heavily. She stepped forward and shook his shoulder. "Mr. Hoag—do you hear me?"

"Yes."

"What is your name?"

"Jonathan . . . Hoag."

"Where do you live?"

"Six-oh-two—Gotham Apartments."

"What do you do?"

"I . . . don't know."

"Try to remember. What is your profession?"

No answer. She tried again. "Are you a hypnotist?"

"No."

"Are you a—magician?"

The answer was delayed a little, but finally came. "No."

"What are you, Jonathan Hoag?"

He opened his mouth, seemed about to answer—then sat up suddenly, his manner brisk and completely free of the lassitude normal to the drug. "I'm sorry, my dear, but this will have to stop—for the present."

He stood up, walked over to the window, and looked out. "Bad," he said, glancing up and down the street. "How distressingly bad." He seemed to be talking to himself rather than to them. Cynthia and Randall looked at him, then to each other for help.

"What is bad, Mr. Hoag?" Cynthia asked, rather

diffidently. She did not have the impression analyzed, but he seemed like another person—younger, more vibrant.

"Eh? Oh, I'm sorry. I owe you an explanation. I was forced to, uh, dispense with the drug."

"Dispense with it?"

"Throw it off, ignore it, make it as nothing. You see, my dear, while you were talking I recalled my profession." He looked at them cheerily, but offered no further explanation.

Randall was the first to recover. "What *is* your profession?"

Hoag smiled at him, almost tenderly. "It wouldn't do to tell you," he said. "Not now, at least." He turned to Cynthia. "My dear, could I trouble you for a pencil and a sheet of paper?"

"Uh—why, certainly." She got them for him; he accepted them graciously and, seating himself, began to write.

When he said nothing to explain his conduct Randall spoke up, "Say, Hoag, look here—" Hoag turned a serene face to him; Randall started to speak, seemed puzzled by what he saw in Hoag's face, and concluded lamely, "Er . . . Mr. Hoag, what's this all about?"

"Are you not willing to trust me?"

Randall chewed his lip for a moment and looked at him; Hoag was patient and serene. "Yes . . . I suppose I am," he said at last.

"Good. I am making a list of some things I want you to buy for me. I shall be quite busy for the next two hours or so."

"You are leaving us?"

"You are worried about the Sons of the Bird, aren't you? Forget them. They will not harm you. I promise it." He resumed writing. Some minutes later he handed the list to Randall. "I've noted at the bottom the place where you are to meet me—a filling station outside Waukegan."

"Waukegan? Why Waukegan?"

"No very important reason. I want to do once more something I am very fond of doing and don't expect to be able to do again. You'll help me, won't you? Some of the things I've asked you to buy may be hard to get, but you will try?"

"I suppose so."

"Good." He left at once.

Randall looked from the closing door back to the list in his hand. "Well, I'll be a— Cyn, what do you suppose he wants us to get for him?—groceries!"

"Groceries? Let me see that list."

X

They were driving north in the outskirts of the city, with Randall at the wheel. Somewhere up ahead lay the place where they were to meet Hoag; behind them in the trunk of the car were the purchases he had directed them to make.

"Teddy?"

"Yeah, kid."

"Can you make a U-turn here?"

"Sure—if you don't get caught. Why?"

"Because that's just what I'd like to do. Let me finish," she went on hurriedly. "We've got the car; we've got all the money we have in the world with us; there isn't anything to stop us from heading south if we want to."

"Still thinking of that vacation? But we're going on it—just as soon as we deliver this stuff to Hoag."

"I don't mean a vacation. I mean go away and never come back—*now!*"

"With eighty dollars' worth of fancy groceries that Hoag ordered and hasn't paid for yet? No soap."

"We could eat them ourselves."

"Humph! Caviar and humming-bird wings. We can't afford it, kid. We're the hamburger type. Anyhow, even if we could, I want to see Hoag again. Some plain talk —and explanations."

She sighed. "That's just what I thought, Teddy, and that's why I want to cut and run. I don't want explanations; I'm satisfied with the world the way it is. Just you and me—and no complications. I don't *want* to know anything about Mr. Hoag's profession—or the Sons of the Bird—or anything like, that."

He fumbled for a cigarette, then scratched a match under the instrument board, while looking at her quizzically out of the corner of his eye. Fortunately the traffic was light. "I think I feel the same way you do about it, kid, but I've got a different angle on it. If we drop it now, I'll be jumpy about the Sons of the Bird the rest of my life, and scared to shave, for fear of looking in a mirror. But there is a rational explanation for the whole thing—bound to be—and I'm going to get it. Then we can sleep."

She made herself small and did not answer.

"Look at it this way," Randall went on, somewhat irritated. "Everything that has happened could have been done in the ordinary way, without recourse to supernatural agencies. As for supernatural agencies— well, out here in the sunlight and the traffic it's a little too much to swallow. Sons of the Bird—rats!"

She did not answer. He went on. "The first significant point is that Hoag is a consummate actor. Instead of being a prissy little Milquetoast, he's a dominant personality of the first water. Look at the way I shut up and said, 'Yes, sir,' when he pretended to throw off the drug and ordered us to buy all those groceries."

"Pretended?"

"Sure. Somebody substituted colored water for my sleepy juice—probably done the same time the phony warning was stuck in the typewriter. But to get back to the point—he's a naturally strong character and almost certainly a clever hypnotist. Pulling that illusion about the thirteenth floor and Detheridge & Co. shows how skillful he is—or somebody is. Probably used drugs on me as well, just as they did on you."

"On me?"

"Sure. Remember that stuff you drank in Potbury's office? Some sort of a delayed-action Mickey Finn."

"But you drank it, too!"

"Not necessarily the same stuff. Potbury and Hoag were in cahoots, which is how they created the atmosphere that made the whole thing possible. Everything else was little stuff, insignificant when taken alone."

Cynthia had her own ideas about that, but she kept them to herself. However, one point bothered her. "How did Potbury get out of the bathroom? You told me he was locked in."

"I've thought about that. He picked the lock while I was phoning Hoag, hid in the closet and just waited his chance to walk out."

"Hm-m-m—" She let it go at that for several minutes.

Randall stopped talking, being busy with the traffic in Waukegan. He turned left and headed out of town.

"Teddy—if you are sure that the whole thing was just a hoax and there are no such things as the Sons, then why can't we drop it and head south? We don't need to keep this appointment."

"I'm sure of my explanation all right," he said, skillfully avoiding a suicide-bent boy on a bicycle, "in its broad outlines, but I'm *not* sure of the motivation —and *that's* why I have to see Hoag. Funny thing, though," he continued thoughtfully, "I don't think Hoag has anything against us; I think he had some reasons of his own and paid us five hundred berries to put up with some discomfort while he carried out his plans. But we'll see. Anyhow, it's too late to turn back; there's the filling station he mentioned—and there's Hoag!"

Hoag climbed in with no more than a nod and a smile; Randall felt again the compulsion to do as he was told which had first hit him some two hours before. Hoag told him where to go.

The way lay out in the country and, presently, off the pavement. In due course they came to a farm gate leading into pasture land, which Hoag instructed Randall to open and drive through. "The owner does not mind," he said. "I've been here many times, on my Wednesdays. A beautiful spot."

It *was* a beautiful spot. The road, a wagon track now, led up a gradual rise to a tree-topped crest. Hoag had him park under a tree, and they got out. Cynthia stood for a moment, drinking it in, and savoring deep breaths of the clean air. To the south Chicago could be seen and beyond it and east of it a silver gleam of the lake. "Teddy, isn't it gorgeous?"

"It is," he admitted, but turned to Hoag. "What I want to know is—why arc we here?"

"Picnic," said Hoag. "I chose this spot for my finale."

"Finale?"

"Food first," said Hoag. "Then, if you must, we'll talk."

It was a very odd menu for a picnic; in place of hearty foods there were some dozens of gourmets' specialties—preserved cumquats, guava jelly, little potted meats, tea—made by Hoag over a spirit lamp —delicate wafers with a famous name on the package. In spite of this both Randall and Cynthia found themselves eating heartily. Hoag tried everything, never passing up a dish—but Cynthia noticed that he actually ate very little, tasting rather than dining.

In due course Randall got his courage up to brace Hoag; it was beginning to appear that Hoag had no intention of broaching the matter himself. "Hoag?"

"Yes, Ed?"

"Isn't it about time you took off the false face and quit kidding us?"

"I have not kidded you, my friend."

"You know what I mean—this whole rat race that has been going on the past few days. You're mixed up in it and know more about it than we do—that's evident. Mind you, not that I'm accusing you of anything," he added hastily. "But I want to know what it means."

"Ask yourself what it means."

"O.K.," Randall accepted the challenge. "I will." He launched into the explanation which he had sketched out to Cynthia, Hoag encouraged him to continue it fully, but, when he was through, said nothing.

"Well," Randall said nervously, "that's how it happened—wasn't it?"

"It seems like a good explanation."

"I thought so. But you've still got to clear some things up. Why did you do it?"

Hoag shook his head thoughtfully. "I'm sorry, Ed. I cannot possibly explain my motives to you."

"But, damn it, that's not fair! The least you could—"

"When did you ever find fairness, Edward?"

"Well—I expected you to play fair with us. You encouraged us to treat you as a friend. You owe us explanations."

"I promised you explanations. But consider, Ed—do you want explanations? I assure you that you will have no more trouble, no more visitations from the Sons."

Cynthia touched his arm. "Don't ask for them, Teddy!"

He brushed her off, not unkindly but decisively. "I've got to *know*. Let's have the explanation."

"You won't like it."

"I'll chance it."

"Very well." Hoag settled back. "Will you serve the wine, my dear? Thank you. I shall have to tell you a little story first. It will be partly allegorical, as there are not the . . . the words, the concepts. Once there was a race, quite unlike the human race—quite. I have no way of describing to you what they looked like or how they lived, but they had one characteristic you can understand: they were creative. The creating and enjoying of works of art was their occupation and their reason for being. I say 'art' advisedly, for art is undefined, undefinable, and without limits. I can use the word without fear of misusing it, for it has no exact meaning. There are as many meanings as there are artists. But remember that these artists are not human and their art is not human.

"Think of one of this race, in your terms—young. He creates a work of art, under the eye and the guidance of his teacher. He has talent, this one, and his creation has many curious and amusing features. The teacher encourages him to go on with it and prepare it for the judging. Mind you, I am speaking in metaphorical terms, as if this were a human artist, preparing his canvases to be judged in the annual showing."

He stopped and said suddenly to Randall, "Are you a religious man? Did it ever occur to you that all this"—he included the whole quietly beautiful countryside in the sweep of his arm—"might have had a Creator? *Must* have had a Creator?"

Randall stared and turned red. "I'm not exactly a

church-going man," he blurted, "but— Yes, I suppose I do believe it."

"And you, Cynthia?"

She nodded, tense and speechless.

"The Artist created this world, after His Own fashion and using postulates which seemed well to Him. His teacher approved on the whole, but—"

"Wait a minute," Randall said insistently. "Are you trying to describe the creation of the world—the Universe?"

"What else?"

"But—damn it, this is preposterous! I asked for an explanation of the things that have just happened to *us.*"

"I told you that you would not like the explanation." He waited for a moment, then continued. "The Sons of the Bird were the dominant feature of the world, at first."

Randall listened to him, feeling that his head would burst. He knew, with sick horror, that the rationalization he had made up on the way to the rendezvous had been sheerest moonshine, thrown together to still the fears that had overcome him. The Sons of the Bird— real, real and horrible—and potent. He felt that he knew now the sort of race of which Hoag spoke. From Cynthia's tense and horrified face she *knew,* also—and there would never again be peace for either of them. "In the Beginning there was the Bird—"

Hoag looked at him with eyes free of malice but without pity. "No," he said serenely, "there was never the Bird. They who call themselves Sons of the Bird there are. But they are stupid and arrogant. Their sacred story is so much superstition. But in their way and by the rules of this world they are powerful. The things, Edward, that you thought you saw you did see."

"You mean that—"

"Wait, let me finish. I must hasten. You saw what you thought you saw, with one exception. Until today you have seen *me* only in your apartment, or mine. The creatures you shadowed, the creature that frightened Cynthia—Sons of the Bird, all of them. Stoles and his friends.

"The teacher did not approve of the Sons of the Bird and suggested certain improvements in the creation. But the Artist was hasty or careless; instead of removing them entirely He merely—painted over them, made them appear to be some of the new creations with which He peopled His world.

"All of which might not have mattered if the work had not been selected for judging. Inevitably the critics noticed them; they were—bad art, and they disfigured the final work. There was some doubt in their minds as to whether or not the creation was worth preserving. That is why I am here."

He stopped, as if there were no more to say. Cynthia looked at him fearfully. "Are you . . . are you—"

He smiled at her. "No, Cynthia, I am not the Creator of your world. You asked me my profession once.

"I am an art critic."

Randall would like to have disbelieved. It was impossible for him to do so; the truth rang in his ears and would not be denied. Hoag continued, "I said to you that I would have to speak to you in terms you use. You must know that to judge a creation such as this, your world, is not like walking up to a painting and looking at it. This world is peopled with *men;* it must be looked at through the eyes of men. I am a man."

Cynthia looked still more troubled. "I don't understand. You act through the body of a man?"

"I *am* a man. Scattered around through the human race are the Critics—men. Each is the projection of a Critic, but each is a man—in every way a man, not knowing that he is also a Critic."

Randall seized on the discrepancy as if his reason depended on it—which, perhaps, it did. "But *you* know—or say you do. It's a contradiction."

Hoag nodded, undisturbed. "Until today, when Cynthia's questioning made it inconvenient to continue as I was—and for other reasons—this *persona*"—he tapped his chest—"had no idea of why he was here. He was a man, and no more. Even now, I have extended my present *persona* only as far as is necessary for my purpose. There are questions which I could not answer —as Jonathan Hoag.

"Jonathan Hoag came into being as a man, for the purpose of examining, *savoring,* certain of the artistic aspects of this world. In the course of that it became convenient to use him to smell out some of the activities of those discarded and painted-over creatures that call themselves the Sons of the Bird. You two happened to be drawn into the activity—innocent and unknowing, like the pigeons used by armies. But it so happened that I observed something else of artistic worth while in contact with you, which is why we are taking the trouble for these explanations."

"What do you mean?"

"Let me speak first of the matters I observed as a critic. Your world has several pleasures. There is eating." He reached out and pulled off from its bunch a muscat grape, fat and sugar-sweet, and ate it appreciatively. "An odd one, that. And very remarkable. No one ever before thought of making an art of the simple business of obtaining the necessary energy. Your Artist has very real talent.

"And there is sleeping. A strange reflexive business in which the Artist's own creations are allowed to create more worlds of their own. You see now, don't you," he said, smiling, "why the critic must be a *man* in truth—else he could not dream as a man does?

"There is drinking—which mixes both eating and dreaming.

"There is the exquisite pleasure of conversing together, friend with friend, as we are doing. That is not new, but it goes to the credit of the Artist that He included it.

"And there is sex. Sex is ridiculous. As a critic I would have disregarded it entirely had not you, my friends, let me see something which had not come to the attention of Jonathan Hoag, something which, in my own artistic creations, I had never had the wit to invent. As I said, your Artist has talent." He looked at them almost tenderly. "Tell me, Cynthia, what do you love in this world and what is it that you hate and fear?"

She made no attempt to answer him, but crept closer to her husband. Randall put a protecting arm around her. Hoag spoke then to Randall. "And you, Edward? Is there something in this world for which you'd surrender your life and your soul if need be? You need not answer—I saw in your face and in your heart, last night, as you bent over the bed. Good art, good art—both of you. I have found several sorts of good and original art in this world, enough to justify encouraging your Artist to try again. But there was so much that was bad, poorly drawn and amateurish, that I could not find it in me to approve the work as a whole until I encountered and savored this, the tragedy of human love."

Cynthia looked at him wildly. "Tragedy? You say 'tragedy'?"

He looked at her with eyes that were not pitying, but serenely appreciative. "What else could it be, my dear?"

She stared at him, then turned and buried her face on the lapel of her husband's coat. Randall patted her head. "Stop it, Hoag!" he said savagely. "You've frightened her again."

"I did not wish to."

"You have. And I can tell you what I think of your story. It's got holes in it you can throw a cat through. You made it up."

"You do not believe that."

It was true; Randall did not. But he went on bravely, his hand still soothing his wife. "The stuff under your nails—how about that? I noticed you left that out. And your fingerprints."

"The stuff under my nails has little to do with the story. It served its purpose, which was to make fearful the Sons of the Bird. They knew what it was."

"But what was it?"

"The ichor of the Sons—planted there by my other *persona*. But what is this about fingerprints? Jonathan Hoag was honestly fearful of having them taken; Jonathan Hoag is a man, Edward. You must remember that."

Randall told him; Hoag nodded. "I see. Truthfully, I do not recall it, even today, although my full *persona* knows of it. Jonathan Hoag had a nervous habit of polishing things with his handkerchief; perhaps he polished the arm of your chair."

"I don't remember it."

"Nor do I."

Randall took up the fight again. "That isn't all and that isn't half of it. What about the rest home you said you were in? And who pays you? Where do you get your money? Why was Cynthia always so darned scared of you?"

Hoag looked out towards the city; a fog was rolling in from the lake. "There is little time for these things," he said, "and it does not matter, even to you, whether you believe or not. But you do believe—you cannot help it. But you have brought up another matter. Here." He pulled a thick roll of bills from his pocket and handed them to Randall. "You might as well take them with you; I shall have no more use for them. I shall be leaving you in a few minutes."

"Where are you going?"

"Back to myself. After I leave, you must do this: Get into your car and drive at once, south, through the city. *Under no circumstances* open a window of your car until you are miles away from the city."

"Why? I don't like this."

"Nevertheless, do it. There will be certain—changes, readjustments going on."

"What do you mean?"

"I told you, did I not, that the Sons of the Bird are being dealt with? They, and all their works."

"How?"

Hoag did not answer, but stared again at the fog. It was creeping up on the city. "I think I must go now. Do as I have told you to do." He started to turn away. Cynthia lifted up her face and spoke to him.

"Don't go! Not yet."

"Yes, my dear?"

"You must tell me one thing: *Will Teddy and I be together?*"

He looked into her eyes and said. "I see what you mean. I don't know."

"But you *must* know!"

"I do not know. If you are both creatures of this

world, then your patterns may run alike. But there are the Critics, you know."

"The Critics? What have *they* to do with *us?*"

"One, or the other, or both of you may *be* Critics. I would not know. Remember, the Critics are men—here. I did not even know myself as one until today." He looked at Randall meditatively. "*He* may be one. I suspected it once today."

"Am—I?"

"I have no way of knowing. It is most unlikely. You see, we can't know each other, for it would spoil our artistic judgment."

"But . . . but . . . if we *are* not the same, then—"

"That is all." He said it, not emphatically, but with such a sound of finality that they were both startled. He bent over the remains of the feast and selected one more grape, ate it, and closed his eyes.

He did not open them. Presently Randall said, "Mr. Hoag?" No answer. "Mr. Hoag!" Still no answer. He separated himself from Cynthia, stood up, and went around to where the quiet figure sat. He shook him. "Mr. Hoag!"

"But we can't just leave him there!" Randall insisted, some minutes later.

"Teddy, he knew what he was doing. The thing for us to do is to follow his instructions."

"Well—we can stop in Waukegan and notify the police."

"Tell them we left a dead man back there on a hillside? Do you think they would say, 'Fine,' and let us drive on? No, Teddy—just what he told us to do."

"Honey—you don't believe all that stuff he was telling us, do you?"

She looked him in his eyes, her own eyes welling with tears, and said, "Do you? Be honest with me, Teddy."

He met her gaze for a moment, then dropped his eyes and said, "Oh, never mind! We'll do what he said. Get in the car."

The fog which appeared to have engulfed the city was not visible when they got down the hill and had

started back toward Waukegan, nor did they see it
again after they had turned south and drove toward
the city. The day was bright and sunny, as it had
started to be that morning, with just enough nip in the
air to make Hoag's injunction about keeping the windows rolled up tight seem like good sense.

They took the lake route south, skipping the Loop
thereby, with the intention of continuing due south
until well out of the city. The traffic had thickened
somewhat over what it had been when they started out
in the middle of the morning; Randall was forced to
give his attention to the wheel. Neither of them felt
like talking and it gave an excuse not to.

They had left the Loop area behind them when Randall spoke up, "Cynthia—"

"Yes."

"We ought to tell somebody. I'm going to ask the
next cop we see to call the Waukegan station."

"Teddy!"

"Don't worry. I'll give him some stall that will make
them investigate without making them suspicious of us.
The old run-around—you know."

She knew his powers of invention were fertile enough
to do such a job; she protested no more. A few blocks
later Randall saw a patrolman standing on the sidewalk, warming himself in the sun, and watching some
boys playing sand-lot football. He pulled up to the
curb beside him. "Run down the window, Cyn."

She complied, then gave a sharp intake of breath
and swallowed a scream. He did not scream, but he
wanted to.

Outside the open window was no sunlight, no cops,
no kids—nothing. Nothing but a gray and formless
mist, pulsing slowly as if with inchoate life. They could
see nothing of the city through it, not because it was
too dense but because it was—empty. No sound came
out of it; no movement showed in it.

It merged with the frame of the window and began
to drift inside. Randall shouted, "Roll up the window!"
She tried to obey, but her hands were nerveless; he
reached across her and cranked it up himself, jamming
it hard into its seat.

The sunny scene was restored; through the glass they saw the patrolman, the boisterous game, the sidewalk, and the city beyond. Cynthia put a hand on his arm. "Drive on, Teddy!"

"Wait a minute," he said tensely, and turned to the window beside him. Very cautiously he rolled it down —just a crack, less than an inch.

It was enough. The formless gray flux was out there, too; through the glass the city traffic and sunny street were plain, through the opening—nothing.

"Drive on, Teddy—*please!*"

She need not have urged him; he was already gunning the car ahead with a jerk.

Their house is not exactly on the Gulf, but the water can be seen from the hilltop near it. The village where they do their shopping has only eight hundred people in it, but it seems to be enough for them. They do not care much for company, anyway, except their own. They get a lot of that. When he goes out to the vegetable patch, or to the fields, she goes along, taking with her such woman's work as she can carry and do in her lap. If they go to town, they go together, hand in hand —always.

He wears a beard, but it is not so much a peculiarity as a necessity, for there is not a mirror in the entire house. They do have one peculiarity which would mark them as odd in any community, if anyone knew about it, but it is of such a nature that no one else *would* know.

When they go to bed at night, before he turns out the light, he handcuffs one of his wrists to one of hers.

THE MAN WHO TRAVELED
IN ELEPHANTS

RAIN STREAMED ACROSS THE BUS'S WINDOW. John Watts peered out at wooded hills, content despite the weather. As long as he was rolling, moving, traveling, the ache of loneliness was somewhat quenched. He could close his eyes and imagine that Martha was seated beside him.

They had always traveled together; they had honeymooned covering his sales territory. In time they had covered the entire country—Route 66, with the Indians' booths by the highway, Route 1, up through the District, the Pennsylvania Turnpike, zipping in and out through the mountain tunnels, himself hunched over the wheel and Martha beside him, handling the maps and figuring the mileage to their next stop.

He recalled one of Martha's friends saying, "But, dear, don't you get tired of it?"

He could hear Martha's bubbly laugh, "With forty-eight wide and wonderful states to see, grow *tired?* Besides, there is always something new—fairs and expositions and things."

"But when you've seen one fair you've seen them all."

"You think there is no difference between the Santa Barbara Fiesta and the Fort Worth Fat Stock Show? Anyhow," Martha had gone on, "Johnny and I are country cousins; we like to stare at the tall buildings and get freckles on the roofs of our mouths."

"Do be sensible, Martha." The woman had turned to him. "John, isn't it time that you two were settling down and making something out of your lives?"

Such people tired him. "It's for the 'possums," he had told her solemnly. "They like to travel."

127

"The opossums? What in the world is he talking about, Martha?"

Martha had shot him a private glance, then deadpanned, "Oh, I'm sorry! You see, Johnny raises baby 'possums in his umbilicus."

"I'm equipped for it," he had confirmed, patting his round stomach.

That had settled her hash! He had never been able to stand people who gave advice "for your own good."

Martha had read somewhere that a litter of newborn opossums would no more than fill a teaspoon and that as many as six in a litter were often orphans through lack of facilities in mother 'possum's pouch to take care of them all.

They had immediately formed the Society for the Rescue and Sustenance of the Other Six 'Possums, and Johnny himself had been unanimously selected—by Martha—as the site of Father Johnny's 'Possum Town.

They had had other imaginary pets, too. Martha and he had hoped for children; when none came, their family had filled out with invisible little animals: Mr. Jenkins, the little gray burro who advised them about motels, Chipmink the chattering chipmunk, who lived in the glove compartment, *Mus Followalongus* the traveling mouse, who never said anything but who would bite unexpectedly, especially around Martha's knees.

They were all gone now; they had gradually faded away for lack of Martha's gay, infectious spirit to keep them in health. Even Bindlestiff, who was not invisible, was no longer with him. Bindlestiff was a dog they had picked up beside the road, far out in the desert, given water and succor and received in return his large uncritical heart. Bindlestiff had traveled with them thereafter, until he, too, had been called away, shortly after Martha.

John Watts wondered about Bindlestiff. Did he roam free in the Dog Star, in a land lush with rabbits and uncovered garbage pails? More likely he was with Martha, sitting on her feet and getting in the way. Johnny hoped so.

He sighed and turned his attention to the passengers.

A thin, very elderly woman leaned across the aisle and said, "Going to the Fair, young man?"

He started. It was twenty years since anyone had called him "young man." "Unh? Yes, certainly." They were *all* going to the Fair: the bus was a special.

"You like going to fairs?"

"Very much." He knew that her inane remarks were formal gambits to start a conversation. He did not resent it; lonely old women have need of talk with strangers—and so did he. Besides, he liked perky old women. They seemed the very spirit of America to him, putting him in mind of church sociables and farm kitchens—and covered wagons.

"I like fairs, too," she went on. "I even used to exhibit—quince jelly and my Crossing-the-Jordan pattern."

"Blue ribbons, I'll bet."

"Some," she admitted, "but mostly I just liked to go to them. I'm Mrs. Alma Hill Evans. Mr. Evans was a great one for doings. Take the exposition when they opened the Panama Canal—but you wouldn't remember that."

John Watts admitted that he had not been there.

"It wasn't the best of the lot, anyway. The Fair of '93, there was a fair for you: There'll never be one that'll even be a patch on that one."

"Until this one, perhaps?"

"This one? Pish and tush! Size isn't everything." The All-American Exposition would certainly be the biggest thing yet—and the best. If only Martha were along, it would seem like heaven. The old lady changed the subject. "You're a traveling man, aren't you?"

He hesitated, then answered, "Yes."

"I can always tell. What line are you in, young man?"

He hesitated longer, then said flatly, "I travel in elephants."

She looked at him sharply and he wanted to explain, but loyalty to Martha kept his mouth shut. Martha had insisted that they treat their calling seriously, never explaining, never apologizing. They had taken it up when he had planned to retire; they had been talking

of getting an acre of ground and doing something useful with radishes or rabbits, or such. Then, during their
final trip over his sales route, Martha had announced
after a long silence. "John, you don't want to stop
traveling."

"Eh? Don't I? You mean we should keep the territory?"

"No, that's done. But we won't settle down, either."

"What do you want to do? Just gypsy around?"

"Not exactly. I think we need some new line to
travel in."

"Hardware? Shoes? Ladies' ready-to-wear?"

"No." She had stopped to think. "We ought to travel
in *something*. It gives point to your movements. I think
it ought to be something that doesn't turn over too fast,
so that we could have a really large territory, say the
whole United States."

"Battleships perhaps?"

"Battleships are out of date, but that's close." Then
they had passed a barn with a tattered circus poster.
"I've got it!" She had shouted. "Elephants! We'll travel
in elephants."

"Elephants, eh? Rather hard to carry samples."

"We don't need to. Everybody knows what an
elephant looks like. Isn't that right, Mr. Jenkins?" The
invisible burro had agreed with Martha, as he always
did; the matter was settled.

Martha had known just how to go about it. "First
we make a survey. We'll have to comb the United
States from corner to corner before we'll be ready to
take orders."

For ten years they had conducted the survey. It was
an excuse to visit every fair, zoo, exposition, stock
show, circus, or punkin doings anywhere, for were they
not all prospective customers? Even national parks and
other natural wonders were included in the survey, for
how was one to tell where a pressing need for an
elephant might turn up? Martha had treated the matter
with a straight face and had kept a dog-eared notebook: "La Brea Tar Pits, Los Angeles—surplus of
elephants, obsolete type, in these parts about 25,000
years ago." "Philadelphia—sell at least six to the Union

League." "Brookfield Zoo, Chicago—African elephants, rare." "Gallup, New Mexico—stone elephants east of town, very beautiful." "Riverside, California, Elephant Barbershop—brace owner to buy mascot." "Portland, Oregon—query Douglas Fir Association. Recite *Road to Mandalay*. Same for Southern Pine group. N.B. this calls for trip to Gulf Coast as soon as we finish with rodeo in Laramie."

Ten years and they had enjoyed every mile of it. The survey was still unfinished when Martha had been taken. John wondered if she had buttonholed Saint Peter about the elephant situation in the Holy City. He'd bet a nickel she had.

But he could not admit to a stranger that traveling in elephants was just his wife's excuse for traveling around the country they loved.

The old woman did not press the matter. "I knew a man once who sold mongooses," she said cheerfully. "Or is it 'mongeese'? He had been in the exterminator business and—what does that driver think he is doing?"

The big bus had been rolling along easily despite the driving rain. Now it was swerving, skidding. It lurched sickeningly—and crashed.

John Watts banged his head against the seat in front. He was picking himself up, dazed, not too sure where he was, when Mrs. Evans' thin, confident soprano oriented him. "Nothing to get excited about, folks. I've been expecting this—and you can see it didn't hurt a bit."

John Watts admitted that he himself was unhurt. He peered near-sightedly around, then fumbled on the sloping floor for his glasses. He found them, broken. He shrugged and put them aside; once they arrived he could dig a spare pair out of his bags.

"Now let's see what has happened," Mrs. Evans went on. "Come along, young man." He followed obediently.

The right wheel of the bus leaned drunkenly against the curb of the approach to a bridge. The driver was standing in the rain, dabbing at a cut on his cheek. "I couldn't help it," he was saying. "A dog ran across the road and I tried to avoid it."

"You might have killed us!" a woman complained.

"Don't cry till you're hurt," advised Mrs. Evans. "Now let's get back into the bus while the driver phones for someone to pick us up."

John Watts hung back to peer over the side of the canyon spanned by the bridge. The ground dropped away steeply; almost under him were large, mean-looking rocks. He shivered and got back into the bus.

The relief car came along very promptly, or else he must have dozed. The latter, he decided, for the rain had stopped and the sun was breaking through the clouds. The relief driver thrust his head in the door and shouted, "Come on, folks! Time's a-wastin'! Climb out and climb in." Hurrying, John stumbled as he got aboard. The new driver gave him a hand. " 'Smatter, Pop? Get shaken up?"

"I'm all right, thanks."

"Sure you are. Never better."

He found a seat by Mrs. Evans, who smiled and said, "Isn't it a heavenly day?"

He agreed. It *was* a beautiful day, now that the storm had broken. Great fleecy clouds tumbling up into warm blue sky, a smell of clean wet pavement, drenched fields and green things growing—he lay back and savored it. While he was soaking it up a great double rainbow formed and blazed in the eastern sky. He looked at them and made two wishes, one for himself and one for Martha. The rainbows' colors seemed to be reflected in everything he saw. Even the other passengers seemed younger, happier, better dressed, now that the sun was out. He felt light-hearted, almost free from his aching loneliness.

They were there in jig time; the new driver more than made up the lost minutes. A great arch stretched across the road: THE ALL-AMERICAN CELEBRATION AND EXPOSITION OF ARTS and under it PEACE AND GOOD WILL TO ALL. They drove through and sighed to a stop.

Mrs. Evans hopped up. "Got a date—must run!" She trotted to the door, then called back, "See you on the midway, young man," and disappeared in the crowd.

John Watts got out last and turned to speak to the driver. "Oh, uh, about my baggage. I want to—"

The driver had started his engine again. "Don't worry about your baggage," he called out. "You'll be taken care of." The huge bus moved away.

"But—" John Watts stopped; the bus was gone. All very well—but what was he to do without his glasses?

But there were sounds of carnival behind him, that decided him. After all, he thought, tomorrow will do. If anything is too far away for me to see, I can always walk closer. He joined the queue at the gate and went in.

It was undeniably the greatest show ever assembled for the wonderment of mankind. It was twice as big as all outdoors, brighter than bright lights, newer than new, stupendous, magnificent, breathtaking, awe inspiring, supercolossal, incredible—and a lot of fun. Every community in America had sent its own best to this amazing show. The marvels of P. T. Barnum, of Ripley, and of all Tom Edison's godsons had been gathered in one spot. From up and down a broad continent the riches of a richly endowed land and the products of a clever and industrious people had been assembled, along with their folk festivals, their annual blowouts, their celebrations, and their treasured carnival customs. The result was as American as strawberry shortcake and as gaudy as a Christmas tree, and it all lay there before him, noisy and full of life and crowded with happy, holiday people.

Johnny Watts took a deep breath and plunged into it.

He started with the Fort Worth Southwestern Exposition and Fat Stock Show and spent an hour admiring gentle, white-faced steers, as wide and square as flat-topped desks, scrubbed and curried, with their hair parted neatly from skull to base of spine, then day-old little black lambs on rubbery stalks of legs, too new to know themselves, fat ewes, their broad backs, paddled flatter and flatter by grave-eyed boys intent on blue ribbons. Next door he found the Pomona Fair with solid matronly Percherons and dainty Palominos from the Kellog Ranch.

And harness racing. Martha and he had always loved harness racing. He picked out a likely looking nag of the famous Dan Patch line, bet and won, then moved on, as there was so much more to see. Other country fairs were just beyond, apples from Yakima, the cherry festival from Beaumont and Banning, Georgia's peaches. Somewhere off beyond him a band was beating out, "Ioway, Ioway, that's where the tall corn grows!"

Directly in front of him was a pink cotton candy booth.

Martha had loved the stuff. Whether at Madison Square Garden or at Imperial County's fair grounds she had always headed first for the cotton candy booth. "The big size, honey?" he muttered to himself. He felt that if he were to look around he would see her nodding. "The large size, please," he said to the vendor.

The carnie was elderly, dressed in a frock coat and stiff shirt. He handled the pink gossamer with dignified grace. "Certainly, sir, there is no other size." He twirled the paper cornucopia and presented it. Johnny handed him a half dollar. The man flexed and opened his fingers; the coin disappeared. That appeared to end the matter.

"The candy is fifty cents?" Johnny asked diffidently.

"Not at all, sir." The old showman plucked the coin from Johnny's lapel and handed it back. "On the house —I see you are with it. After all, what is money?"

"Why, thank you, but, uh, I'm not really 'with it,' you know."

The old man shrugged. "If you wish to go incognito, who am I to dispute you? But your money is no good here."

"Uh, if you say so."

"You will see."

He felt something brush against his leg. It was a dog of the same breed, or lack of breed, as Bindlestiff had been. It looked amazingly like Bindlestiff. The dog looked up and waggled its whole body.

"Why, hello, old fellow!" He patted it—then his eyes blurred; it even felt like Bindlestiff. "Are you lost,

boy? Well, so am I. Maybe we had better stick together, eh? Are you hungry?"

The dog licked his hand. He turned to the cotton
candy man. "Where can I buy hot dogs?"

"Just across the way, sir."

He thanked him, whistled to the dog, and hurried
across. "A half dozen hot dogs, please."

"Coming up! Just mustard, or everything on?"

"Oh, I'm sorry. I want them raw, they are for a
dog."

"I getcha. Just a sec."

Presently he was handed six wienies, wrapped in
paper. "How much are they?"

"Compliments of the house."

"I beg pardon?"

"Every dog has his day. This is his."

"Oh. Well, thank you." He became aware of increased noise and excitement behind him and looked
around to see the first of the floats of the Priests of
Pallas, from Kansas City, coming down the street. His
friend the dog saw it, too, and began to bark.

"Quiet, old fellow." He started to unwrap the meat.
Someone whistled across the way; the dog darted between the floats and was gone. Johnny tried to follow,
but was told to wait until the parade had passed. Between floats he caught glimpses of the dog, leaping up
on a lady across the way. What with the dazzling lights
of the floats and his own lack of glasses he could not
see her clearly, but it was plain that the dog knew her;
he was greeting her with the all-out enthusiasm only a
dog can achieve.

He held up the package and tried to shout to her;
she waved back, but the band music and the noise of
the crowd made it impossible to hear each other. He
decided to enjoy the parade, then cross and find the
pooch and its mistress as soon as the last float had
passed.

It seemed to him the finest Priests of Pallas parade
he had ever seen. Come to think about it, there hadn't
been a Priests of Pallas parade in a good many years.
Must have revived it just for this.

That was like Kansas City—a grand town. He didn't

know of any he liked as well. Possibly Seattle. And
New Orleans, of course.

And Duluth—Duluth was swell. And so was Memphis. He would like to own a bus someday that ran
from Memphis to Saint Joe, from Natchez to Mobile,
wherever the wide winds blow.

Mobile—there was a town.

The parade was past now, with a swarm of small
boys tagging after it. He hurried across.

The lady was not there, neither she, nor the dog.
He looked quite thoroughly. No dog. No lady with a
dog.

He wandered off, his eyes alert for marvels, but his
thoughts on the dog. It really had been a great deal
like Bindlestiff . . . and he wanted to know the lady it
belonged to—anyone who could love that sort of a dog
must be a pretty good sort herself. Perhaps he could
buy her ice cream, or persuade her to go the midway
with him. Martha would approve he was sure. Martha
would know he wasn't up to anything.

Anyhow, no one ever took a little fat man seriously.

But there was too much going on to worry about it.
He found himself at St. Paul's Winter Carnival, marvelously constructed in summer weather through the
combined efforts of York and American. For fifty years
it had been held in January, yet here it was, rubbing
shoulders with the Pendleton Round-Up, the Fresno
Raisin Festival, and Colonial Week in Annapolis. He
got in at the tail end of the ice show, but in time for
one of his favorite acts, the Old Smoothies, out of
retirement for the occasion and gliding as perfectly as
ever to the strains of *Shine On, Harvest Moon.*

His eyes blurred again and it was not his lack of
glasses.

Coming out he passed a large sign: SADIE HAWKINS
DAY—STARTING POINT FOR BACHELORS. He was
tempted to take part; perhaps the lady with the dog
might be among the spinsters. But he was a little tired
by now; just ahead there was an outdoor carnival of
the pony-ride-and-ferris-wheel sort; a moment later he
was on the merry-go-round and was climbing gratefully into one of those swan gondolas so favored by

parents. He found a young man already seated there, reading a book.

"Oh, excuse me," said Johnny. "Do you mind?"

"Not at all," the young man answered and put his book down. "Perhaps you are the man I'm looking for."

"You are looking for someone?"

"Yes. You see, I'm a detective. I've always wanted to be one and now I am."

"Indeed?"

"Quite. Everyone rides the merry-go-round eventually, so it saves trouble to wait here. Of course, I hang around Hollywood and Vine, or Times Square, or Canal Street, but here I can sit and read."

"How can you read while watching for someone?"

"Ah, I know what is in the book—" He held it up; it was *The Hunting of the Snark*. "—so that leaves my eyes free for watching."

Johnny began to like this young man. "Are there boo-jums about?"

"No, for we haven't softly and silently vanished away. But would we notice it if we did? I must think it over. Are you a detective, too?"

"No, I—uh—I travel in elephants."

"A fine profession. But not much for you here. We have giraffes—" He raised his voice above the music of the calliope and let his eyes rove around the carousel. "—camels, two zebras, plenty of horses, but no elephants. Be sure to see the Big Parade; there will be elephants."

"Oh, I wouldn't miss it!"

"You musn't. It will be the most amazing parade in all time, so long that it will never pass a given point and every mile choked with wonders more stupendous than the last. You're sure you're not the man I'm looking for?"

"I don't think so. But see here—how would you go about finding a lady with a dog in this crowd?"

"Well, if she comes here, I'll let you know. Better go down on Canal Street. Yes, I think if I were a lady with a dog I'd be down on Canal Street. Women love to mask; it means they can unmask."

Johnny stood up. "How do I get to Canal Street?"

"Straight through Central City past the opera house, then turn right at the Rose Bowl. Be careful then, for you pass through the Nebraska section with Ak-Sar-Ben in full sway. Anything could happen. After that, Calaveras County—Mind the frogs!—then Canal Street."

"Thank you so much." He followed the directions, keeping an eye out for the lady with a dog. Nevertheless he stared with wonder at the things he saw as he threaded through the gay crowds. He did see a dog, but it was a seeing-eye dog—and that was a great wonder, too, for the live clear eyes of the dog's master could and did see anything that was going on around him, yet the man and the dog traveled together with the man letting the dog direct their way, as if no other way of travel were conceivable, or desired, by either one.

He found himself in Canal Street presently and the illusion was so complete that it was hard to believe that he had not been transported to New Orleans. Carnival was at height; it was Fat Tuesday here; the crowds were masked. He got a mask from a street vendor and went on.

The hunt seemed hopeless. The street was choked by merry-makers watching the parade of the Krewe of Venus. It was hard to breathe, much harder to move and search. He eased into Bourbon Street—the entire French Quarter had been reproduced—when he saw the dog.

He was sure it was the dog. It was wearing a clown suit and a little peaked hat, but it looked like his dog. He corrected himself; it looked like Bindlestiff.

And it accepted one of the frankfurters gratefully. "Where is she, old fellow?" The dog woofed once, then darted away into the crowd. He tried to follow, but could not; he required more clearance. But he was not downhearted; he had found the dog once, he would find him again. Besides, it had been at a masked ball that he had first met Martha, she a graceful Pierrette, he a fat Pierrot. They had watched the dawn come up after the ball and before the sun had set again they had agreed to marry.

He watched the crowd for Pierrettes, sure somehow that the dog's mistress would costume so.

Everything about this fair made him think even more about Martha, if that were possible. How she had traveled his territory with him, how it had been their habit to start out, anywhere, whenever a vacation came along. Chuck the Duncan Hines guide and some bags in the car and be off. Martha . . . sitting beside him with the open highway a broad ribbon before them . . . singing their road song *America the Beautiful* and keeping him on key: "—thine alabaster cities gleam, undimmed by human tears—"

Once she had said to him, while they were bowling along through—where was it? The Black Hills? The Ozarks? The Poconos? No matter. She had said, "Johnny, you'll never be President and I'll never be First Lady, but I'll bet we know more about the United States than any President ever has. Those busy, useful people never have time to *see* it, not really."

"It's a wonderful country, darling."

"It is, it is indeed. I could spend all eternity just traveling around in it—traveling in elephants, Johnny, with you."

He had reached over and patted her knee; he remembered how it felt.

The revelers in the mock French Quarter were thinning out; they had drifted away while he daydreamed. He stopped a red devil. "Where is everyone going?"

"To the parade, of course."

"The Big Parade?"

"Yes, it's forming now." The red devil moved on, he followed.

His own sleeve was plucked. "Did you find her?" It was Mrs. Evans, slightly disguised by a black domino and clinging to the arm of a tall and elderly Uncle Sam.

"Eh? Why, hello, Mrs. Evans! What do you mean?"

"Don't be silly. Did you find her?"

"How did you know I was looking for anyone?"

"Of course you were. Well, keep looking. We must go now." They trailed after the mob.

The Big Parade was already passing by the time he reached its route. It did not matter, there was endlessly more to come. The Holly, Colorado, Boosters were passing; they were followed by the prize Shriner drill team. Then came the Veiled Prophet of Khorassan and his Queen of Love and Beauty, up from their cave in the bottom of the Mississippi . . . the Anniversary Day Parade from Brooklyn, with the school children carrying little American flags . . . the Rose Parade from Pasadena, miles of flowered-covered floats . . . the Indian Powwow from Flagstaff, twenty-two nations represented and no buck in the march wearing less than a thousand dollars' worth of hand-wrought jewelry. After the indigenous Americans rode Buffalo Bill, goatee jutting out and hat in hand, locks flowing in the breeze. Then was the delegation from Hawaii with King Kamehamela himself playing Alii, Lord of Carnival, with royal abandon, while his subjects in dew-fresh leis pranced behind him, giving aloha to all.

There was no end. Square dancers from Ojai and from upstate New York, dames and gentlemen from Annapolis, the Cuero, Texas, Turkey Trot, all the Krewes and marching clubs of old New Orleans, double flambeaux blazing, nobles throwing favors to the crowd —the King of Zulus and his smooth brown court, singing: "Everybody who was anybody doubted it—"

And the Mummers came, "taking a suit up the street" to *Oh Dem Golden Slippers.* Here was something older than the country celebrating it, the shuffling jig of the masquers, a step that was young when mankind was young and first celebrating the birth of spring. First the fancy clubs, whose captains wore capes worth a king's ransom—or a mortgage on a row house— with fifty pages to bear them. Then the Liberty Clowns and the other comics and lastly the ghostly, sweet string bands whose strains bring tears.

Johnny thought back to '44 when he had first seen them march, old men and young boys, because the proper "shooters" were away to war. And of something that should not be on Broad Street in Philadelphia on the first day of January, men riding in the parade because, merciful Heaven forgive us, they could not walk.

He looked and saw that there were indeed automobiles in the line of march—wounded of the last war, and one G.A.R., hat square, hands folded over the head of his cane. Johnny held his breath and waited. When each automobile approached the judges' stand, it stopped short of it, and everyone got out. Somehow, with each other's help, they hobbled or crawled past the judging line, under their own power—and each club's pride was kept intact.

There followed another wonder—they did not get back into the automobiles, but marched up Broad Street.

Then it was Hollywood Boulevard, disguised as Santa Claus Lane, in a production more stupendous than movieland had ever attempted before. There were baby stars galore and presents and favors and candy for all the children and all the grown-up children, too. When, at last, Santa Claus's own float arrived, it was almost too large to be seen, a veritable iceberg, almost the North Pole itself, with John Barrymore and Mickey Mouse riding one on each side of Saint Nicholas.

On the tail end of the great, icy float was a pathetic little figure. Johnny squinted and recognized Mr. Emmett Kelly, dean of all clowns, in his role as Weary Willie. Willie was not merry—oh, no, he was shivering. Johnny did not know whether to laugh or to cry. Mr. Kelly had always affected him that way.

And the elephants came.

Big elephants, little elephants, middle-sized elephants, from pint-sized Wrinkles to mighty Jumbo . . . and with them the bull men, Chester Conklin, P. T. Barnum, Wallie Beery, Mowgli. "This," Johnny said to himself, "must be Mulberry Street."

There was a commotion on the other side of the column; one of the men was shooing something away. Then Johnny saw what it was—the dog. He whistled; the animal seemed confused, then it spotted him, scampered up, and jumped into Johnny's arms. "You stay with me," Johnny told him. "You might have gotten stepped on."

The dog licked his face. He had lost his clown suit, but the little peaked cap hung down under his neck. "What have you been up to?" asked Johnny. "And where is your mistress?"

The last of the elephants were approaching, three abreast, pulling a great carriage. A bugle sounded up front and the procession stopped. "Why are they stopping?" Johnny asked a neighbor.

"Wait a moment. You'll see."

The Grand Marshal of the march came trotting back down the line. He rode a black stallion and was himself brave in villain's boots, white pegged breeches, cutaway, and top hat. He glanced all around.

He stopped immediately in front of Johnny. Johnny held the dog more closely to him. The Grand Marshal dismounted and bowed. Johnny looked around to see who was behind him. The Marshal removed his tall silk hat and caught Johnny's eye. "You, sir, are the Man Who Travels in Elephants?" It was more a statement than a question.

"Uh? Yes."

"Greetings, Rex! Serene Majesty, your Queen and your court await you." The man turned slightly, as if to lead the way.

Johnny gulped and gathered Bindlestiff under one arm. The Marshal led him to the elephant-drawn carriage. The dog slipped out of his arms and bounded up into the carriage and into the lap of the lady. She patted it and looked proudly, happily, down at Johnny Watts. "Hello, Johnny! Welcome home, darling!"

"Martha!" he sobbed—and Rex stumbled and climbed into his carriage to embrace his queen.

The sweet voice of a bugle sounded up ahead, the parade started up again, wending its endless way—

"—ALL YOU ZOMBIES—"

2217 Time Zone V (EST) 7 Nov 1970 NYC—
"Pop's Place": I was polishing a brandy snifter when
the Unmarried Mother came in. I noted the time—
10.17 P.M. zone five or eastern time November 7th,
1970. Temporal agents always notice time & date; we
must.

The Unmarried Mother was a man twenty-five years
old, no taller than I am, immature features and a
touchy temper. I didn't like his looks—I never had—
but he was a lad I was here to recruit, he was my boy.
I gave him my best barkeep's smile.

Maybe I'm too critical. He wasn't swish; his nick-
name came from what he always said when some nosy
type asked him his line: "I'm an unmarried mother."
If he felt less than murderous he would add: "—at four
cents a word. I write confession stories."

If he felt nasty, he would wait for somebody to make
something of it. He had a lethal style of in-fighting, like
a female cop—one reason I wanted him. Not the only
one.

He had a load on and his face showed that he
despised people more than usual. Silently I poured a
double shot of Old Underwear and left the bottle. He
drank, poured another.

I wiped the bar top. "How's the 'Unmarried Mother'
racket?"

His fingers tightened on the glass and he seemed
about to throw it at me; I felt for the sap under the
bar. In temporal manipulation you try to figure everything, but there are so many factors that you never
take needless risks.

I saw him relax that tiny amount they teach you to

143

watch for in the Bureau's training school. "Sorry," I said. "Just asking, 'How's business?' Make it 'How's the weather?' "

He looked sour. "Business is O.K. I write 'em, they print 'em, I eat."

I poured myself one, leaned toward him. "Matter of fact," I said, "you write a nice stick—I've sampled a few. You have an amazingly sure touch with the woman's angle."

It was a slip I had to risk; he never admitted what pennames he used. But he was boiled enough to pick up only the last. " 'Woman's angle!' " he repeated with a snort. "Yeah, I know the woman's angle. I should."

"So?" I said doubtfully. "Sisters?"

"No. You wouldn't believe me if I told you."

"Now, now," I answered mildly, "bartenders and psychiatrists learn that nothing is stranger than the truth. Why, son, if you heard the stories I do—well, you'd make yourself rich. Incredible."

"You don't know what 'incredible' means!"

"So? Nothing astonishes me. I've always heard worse."

He snorted again. "Want to bet the rest of the bottle?"

"I'll bet a full bottle." I placed one on the bar.

"Well—" I signaled my other bartender to handle the trade. We were at the far end, a single-stool space that I kept private by loading the bar top by it with jars of pickled eggs and other clutter. A few were at the other end watching the fights and somebody was playing the juke box—private as a bed where we were. "O.K.," he began, "to start with, I'm a bastard."

"I mean it," he snapped. "My parents weren't married."

"Still no distinction," I insisted. "Neither were mine."

"When—" He stopped, gave me the first warm look I ever saw on him. "You mean that?"

"I do. A one-hundred-percent bastard. In fact," I added, "No one in my family ever marries. All bastards."

"Don't try to top me—you're married." He pointed at my ring.

"Oh, that." I showed it to him. "It just looks like a wedding ring; I wear it to keep women off." That ring is an antique I bought in 1985 from a fellow operative —he had fetched it from pre-Christian Crete. "The Worm Ouroboros . . . the World Snake that eats its own tail, forever without end. A symbol of the Great Paradox."

He barely glanced at it. "If you're really a bastard, you know how it feels. When I was a little girl—"

"Wups!" I said. "Did I hear you correctly?"

"Who's telling this story? When I was a little girl— Look, ever hear of Christine Jorgenson? Or Roberta Cowell?"

"Uh, sex change cases? You're trying to tell me—"

"Don't interrupt or swelp me, I won't talk. I was a foundling, left at an orphanage in Cleveland in 1945 when I was a month old. When I was a little girl, I envied kids with parents. Then, when I learned about sex—and, believe me, Pop, you learn fast in an orphanage—"

"I know."

"I made a solemn vow that any kid of mine would have both a pop and a mom. It kept me 'pure,' quite a feat in that vicinity—I had to learn to fight to manage it. Then I got older and realized I stood darned little chance of getting married—for the same reason I hadn't been adopted." He scowled. "I was horse-faced and buck-toothed, flat-chested and straight-haired."

"You don't look any worse than I do."

"Who cares how a barkeep looks? Or a writer? But people wanting to adopt pick little blue-eyed golden-haired morons. Later on, the boys want bulging breasts, a cute face, and an Oh-you-wonderful-male manner." He shrugged. "I couldn't compete. So I decided to join the W.E.N.C.H.E.S."

"Eh?"

"Women's Emergency National Corps, Hospitality & Entertainment Section, what they now call 'Space Angels'—Auxiliary Nursing Group, Extraterrestrial Legions."

I knew both terms, once I had them chronized. Although we now use still a third name; it's that elite

military service corps: Women's Hospitality Order Re-
fortifying & Encouraging Spacemen. Vocabulary shift
is the worst hurdle in time-jumps—did you know that
"service station" once meant a dispensary for petroleum fractions? Once on an assignment in the Churchill
Era a woman said to me, "Meet me at the service
station next door"—which is *not* what it sounds; a
"service station" (then) wouldn't have a bed in it.

He went on: "It was when they first admitted you
can't send men into space for months and years and
not relieve the tension. You remember how the wowsers
screamed?—that improved my chances, volunteers were
scarce. A gal had to be respectable, preferably virgin
(they liked to train them from scratch), above average
mentally, and stable emotionally. But most volunteers
were old hookers, or neurotics who would crack up ten
days off Earth. So I didn't need looks; if they accepted
me, they would fix my buck teeth, put a wave in my
hair, teach me to walk and dance and how to listen to
a man pleasingly, and everything else—plus training
for the prime duties. They would even use plastic
surgery if it would help—nothing too good for Our
Boys.

"Best yet, they made sure you didn't get pregnant
during your enlistment—and you were almost certain
to marry at the end of your hitch. Same way today,
A.N.G.E.L.S. marry spacers—they talk the language.

"When I was eighteen I was placed as a 'mother's
helper.' This family simply wanted a cheap servant
but I didn't mind as I couldn't enlist till I was twenty-
one. I did housework and went to night school—pre-
tending to continue my high school typing and short-
hand but going to a charm class instead, to better my
chances for enlistment.

"Then I met this city slicker with his hundred dollar
bills." He scowled. "The no-good actually did have a
wad of hundred dollar bills. He showed me one night,
told me to help myself.

"But I didn't. I liked him. He was the first man I
ever met who was nice to me without trying to take
my pants off. I quit night school to see him oftener. It
was the happiest time of my life.

"Then one night in the park my pants did come off."
He stopped. I said, "And then?"

"And then *nothing!* I never saw him again. He walked me home and told me he loved me—and kissed me good-night and never came back." He looked grim. "If I could find him, I'd kill him!"

"Well," I sympathized, "I know how you feel. But killing him—just for doing what comes naturally—hmm . . . Did you struggle?"

"Huh? What's that got to do with it?"

"Quite a bit. Maybe he deserves a couple of broken arms for running out on you, but—"

"He deserves worse than that! Wait till you hear. Somehow I kept anyone from suspecting and decided it was all for the best. I hadn't really loved him and probably would never love anybody—and I was more eager to join the W.E.N.C.H.E.S. than ever. I wasn't disqualified, they didn't insist on virgins. I cheered up.

"It wasn't until my skirts got tight that I realized."

"Pregnant?"

"The bastard had me higher'n a kite! Those skinflints I lived with ignored it as long as I could work—then kicked me out and the orphanage wouldn't take me back. I landed in a charity ward surrounded by other big bellies and trotted bedpans until my time came.

"One night I found myself on an operating table, with a nurse saying, 'Relax. Now breathe deeply.'

"I woke up in bed, numb from the chest down. My surgeon came in. 'How do you feel?' he says cheerfully.

" 'Like a mummy.'

" 'Naturally. You're wrapped like one and full of dope to keep you numb. You'll get well—but a Caesarian isn't a hangnail.'

" 'Caesarian?' " I said, 'Doc—*did I lose the baby?*'

" 'Oh, no. Your baby's fine.'

" 'Oh. Boy or girl?'

" 'A healthy little girl. Five pounds, three ounces.'

"I relaxed. It's something, to have made a baby. I told myself I would go somewhere and tack 'Mrs.' on my name and let the kid think her papa was dead—no orphanage for *my* kid!

"But the surgeon was talking. 'Tell me, uh—' He avoided my name. '—did you ever think your glandular setup was odd?'

"I said, 'Huh? Of course not. What are you driving at?'

"He hesitated. 'I'll give you this in one dose, then a hypo to let you sleep off your jitters. You'll have 'em.'

" 'Why?' I demanded.

" 'Ever hear of that Scottish physician who was female until she was thirty-five?—then had surgery and became legally and medically a man? Got married. All okay.'

" 'What's that got to do with me?'

" 'That's what I'm saying. You're a man.'

"I tried to sit up. '*What?*'

" 'Take it easy. When I opened you, I found a mess. I sent for the Chief of Surgery while I got the baby out, then we held a consultation with you on the table— and worked for hours to salvage what we could. You had two full sets of organs, both immature, but with the female set well enough developed that you had a baby. They could never be any use to you again, so we took them out and rearranged things so that you can develop properly as a man.' He put a hand on me. 'Don't worry. You're young, your bones will readjust, we'll watch your glandular balance—and make a fine young man out of you.'

"I started to cry. 'What about my *baby?*'

" 'Well, you can't nurse her, you haven't milk enough for a kitten. If I were you, I wouldn't see her —put her up for adoption.'

" '*No!*'

"He shrugged. 'The choice is yours; you're her mother—well, her parent. But don't worry now; we'll get you well first.'

"Next day they let me see the kid and I saw her daily—trying to get used to her. I had never seen a brand-new baby and had no idea how awful they look— my daughter looked like an orange monkey. My feeling changed to cold determination to do right by her. But four weeks later that didn't mean anything."

"Eh?"

"She was snatched."

" 'Snatched?' "

The unmarried mother almost knocked over the bottle we had bet. "Kidnapped—stolen from the hospital nursery!" He breathed hard. "How's that for taking the last thing a man's got to live for?"

"A bad deal," I agreed. "Let's pour you another. No clues?"

"Nothing the police could trace. Somebody came to see her, claimed to be her uncle. While the nurse had her back turned, he walked out with her."

"Description?"

"Just a man, with a face-shaped face, like yours or mine." He frowned. "I think it was the baby's father. The nurse swore it was an older man but he probably used make-up. Who else would swipe my baby? Childless women pull such stunts—but whoever heard of a man doing it?"

"What happened to you then?"

"Eleven more months of that grim place and three operations. In four months I started to grow a beard; before I was out I was shaving regularly . . . and no longer doubted that I was male." He grinned wryly. "I was staring down nurses' necklines."

"Well," I said, "seems to me you came through okay. Here you are, a normal man, making good money, no real troubles. And the life of a female is not an easy one."

He glared at me. "A lot you know about it!"

"So?"

"Ever hear the expression 'a ruined woman'?"

"Mmm, years ago. Doesn't mean much today."

"I was as ruined as a woman can be; that bastard *really* ruined me—I was no longer a woman . . . and I didn't know *how* to be a man."

"Takes getting used to, I suppose."

"You have no idea. I don't mean learning how to dress, or not walking into the wrong rest room; I learned those in the hospital. But how could I *live*? What job could I get? Hell, I couldn't even drive a car. I didn't know a trade; I couldn't do manual labor—too much scar tissue, too tender.

"I hated him for having ruined me for the W.E.N.-
C.H.E.S., too, but I didn't know how much until I
tried to join the Space Corps instead. One look at my
belly and I was marked unfit for military service. The
medical officer spent time on me just from curiosity;
he had read about my case.

"So I changed my name and came to New York. I
got by as a fry cook, then rented a typewriter and set
myself up as a public stenographer—what a laugh! In
four months I typed four letters and one manuscript.
The manuscript was for *Real Life Tales* and a waste
of paper, but the goof who wrote it, sold it. Which
gave me an idea; I bought a stack of confession mag-
azines and studied them." He looked cynical. "Now
you know how I get the authentic woman's angle on
an unmarried-mother story . . . through the only ver-
sion I haven't sold—the true one. Do I win the bottle?"

I pushed it toward him. I was upset myself, but there
was work to do. I said, "Son, you still want to lay
hands on that so-and-so?"

His eyes lighted up—a feral gleam.

"Hold it!" I said. "You wouldn't kill him?"

He chuckled nastily. "Try me."

"Take it easy. I know more about it than you think
I do. I can help you. I know where he is."

He reached across the bar. *"Where is he?"*

I said softly, "Let go my shirt, sonny—or you'll land
in the alley and we'll tell the cops you fainted." I
showed him the sap.

He let go. "Sorry. But where is he?" He looked at
me. "And how do you know so much?"

"All in good time. There are records—hospital records, orphanage records, medical records. The matron
of your orphanage was Mrs. Fetherage—right? She
was followed by Mrs. Gruenstein—right? Your name,
as a girl, was 'Jane'—right? And you didn't tell me any
of this—right?"

I had him baffled and a bit scared. "What's this?
You trying to make trouble for me?"

"No indeed. I've your welfare at heart. I can put this
character in your lap. You do to him as you see fit—
and I guarantee that you'll get away with it. But I don't

think you'll kill him. You'd be nuts to—and you aren't nuts. Not quite."

He brushed it aside. "Cut the noise. *Where is he?*"

I poured him a short one; he was drunk but anger was offsetting it. "Not so fast. I do something for you —you do something for me."

"Uh . . . what?"

"You don't like your work. What would you say to high pay, steady work, unlimited expense account, your own boss on the job, and lots of variety and adventure?"

He stared. "I'd say, 'Get those goddam reindeer off my roof!' Shove it, Pop—there's no such job."

"Okay, put it this way: I hand him to you, you settle with him, then try my job. If it's not all I claim—well, I can't hold you."

He was wavering, the last drink did it. "When d'yuh d'liver 'im?" he said thickly.

"If it's a deal—*right now!*"

He shoved out his hand. "It's a deal!"

I nodded to my assistant to watch both ends, noted the time—2300—started to duck through the gate under the bar—when the juke box blared out: *"I'm My Own Granpaw!"* The service man had orders to load it with old Americana and classics because I couldn't stomach the "music" of 1970, but I hadn't known that tape was in it. I called out, "Shut that off! Give the customer his money back." I added, "Storeroom, back in a moment," and headed there with my Unmarried Mother following.

It was down the passage across from the johns, a steel door to which no one but my day manager and myself had a key; inside was a door to an inner room to which only I had a key. We went there.

He looked blearily around at windowless walls. "Where is 'e?"

"Right away." I opened a case, the only thing in the room; it was a U.S.F.F. Co-ordinates Transformer Field Kit, series 1992, Mod. II—a beauty, no moving parts, weight twenty-three kilos fully charged, and shaped to pass as a suitcase. I had adjusted it precisely earlier that day; all I had to do was to shake the metal net which limits the transformation field.

Which I did. "Wha's that?" he demanded.

"Time machine," I said and tossed the net over us.

"Hey!" he yelled and stepped back. There is a technique to this; the net has to be thrown so that the subject will instinctively step back *onto* the metal mesh, then you close the net with both of you inside completely—else you might leave shoe soles behind or a piece of foot, or scoop up a slice of floor. But that's all the skill it takes. Some agents con a subject into the net; I tell the truth and use that instant of utter astonishment to flip the switch. Which I did.

1030-V-3 April 1963-Cleveland, Ohio-Apex Bldg.: "Hey!" he repeated. "Take this damn thing off!"

"Sorry," I apologized and did so, stuffed the net into the case, closed it. "You said you wanted to find him."

"But—You said that was a time machine!"

I pointed out a window. "Does that look like November? Or New York?" While he was gawking at new buds and spring weather, I reopened the case, took out a packet of hundred dollar bills, checked that the numbers and signatures were compatible with 1963. The Temporal Bureau doesn't care how much you spend (it costs nothing) but they don't like unnecessary anachronisms. Too many mistakes and a general court martial will exile you for a year in a nasty period, say 1974 with its strict rationing and forced labor. I never make such mistakes, the money was okay. He turned around and said, "What happened?"

"He's here. Go outside and take him. Here's expense money." I shoved it at him and added, "Settle him, then I'll pick you up."

Hundred dollar bills have a hypnotic effect on a person not used to them. He was thumbing them unbelievingly as I eased him into the hall, locked him out. The next jump was easy, a small shift in era.

1700-V-10 March 1964-Cleveland-Apex Bldg.: There was a notice under the door saying that my lease expired next week; otherwise the room looked as it had a moment before. Outside, trees were bare and snow threatened; I hurried, stopping only for contemporary money and a coat, hat and topcoat I had left there when I leased the room. I hired a car, went to the hospital. It took twenty minutes to bore the nursery attendant to the point where I could swipe the baby without being noticed; we went back to the Apex Building. This dial setting was more involved as the building did not yet exist in 1945. But I had precalculated it.

0100-V-20 Sept 1945-Cleveland-Skyview Motel: Field kit, baby, and I arrived in a motel outside town. Earlier I had registered as "Gregory Johnson, Warren, Ohio," so we arrived in a room with curtains closed, windows locked, and doors bolted, and the floor cleared to allow for waver as the machine hunts. You can get a nasty bruise from a chair where it shouldn't be—not the chair of course, but backlash from the field.

No trouble. Jane was sleeping soundly; I carried her out, put her in a grocery box on the seat of a car I had provided earlier, drove to the orphanage, put her on the steps, drove two blocks to a "service station" (the petroleum products sort) and phoned the orphanage, drove back in time to see them taking the box inside, kept going and abandoned the car near the motel— walked to it and jumped forward to the Apex Building in 1963.

2200-V-24 April 1963-Cleveland-Apex Bldg.: I had cut the time rather fine—temporal accuracy depends on span, except on return to zero. If I had it right, Jane was discovering, out in the park this balmy spring night, that she wasn't quite as "nice" a girl as she had thought. I grabbed a taxi to the home of those skinflints, had the hackie wait around a corner while I lurked in shadows.

Presently I spotted them down the street, arms around each other. He took her up on the porch and made a long job of kissing her good-night—longer than I had thought. Then she went in and he came down the walk, turned away. I slid into step and hooked an arm in his. "That's all, son," I announced quietly. "I'm back to pick you up."

"*You!*" He gasped and caught his breath.

"Me. Now you know who *he* is—and after you think it over you'll know who *you* are . . . and if you think hard enough, you'll figure out who the baby is . . . and who *I* am."

He didn't answer, he was badly shaken. It's a shock to have it proved to you that you can't resist seducing yourself. I took him to the Apex Building and we jumped again.

2300-VII-12 Aug 1985-Sub Rockies Base: I woke the duty sergeant, showed my I.D., told the sergeant to bed him down with a happy pill and recruit him in the morning. The sergeant looked sour but rank is rank, regardless of era; he did what I said—thinking no doubt, that the next time we met he might be the colonel and I the sergeant. Which can happen in our corps. "What name?" he asked.

I wrote it out. He raised his eyebrows. "Like so, eh? *Hmm—*"

"You just do your job, Sergeant." I turned to my companion. "Son, your troubles are over. You're about to start the best job a man ever held—and you'll do well. I *know.*"

"But—"

" 'But' nothing. Get a night's sleep, then look over the proposition. You'll like it."

"That you will!" agreed the sergeant. "Look at me —born in 1917—still around, still young, still enjoying life." I went back to the jump room, set everything on preselected zero.

2301-V-7 Nov 1970-NYC-"Pop's Place": I came out of the storeroom carrying a fifth of Drambuie to account for the minute I had been gone. My assistant was arguing with the customer who had been playing *"I'm My Own Granpaw!"* I said, "Oh, let him play it, then unplug it." I was very tired.

It's rough, but somebody must do it and it's very

hard to recruit anyone in the later years, since the Mistake of 1972. Can you think of a better source than to pick people all fouled up where they are and give them well-paid, interesting (even though dangerous) work in a necessary cause? Everybody knows now why the Fizzle War of 1963 fizzled. The bomb with New York's number on it didn't go off, a hundred other things didn't go as planned—all arranged by the likes of me.

But not the Mistake of '72; that one is not our fault —and can't be undone; there's no paradox to resolve. A thing either is, or it isn't, now and forever amen. But there won't be another like it; an order dated "1992" takes precedence any year.

I closed five minutes early, leaving a letter in the cash register telling my day manager that I was accepting his offer, so see my lawyer as I was leaving on a long vacation. The Bureau might or might not pick up his payments, but they want things left tidy. I went to the room back of the storeroom and forward to 1993.

2200-VII-12 Jan 1993-Sub Rockies Annex-HQ Temporal DOL: I checked in with the duty officer and went to my quarters, intending to sleep for a week. I had fetched the bottle we bet (after all, I won it) and took a drink before I wrote my report. It tasted foul and I wondered why I had ever liked Old Underwear. But it was better than nothing; I don't like to be cold sober, I think too much. But I don't really hit the bottle either; other people have snakes—*I* have people.

I dictated my report: forty recruitments all okayed by the Psych Bureau—counting my own, which I knew would be okayed. I was here, wasn't I? Then I taped a request for assignment to operations; I was sick of recruiting. I dropped both in the slot and headed for bed.

My eye fell on "The By-Laws of Time," over my bed:

> *Never Do Yesterday What Should be Done Tomorrow.*
> *If At Last You Do Succeed, Never Try Again.*

A Stitch In Time Saves Nine Billion.
A Paradox May be Paradoctored.
It is Earlier When You Think.
Ancestors Are Just People.
Even Jove Nods.

They didn't inspire me the way they had when I was a recruit; thirty subjective years of time-jumping wears you down. I undressed and when I got down to the hide I looked at my belly. A Caesarian leaves a big scar but I'm so hairy now that I don't notice it unless I look for it.

Then I glanced at the ring on my finger.

The Snake That Eats Its Own Tail, Forever and Ever . . . I *know* where *I* came from—but *where did all you zombies come from?*

I felt a headache coming on, but a headache powder is one thing I do not take. I did it once—and you all went away.

So I crawled into bed and whistled out the light.

You aren't really there at all. There isn't anybody but me—Jane—here alone in the dark.

I miss you dreadfully!

THEY

THEY WOULD NOT LET HIM ALONE.

They would never let him alone. He realized that that was part of the plot against him—never to leave him in peace, never to give him a chance to mull over the lies they had told him, time enough to pick out the flaws, and to figure out the truth for himself.

That damned attendant this morning! He had come busting in with his breakfast tray, waking him, and causing him to forget his dream. If only he could remember that dream—

Someone was unlocking the door. He ignored it.

"Howdy, old boy. They tell me you refused your breakfast?" Dr. Hayward's professionally kindly mask hung over his bed.

"I wasn't hungry."

"But we can't have that. You'll get weak, and then I won't be able to get you well completely. Now get up and get your clothes on and I'll order an eggnog for you. Come on, that's a good fellow!"

Unwilling, but still less willing at that moment to enter into any conflict of wills, he got out of bed and slipped on his bathrobe. "That's better," Hayward approved. "Have a cigarette?"

"No, thank you."

The doctor shook his head in a puzzled fashion. "Darned if I can figure you out. Loss of interest in physical pleasures does not fit your type of case."

"What is my type of case?" he inquired in flat tones.

"Tut! Tut!" Hayward tried to appear roguish. "If medicos told their professional secrets, they might have to work for a living."

"What is my type of case?"

"Well—the label doesn't matter, does it? Suppose you tell me. I really know nothing about your case as yet. Don't you think it is about time you talked?"

"I'll play chess with you."

"All right, all right." Hayward made a gesture of impatient concession. "We've played chess every day for a week. If you will talk, I'll play chess."

What could it matter? If he was right, they already understood perfectly that he had discovered their plot; there was nothing to be gained by concealing the obvious. Let them try to argue him out of it. Let the tail go with the hide! To hell with it!

He got out the chessmen and commenced setting them up. "What do you know of my case so far?"

"Very little. Physical examination, negative. Past history, negative. High intelligence, as shown by your record in school and your success in your profession. Occasional fits of moodiness, but nothing exceptional. The only positive information was the incident that caused you to come here for treatment."

"To be brought here, you mean. Why should it cause comment?"

"Well, good gracious, man—if you barricade yourself in your room and insist that your wife is plotting against you, don't you expect people to notice?"

"But she was plotting against me—and so are you. White, or black?"

"Black—it's your turn to attack. Why do you think we are plotting against you?"

"It's an involved story, and goes way back into my early childhood. There was an immediate incident, however—" He opened by advancing the white king's knight to KB3. Hayward's eyebrows raised.

"You make a piano attack?"

"Why not? You know that it is not safe for me to risk a gambit with you."

The doctor shrugged his shoulders and answered the opening. "Suppose we start with your early childhood. It may shed more light than more recent incidents. Did you feel that you were being persecuted as a child?"

"No!" He half rose from his chair. "When I was a child I was sure of myself. I knew then, I tell you; I knew! Life was worth while, and I knew it. I was at peace with myself and my surroundings. Life was good and I assumed that the creatures around me were like myself."

"And weren't they?"

"Not at all! Particularly the children. I didn't know what viciousness was until I was turned loose with other children. The little devils! And I was expected to be like them and play with them."

The doctor nodded. "I know. The herd compulsion. Children can be pretty savage at times."

"You've missed the point. This wasn't any healthy roughness; these creatures were different—not like myself at all. They looked like me, but they were not like me. If I tried to say anything to one of them about anything that mattered to me, all I could get was a stare and a scornful laugh. Then they would find some way to punish me for having said it."

Hayward nodded. "I see what you mean. How about grown-ups?"

"That is somewhat different. Adults don't matter to children at first—or, rather they did not matter to me. They were too big, and they did not bother me, and they were busy with things that did not enter into my considerations. It was only when I noticed that my presence affected them that I began to wonder about them."

"How do you mean?"

"Well, they never did the things when I was around that they did when I was not around."

Hayward looked at him carefully. "Won't that statement take quite a lot of justifying? How do you know what they did when you weren't around?"

He acknowledged the point. "But I used to catch them just stopping. If I came into a room, the conversation would stop suddenly, and then it would pick up about the weather or something equally inane. Then I took to hiding and listening and looking. Adults did not behave the same way in my presence as out of it."

"Your move, I believe. But see here, old man—that was when you were a child. Every child passes through that phase. Now that you are a man, you must see the adult point of view. Children are strange creatures and have to be protected—at least, we do protect them—from many adult interests. There is a whole code of conventions in the matter that—"

"Yes, yes," he interrupted impatiently, "I know all that. Nevertheless, I noticed enough and remembered enough that was never clear to me later. And it put me on my guard to notice the next thing."

"Which was?" He noticed that the doctor's eyes were averted as he adjusted a castle's position.

"The things I saw people doing and heard them talking about were never of any importance. They must be doing something else."

"I don't follow you."

"You don't choose to follow me. I'm telling this to you in exchange for a game of chess."

"Why do you like to play chess so well?"

"Because it is the only thing in the world where I can see all the factors and understand all the rules. Never mind—I saw all around me this enormous plant, cities, farms, factories, churches, schools, homes, railroads, luggage, roller coasters, trees, saxophones, libraries, people and animals. People that looked like me and who should have felt very much like me, if what I was told was the truth. But what did they appear to be doing? 'They went to work to earn the money to buy the food to get the strength to go to work to earn the money to buy the food to get the strength to go to work to get the strength to buy the food to earn the money to go to—' until they fell over dead. Any slight variation in the basic pattern did not matter, for they always fell over dead. And everybody tried to tell me that I should be doing the same thing. I knew better!"

The doctor gave him a look apparently intended to denote helpless surrender and laughed. "I can't argue with you. Life does look like that, and maybe it is just that futile. But it is the only life we have. Why not make up your mind to enjoy it as much as possible?"

"Oh, no!" He looked both sulky and stubborn. "You can't peddle nonsense to me by claiming to be fresh out of sense. How do I know? Because all this complex stage setting, all these swarms of actors, could not have been put here just to make idiot noises at each other. Some other explanation, but not that one. An insanity as enormous, as complex, as the one around me had to be planned. I've found the plan!"

"Which is?"

He noticed that the doctor's eyes were again averted.

"It is a play intended to divert me, to occupy my mind and confuse me, to keep me so busy with details that I will not have time to think about the meaning. You are all in it, every one of you." He shook his finger in the doctor's face. "Most of them may be helpless automatons, but you're not. You are one of the conspirators. You've been sent in as a troubleshooter to try to force me to go back to playing the role assigned to me!"

He saw that the doctor was waiting for him to quiet down.

"Take it easy," Hayward finally managed to say. "Maybe it is all a conspiracy, but why do you think that you have been singled out for special attention? Maybe it is a joke on all of us. Why couldn't I be one of the victims as well as yourself?"

"Got you!" He pointed a long finger at Hayward. "That is the essence of the plot. All of these creatures have been set up to look like me in order to prevent me from realizing that I was the center of the arrangements. But I have noticed the key fact, the mathematically inescapable fact, that I am unique. Here am I, sitting on the inside. The world extends outward from me. I am the center—"

"Easy, man, easy! Don't you realize that the world looks that way to me, too. We are each the center of the universe—"

"Not so! That is what you have tried to make me believe, that I am just one of millions more just like me. Wrong! If they were like me, then I could get into communication with them. I can't. I have tried and tried and I can't. I've sent out my inner thoughts, seeking some one other being who has them, too. What have I gotten back? Wrong answers, jarring incongruities, meaningless obscenity. I've tried. I tell you. God!

—how I've tried! But there is nothing out there to speak to me—nothing but emptiness and otherness!"

"Wait a minute. Do you mean to say that you think there is nobody home at my end of the line? Don't you believe that I am alive and conscious?"

He regarded the doctor soberly. "Yes, I think you are probably alive, but you are one of the others—my antagonists. But you have set thousands of others around me whose faces are blank, not lived in, and whose speech is a meaningless reflex of noise."

"Well, then, if you concede that I am an ego, why do you insist that I am so very different from yourself?"

"Why? Wait!" He pushed back from the chess table and strode over to the wardrobe, from which he took out a violin case.

While he was playing, the lines of suffering smoothed out of his face and his expression took a relaxed beatitude. For a while he recaptured the emotions, but not the knowledge, which he had possessed in dreams. The melody proceeded easily from proposition to proposition with inescapable, unforced logic. He finished with a triumphant statement of the essential thesis and turned to the doctor. "Well?"

"Hm-m-m." He seemed to detect an even greater degree of caution in the doctor's manner. "It's an odd bit, but remarkable. 'S pity you didn't take up the violin seriously. You could have made quite a reputation. You could even now. Why don't you do it? You could afford to, I believe."

He stood and stared at the doctor for a long moment, then shook his head as if trying to clear it. "It's no use," he said slowly, "no use at all. There is no possibility of communication. I am alone." He replaced the instrument in its case and returned to the chess table. "My move, I believe?"

"Yes. Guard your queen."

He studied the board. "Not necessary. I no longer need my queen. Check."

The doctor interposed a pawn to parry the attack.

He nodded. "You use your pawns well, but I have

learned to anticipate your play. Check again—and mate, I think."

The doctor examined the new situation. "No," he decided, "no—not quite." He retreated from the square under attack. "Not checkmate—stalemate at the worst. Yes, another stalemate."

He was upset by the doctor's visit. He couldn't be wrong, basically, yet the doctor had certainly pointed out logical holes in his position. From a logical standpoint the whole world might be a fraud perpetrated on everybody. But logic meant nothing—logic itself was a fraud, starting with unproved assumptions and capable of proving anything. The world is what it is!—and carries its own evidence of trickery.

But does it? What did he have to go on? Could he lay down a line between known facts and everything else and then make a reasonable interpretation of the world, based on facts alone—an interpretation free from complexities of logic and no hidden assumptions of points not certain. Very well—

First fact, himself. He knew himself directly. He existed.

Second facts, the evidence of his "five senses," everything that he himself saw and heard and smelled and tasted with his physical senses. Subject to their limitations, he must believe his senses. Without them he was entirely solitary, shut up in a locker of bone, blind, deaf, cut off, the only being in the world.

And that was not the case. He knew that he did not invent the information brought to him by his senses. There had to be something else out there, some otherness that produced the things his senses recorded. All philosophies that claimed that the physical world around him did not exist except in his imagination were sheer nonsense.

But beyond that, what? Were there any third facts on which he could rely? No, not at this point. He could not afford to believe anything that he was told, or that he read, or that was implicitly assumed to be true about the world around him. No, he could not believe any of it, for the sum total of what he had been told and read and been taught in school was so contradic-

tory, so senseless, so wildly insane that none of it could
be believed unless he personally confirmed it.

Wait a minute—The very telling of these lies, these
senseless contradictions, was a fact in itself, known to
him directly. To that extent they were data, probably
very important data.

The world as it had been shown to him was a piece
of unreason, an idiot's dream. Yet it was on too mam-
moth a scale to be without some reason. He came
wearily back to his original point: Since the world
could not be as crazy as it appeared to be, it must
necessarily have been arranged to appear crazy in order
to deceive him as to the truth.

Why had they done it to him? And what was the
truth behind the sham? There must be some clue in the
deception itself. What thread ran through it all? Well,
in the first place he had been given a superabundance
of explanations of the world around him, philosophies,
religions, "common sense" explanations. Most of them
were so clumsy, so obviously inadequate, or meaningless, that they could hardly have expected him to take
them seriously. They must have intended them simply
as misdirection.

But there were certain basic assumptions running
through all the hundreds of explanations of the crazi-
ness around him. It must be these basic assumptions
that he was expected to believe. For example, there
was the deepseated assumption that he was a "human
being," essentially like millions of others around him
and billions more in the past and the future.

That was nonsense! He had never once managed to
get into real communication with all those things that
looked so much like him but were so different. In the
agony of his loneliness, he had deceived himself that
Alice understood him and was a being like him. He
knew now that he had suppressed and refused to examine thousands of little discrepancies because he could
not bear the thought of returning to complete loneliness. He had needed to believe that his wife was a
living, breathing being of his own kind who understood
his inner thoughts. He had refused to consider the pos-

sibility that she was simply, a mirror, an echo—or something unthinkably worse.

He had found a mate, and the world was tolerable, even though dull, stupid, and full of petty annoyance. He was moderately happy and had put away his suspicions. He had accepted, quite docilely, the treadmill he was expected to use, until a slight mischance had momentarily cut through the fraud—then his suspicions had returned with impounded force; the bitter knowledge of his childhood had been confirmed.

He supposed that he had been a fool to make a fuss about it. If he had kept his mouth shut they would not have locked him up. He should have been as subtle and as shrewd as they, kept his eyes and ears open and learned the details of and the reasons for the plot against him. He might have learned how to circumvent it.

But what if they had locked him up—the whole world was an asylum and all of them his keepers.

A key scraped in the lock, and he looked up to see an attendant entering with a tray. "Here's your dinner, sir."

"Thanks, Joe," he said gently. "Just put it down."

"Movies tonight, sir," the attendant went on. "Wouldn't you like to go? Dr. Hayward said you could—"

"No, thank you. I prefer not to."

"I wish you would, sir." He noticed with amusement the persuasive intentness of the attendant's manner. "I think the doctor wants you to. It's a good movie. There's a Mickey Mouse cartoon—"

"You almost persuade me, Joe," he answered with passive agreeableness. "Mickey's trouble is the same as mine, essentially. However, I'm not going. They need not bother to hold movies tonight."

"Oh, there will be movies in any case, sir. Lots of our other guests will attend."

"Really? Is that an example of thoroughness, or are you simply keeping up the pretense in talking to me? It isn't necessary, Joe, if it's any strain on you. I know the game. If I don't attend, there is no point in holding movies."

He liked the grin with which the attendant answered this thrust. Was it possible that this being was created just as he appeared to be—big muscles, phlegmatic disposition, tolerant, doglike? Or was there nothing going on behind those kind eyes, nothing but robot reflex? No, it was more likely that he was one of them, since he was so closely in attendance on him.

The attendant left and he busied himself at his supper tray, scooping up the already-cut bites of meat with a spoon, the only implement provided. He smiled again at their caution and thoroughness. No danger of that—he would not destroy this body as long as it served him in investigating the truth of the matter. There were still many different avenues of research available before taking that possibly irrevocable step.

After supper he decided to put his thoughts in better order by writing them; he obtained paper. He should start with a general statement of some underlying postulate of the credos that had been drummed into him all his "life." Life? Yes, that was a good one. He wrote:

"I am told that I was born a certain number of years ago and that I will die a similar number of years hence. Various clumsy stories have been offered me to explain to me where I was before birth and what becomes of me after death, but they are rough lies, not intended to deceive, except as misdirection. In every other possible way the world around me assures me that I am mortal, here but a few years, and a few years hence gone completely—nonexistent.

"WRONG—I am immortal. I transcend this little time axis; a seventy-year span on it is but a casual phase in my experience. Second only to the prime datum of my own existence is the emotionally convincing certainty of my own continuity. I may be a closed curve, but, closed or open, I neither have a beginning nor an end. Self-awareness is not relational; it is absolute, and cannot be reached to be destroyed, or created. Memory, however, being a relational aspect of consciousness, may be tampered with and possibly destroyed.

"It is true that most religions which have been offered me teach immortality, but note the fashion in which they teach it. The surest way to lie convincingly is to tell the truth unconvincingly. They did not wish me to believe.

"Caution: Why have they tried so hard to convince me that I am going to die in a few years? There must be a very important reason. I infer that they are preparing me for some sort of a major change. It may be crucially important for me to figure out their intentions about this—probably I have several years in which to reach a decision. Note: Avoid using the types of reasoning they have taught me."

The attendant was back. "Your wife is here, sir."

"Tell her to go away."

"Please, sir—Dr. Hayward is most anxious that you should see her."

"Tell Dr. Hayward that I said that he is an excellent chess player."

"Yes, sir." The attendant waited for a moment. "Then you won't see her, sir?"

"No, I won't see her."

He wandered around the room for some minutes after the attendant had left, too distrait to return to his recapitulation. By and large they had played very decently with him since they had brought him here. He was glad that they had allowed him to have a room alone, and he certainly had more time free for contemplation than had ever been possible on the outside. To be sure, continuous effort to keep him busy and to distract him was made, but, by being stubborn, he was able to circumvent the rules and gain some hours each day for introspection.

But, damnation!—he did wish they would not persist in using Alice in their attempts to divert his thoughts. Although the intense terror and revulsion which she had inspired in him when he had first rediscovered the truth had now aged into a simple feeling of repugnance and distaste for her company, nevertheless it was emotionally upsetting to be reminded of her, to be forced into making decisions about her.

After all, she had been his wife for many years. Wife? What was a wife? Another soul like one's own,

a complement, the other necessary pole to the couple,
a sanctuary of understanding and sympathy in the
boundless depths of aloneness. That was what he had
thought, what he had needed to believe and had believed fiercely for years. The yearning need for com-
panionship of his own kind had caused him to see himself reflected in those beautiful eyes and had made him
quite uncritical of occasional incongruities in her re-
sponses.

He sighed. He felt that he had sloughed off most of
the typed emotional reactions which they had taught
him by precept and example, but Alice had gotten
under his skin, 'way under, and it still hurt. He had
been happy—what if it had been a dope dream? They
had given him an excellent, a beautiful mirror to play
with—the more fool he to have looked behind it!

Wearily he turned back to his summing up:

"The world is explained in either one of two ways;
the comon-sense way which says that the world is
pretty much as it appears to be and that ordinary
human conduct and motivations are reasonable, and
the religio-mystic solution which states that the world
is dream stuff, unreal, insubstantial, with reality somewhere beyond.

"WRONG—both of them. The common-sense
scheme has no sense to it of any sort. Life is short and
full of trouble. Man born of woman is born to trouble as the sparks fly upward. His days are few and
they are numbered. All is vanity and vexation. Those
quotations may be jumbled and incorrect, but that is a
fair statement of the common-sense world is-as-it-
seems in its only possible evaluation. In such a world,
human striving is about as rational as the blind darting
of a moth against a light bulb. The common-sense
world is a blind insanity, out of nowhere, going nowhere, to no purpose.

"As for the other solution, it appears more rational
on the surface, in that it rejects the utterly irrational
world of common sense. But it is not a rational solution, it is simply a flight from reality of any sort, for it
refuses to believe the results of the only available direct
communication between the ego and the Outside. Cert-

ainly the 'five senses' are poor enough channels of communication, but they are the only channels."

He crumpled up the paper and flung himself from the chair. Order and logic were no good—his answer was right because it smelled right. But he still did not know all the answer. Why the grand scale to the deception, countless creatures, whole continents, an enormously involved and minutely detailed matrix of insane history, insane tradition, insane culture? Why bother with more than a cell and a strait jacket?

It must be, it had to be, because it was supremely important to deceive him completely, because a lesser deception would not do. Could it be that they dare not let him suspect his real identity no matter how difficult and involved the fraud?

He had to know. In some fashion he must get behind the deception and see what went on when he was not looking. He had had one glimpse; this time he must see the actual workings, catch the puppet masters in their manipulations.

Obviously the first step must be to escape from this asylum, but to do it so craftily that they would never see him, never catch up with him, not have a chance to set the stage before him. That would be hard to do. He must excel them in shrewdness and subtlety.

Once decided, he spent the rest of the evening in considering the means by which he might accomplish his purpose. It seemed almost impossible—he must get away without once being seen and remain in strict hiding. They must lose track of him completely in order that they would not know where to center their deceptions. That would mean going without food for several days. Very well—he could do it. He must not give them any warning by unusual action or manner.

The lights blinked twice. Docilely he got up and commenced preparations for bed. When the attendant looked through the peephole he was already in bed, with his face turned to the wall.

Gladness! Gladness everywhere! It was good to be with his own kind, to hear the music swelling out of every living thing, as it always had and always would

—good to know that everything was living and aware of him, participating in him, as he participated in them. It was good to be, good to know the unity of many and the diversity of one. There had been one bad thought—the details escaped him—but it was gone— it had never been; there was no place for it.

The early-morning sounds from the adjacent ward penetrated the sleepladen body which served him here and gradually recalled him to awareness of the hospital room. The transition was so gentle that he carried over full recollection of what he had been doing and why. He lay still, a gentle smile on his face, and savored the uncouth, but not unpleasant, languor of the body he wore. Strange that he had ever forgotten despite their tricks and stratagems. Well, now that he had recalled the key, he would quickly set things right in this odd place. He would call them in at once and announce the new order. It would be amusing to see old Glaroon's expression when he realized that the cycle had ended—

The click of the peephole and the rasp of the door being unlocked guillotined his line of thought. The morning attendant pushed briskly in with the breakfast tray and placed it on the tip table. "Morning, sir. Nice, bright day—want it in bed, or will you get up?"

Don't answer! Don't listen! Suppress this distraction! This is part of their plan—But it was too late, too late. He felt himself slipping, falling, wrenched from reality back into the fraud world in which they had kept him. It was gone, gone completely, with no single association around him to which to anchor memory. There was nothing left but the sense of heart-breaking loss and the acute ache of unsatisfied catharsis.

"Leave it where it is. I'll take care of it."

"Okey-doke." The attendant bustled out, slamming the door, and noisily locked it.

He lay quite still for a long time, every nerve end in his body screaming for relief.

At last he got out of bed, still miserably unhappy, and attempted to concentrate on his plans for escape. But the psychic wrench he had received in being recalled so suddenly from his plane of reality had left him bruised and emotionally disturbed. His mind insisted on rechewing its doubts, rather than engage in constructive thought. Was it possible that the doctor was right, that he was not alone in his miserable dilemma? Was he really simply suffering from paranoia, delusions of self-importance?

Could it be that each unit in this yeasty swarm around him was the prison of another lonely ego—helpless, blind, and speechless, condemned to an eternity of miserable loneliness? Was the look of suffering which he had brought to Alice's face a true reflection of inner torment and not simply a piece of play acting intended to maneuver him into compliance with their plans?

A knock sounded at the door. He said "Come in," without looking up. Their comings and goings did not matter to him.

"Dearest—" A well-known voice spoke slowly and hesitantly.

"Alice!" He was on his feet at once, and facing her. "Who let you in here?"

"Please, dear, please—I had to see you."

"It isn't fair. It isn't fair." He spoke more to himself than to her. Then: "Why did you come?"

She stood up to him with a dignity he had hardly expected. The beauty of her childlike face had been marred by line and shadow, but it shone with an unexpected courage. "I love you," she answered quietly. "You can tell me to go away, but you can't make me stop loving you and trying to help you."

He turned away from her in an agony of indecision. Could it be possible that he had misjudged her? Was there, behind that barrier of flesh and sound symbols, a spirit that truly yearned toward his? Lovers whispering in the dark— *"You do understand, don't you?"*

"Yes, dear heart, I understand."

"Then nothing that happens to us can matter, as long as we are together and understand—" Words, words, rebounding hollowly from an unbroken wall—

No, he couldn't be wrong! Test her again— "Why did you keep me on that job in Omaha?"

"But I didn't make you keep that job. I simply pointed out that we should think twice before—"

"Never mind. Never mind." Soft hands and a sweet face preventing him with mild stubbornness from ever doing the thing that his heart told him to do. Always with the best of intentions, the best of intentions, but always so that he had never quite managed to do the silly, unreasonable things that he knew were worth while. Hurry, hurry, hurry, and strive, with an angel-faced jockey to see that you don't stop long enough to think for youself—

"Why did you try to stop me from going back upstairs that day?"

She managed to smile, although her eyes were already spilling over with tears. "I didn't know it really mattered to you. I didn't want us to miss the train."

It had been a small thing, an unimportant thing. For some reason not clear to him he had insisted on going back upstairs to his study when they were about to leave the house for a short vacation. It was raining, and she had pointed out that there was barely enough time to get to the station. He had surprised himself and her, too, by insisting on his own way in circumstances in which he had never been known to be stubborn.

He had actually pushed her to one side and forced his way up the stairs. Even then nothing might have come of it had he not—quite unnecessarily—raised the shade of the window that faced toward the rear of the house.

It was a very small matter. It had been raining, hard, out in front. From this window the weather was clear and sunny, with no sign of rain.

He had stood there quite a long while, gazing out at the impossible sunshine and rearranging his cosmos in his mind. He re-examined long-suppressed doubts in the light of this one small but totally unexplainable discrepancy. Then he had turned and had found that she was standing behind him.

He had been trying ever since to forget the expression that he had surprised on her face.

"What about the rain?"

"The rain?" she repeated in a small, puzzled voice. "Why, it was raining, of course. What about it?"

"But it was not raining out my study window."

"What? But of course it was. I did notice the sun break through the clouds for a moment, but that was all."

"Nonsense!"

"But darling, what has the weather to do with you and me? What difference does it make whether it rains or not—to us?" She approached him timidly and slid a small hand between his arm and side. "Am I responsible for the weather?"

"I think you are. Now please go."

She withdrew from him, brushed blindly at her eyes, gulped once, then said in a voice held steady: "All right. I'll go. But remember—you can come home if you want to. And I'll be there, if you want me." She waited a moment, then added hesitantly: "Would you . . . would you kiss me good-bye?"

He made no answer of any sort, neither with voice nor eyes. She looked at him, then turned, fumbled blindly for the door, and rushed through it.

The creature he knew as Alice went to the place of assembly without stopping to change form. "It is necessary to adjourn this sequence. I am no longer able to influence his decisions."

They had expected it, nevertheless they stirred with dismay.

The Glaroon addressed the First for Manipulation. "Prepare to graft the selected memory track at once."

Then, turning to the First for Operations, the Glaroon said: "The extrapolation shows that he will tend to escape within two of his days. This sequence degenerated primarily through your failure to extend that rainfall all around him. Be advised."

"It would be simpler if we understood his motives."

"In my capacity as Dr. Hayward, I have often thought so," commented the Glaroon acidly, "but if we understood his motives, we would be part of him. Bear in mind the Treaty! He almost remembered."

The creature known as Alice spoke up. "Could he

not have the Taj Mahal next sequence? For some reason he values it."

"You are becoming assimilated!"

"Perhaps. I am not in fear. Will he receive it?"

"It will be considered."

The Glaroon continued with orders: "Leave structures standing until adjournment. New York City and Harvard University are now dismantled. Divert him from those sectors.

"Move!"

OUR FAIR CITY

PETE PERKINS TURNED INTO THE ALL-NITE PARKing lot and called out, "Hi, Pappy!"

The old parking lot attendant looked up and answered, "Be with you in a moment, Pete." He was tearing a Sunday comic sheet in narrow strips. A little whirlwind waltzed near him, picking up pieces of old newspaper and bits of dirt and flinging them in the faces of passing pedestrians. The old man held out to it a long streamer of the brightly colored funny-paper. "Here, Kitten," he coaxed. "Come, Kitten—"

The whirlwind hesitated, then drew itself up until it was quite tall, jumped two parked cars, and landed *sur le point* near him.

It seemed to sniff at the offering.

"Take it, Kitten," the old man called softly and let the gay streamer slip from his fingers. The whirlwind whipped it up and wound it around its middle. He tore off another and yet another; the whirlwind wound them in corkscrew through the loose mass of dirty paper and trash that constituted its visible body. Renewed by cold gusts that poured down the canyon of tall buildings, it swirled faster and even taller, while it lifted the colored paper ribbons in a fantastic upswept hair-do. The old man turned, smiling. "Kitten does like new clothes."

"Take it easy, Pappy, or you'll have me believing in it."

"Eh? You don't have to believe in Kitten—you can *see* her."

"Yeah, sure—but you act as if she—I mean 'it'—could understand what you say."

175

"You still don't think so?" His voice was gently tolerant.

"Now, Pappy!"

"IImm . . . lend me your hat." Pappy reached up and took it. "Here, Kitten," he called. "Come back, Kitten!" The whirlwind was playing around over their heads, several stories high. It dipped down.

"Hey! Where you going with that chapeau?" demanded Perkins.

"Just a moment— Here, Kitten!" The whirlwind sat down suddenly, spilling its load. The old man handed it the hat. The whirlwind snatched it and started it up a fast, long spiral.

"Hey!" yelped Perkins. "What do you think you're doing? That's not funny—that hat cost me six bucks only three years ago."

"Don't worry," the old man soothed. "Kitten will bring it back."

"She will, huh? More likely she'll dump it in the river."

"Oh, no! Kitten never drops anything she doesn't want to drop. Watch." The old man looked up to where the hat was dancing near the penthouse of the hotel across the street. "Kitten! Oh, Kitten! Bring it back."

The whirlwind hesitated, the hat fell a couple of stories. It swooped, caught it, and juggled it reluctantly. "Bring it *here,* Kitten."

The hat commenced a downward spiral, finishing in a long curving swoop. It hit Perkins full in the face. "She was trying to put it on your head," the attendant explained. "Usually she's more accurate."

"She is, eh?" Perkins picked up his hat and stood looking at the whirlwind, mouth open.

"Convinced?" asked the old man.

" 'Convinced?' Oh, sho' sho'." He looked back at his hat, then again at the whirlwind. "Pappy, this calls for a drink."

They went inside the lot's little shelter shack; Pappy found glasses; Perkins produced a pint, nearly full, and poured two generous slugs. He tossed his down, poured another, and sat down. "The first was in honor of

Kitten," he announced. "This one is to fortify me for the Mayor's banquet."

Pappy cluck-clucked sympathetically. "You have to cover that?"

"Have to write a column about *something*, Pappy. 'Last night Hizzoner the Mayor, surrounded by a glittering galaxy of highbinders, grifters, sycophants, and ballot thieves, was the recipient of a testimonial dinner celebrating—' Got to write something, Pappy, the cash customers expect it. Why don't I brace up like a man and go on relief?"

"Today's column was good, Pete," the old man comforted him. He picked up a copy of the *Daily Forum;* Perkins took it from him and ran his eye down his own column.

"OUR FAIR CITY, by Peter Perkins," he read, and below that "What, No Horsecars? It is the tradition of our civic paradise that what was good enough for the founding fathers is good enough for us. We stumble over the very chuckhole in which Great-uncle Tozier broke his leg in '09. It is good to know that the bath water, running out, is not gone forever, but will return through the kitchen faucet, thicker and disguised with chlorine, but the same. (Memo—Hizzoner uses bottled spring water. Must look into this.)

"But I must report a dismaying change. Someone has done away with the horsecars!

"You may not believe this. Our public conveyances run so seldom and slowly that you may not have noticed it; nevertheless I swear that I saw one wobbling down Grand Avenue with no horses of any sort. It seemed to be propelled by some new-fangled electrical device.

"Even in the atomic age some changes are too much. I urge all citizens—" Perkins gave a snort of disgust. "It's tackling a pillbox with a beanshooter, Pappy. This town is corrupt; it'll stay corrupt. Why should I beat out my brains on such piffle? Hand me the bottle."

"Don't be discouraged, Peter. The tyrant fears the laugh more than the assassin's bullet."

"Where'd you pick that up? Okay, so I'm not funny.

I've tried laughing them out of office and it hasn't worked. My efforts are as pointless as the activities of your friend the whirling dervish."

The windows rattled under a gusty impact. "Don't talk that way about Kitten," the old man cautioned. "She's sensitive."

"I apologize." He stood up and bowed toward the door. "Kitten, I apologize. Your activities are *more* useful than mine." He turned to his host. "Let's go out and talk to her, Pappy. I'd rather do that than go to the Mayor's banquet, if I had my druthers."

They went outside, Perkins bearing with him the remains of the colored comic sheet. He began tearing off streamers. "Here, Kitty! Here, Kitty! Soup's on!"

The whirlwind bent down and accepted the strips as fast as he tore them. "She's still got the ones you gave her."

"Certainly," agreed Pappy. "Kitten is a pack rat. When she likes something she'll keep it indefinitely."

"Doesn't she ever get tired? There must be some calm days."

"It's never really calm here. It's the arrangement of the buildings and the way Third Street leads up from the river. But I think she hides her pet playthings on tops of buildings."

The newspaperman peered into the swirling trash. "I'll bet she's got newspapers from months back. Say, Pappy, I see a column in this, one about our trash collection service and how we don't clean our streets. I'll dig up some papers a couple of years old and claim that they have been blowing around town since publication."

"Why fake it?" answered Pappy, "let's see what Kitten has." He whistled softly. "Come, baby—let Pappy see your playthings." The whirlwind bulged out; its contents moved less rapidly. The attendant plucked a piece of old newspaper from it in passing. "Here's one three months old."

"We'll have to do better than that."

"I'll try again." He reached out and snatched another. "Last June."

"That's better."

A car honked for service and the old man hurried away. When he returned Perkins was still watching the hovering column. "Any luck?" asked Pappy.

"She won't let me have them. Snatches them away."

"Naughty Kitten," the old man said. "Pete is a friend of ours. You be nice to him." The whirlwind fidgeted uncertainly.

"It's all right," said Perkins. "She didn't know. But look, Pappy—see that piece up there? A front page."

"You want it?"

"Yes. Look closely—the headline reads 'DEWEY' something. You don't suppose she's been hoarding it since the '48 campaign?"

"Could be. Kitten has been around here as long as I can remember. And she does hoard things. Wait a second." He called out softly. Shortly the paper was in his hands. "Now we'll see."

Perkins peered at it. "I'll be a short-term Senator! Can you top that, Pappy?"

The headline read: DEWEY CAPTURES MANILA; the date was "1898."

Twenty minutes later they were still considering it over the last of Perkins' bottle. The newspaperman stared at the yellowed, filthy sheet. "Don't tell me this has been blowing around town for the last half century."

"Why not?"

"'Why not?' Well, I'll concede that the streets haven't been cleaned in that time, but this paper wouldn't last. Sun and rain and so forth."

"Kitten is very careful of her toys. She probably put it under cover during bad weather."

"For the love of Mike, Pappy, you don't really believe— But you do. Frankly, I don't care where she got it; the official theory is going to be that this particular piece of paper has been kicking around our dirty streets, unnoticed and uncollected, for the past fifty years. Boy, am I going to have fun!" He rolled the fragment carefully and started to put it in his pocket.

"Say, don't do that!" his host protested.

"Why not? I'm going to take it down and get a pic of it."

"You mustn't! It belongs to Kitten—I just borrowed it."

"Huh? Are you nuts?"

"She'll be upset if she doesn't get it back. Please, Pete—she'll let you look at it any time you want to."

The old man was so earnest that Perkins was stopped. "Suppose we never see it again? My story hangs on it."

"It's no good to *you*—*she* has to keep it, to make your story stand up. Don't worry—I'll tell her that she mustn't lose it under any circumstances."

"Well—okay." They stepped outside and Pappy talked earnestly to Kitten, then gave her the 1898 fragment. She promptly tucked it into the top column. Perkins said good-bye to Pappy, and started to leave the lot. He paused and turned around, looking a little befuddled. "Say, Pappy—"

"Yes, Pete?"

"You don't really think that whirlwind is alive, do you?"

"Why not?"

" 'Why not?' Why not, the man says?"

"Well," said Pappy reasonably, "how do you know *you* are alive?"

"But . . . why, because I—well, now if you put it—" He stopped. "I don't know. You got me, pal."

Pappy smiled. "You see?"

"Uh, I guess so. G'night, Pappy. G'night, Kitten." He tipped his hat to the whirlwind. The column bowed.

The managing editor sent for Perkins.

"Look, Pete," he said, chucking a sheaf of gray copy paper at him, "whimsy is all right, but I'd like to see some copy that wasn't dashed off in a gin mill."

Perkins looked over the pages shoved at him. "OUR FAIR CITY by Peter Perkins. Whistle Up The Wind. Walking our streets always is a piquant, even adventurous, experience. We pick our way through the assorted trash, bits of old garbage, cigarette butts, and other less appetizing items that stud our sidewalks while our faces are assaulted by more buoyant souvenirs, the confetti of last Hallowe'en, shreds of dead leaves, and other items too weather-beaten to be identified. However, I had always assumed that a constant turn-over in the riches of our streets caused them to renew themselves at least every seven years—" The column then told of the whirlwind that contained the fifty-year-old newspaper and challenged any other city in the country to match it.

" 'Smatter with it?" demanded Perkins.

"Beating the drum about the filth in the streets is fine, Pete, but give it a factual approach."

Perkins leaned over the desk. "Boss, this *is* factual."

"Huh? Don't be silly, Pete."

"Silly, he says. Look—" Perkins gave him a circum-stantial account of Kitten and the 1898 newspaper.

"Pete, you must have been drinking."

"Only Java and tomato juice. Cross my heart and hope to die."

"How about yesterday? I'll bet the whirlwind came right up to the bar with you."

"I was cold, stone—" Perkins stopped himself and stood on his dignity. "That's my story. Print it, or fire me."

"Don't be like that, Pete. I don't want your job; I just want a column with some meat. Dig up some facts on man-hours and costs for street cleaning, compared with other cities."

"Who'd read that junk? Come down the street with me. I'll *show* you the facts. Wait a moment—I'll pick up a photographer."

A few minutes later Perkins was introducing the managing editor and Clarence V. Weems to Pappy. Clarence unlimbered his camera. "Take a pic of him?"

"Not yet, Clarence. Pappy, can you get Kitten to give us back the museum piece?"

"Why, sure." The old man looked up and whistled. "Oh, Kitten! Come to Pappy." Above their heads a tiny gust took shape, picked up bits of paper and stray leaves, and settled on the lot. Perkins peered into it.

"She hasn't got it," he said in aggrieved tones.

"She'll get it." Pappy stepped forward until the

whirlwind enfolded him. They could see his lips move, but the words did not reach them.

"Now?" said Clarence.

"Not yet." The whirlwind bounded up and leapt over an adjoining building. The managing editor opened his mouth, closed it again.

Kitten was soon back. She had dropped everything else and had just one piece of paper—*the* paper. "Now!" said Perkins. "Can you get a shot of that paper, Clarence—while it's in the air?"

"Natch," said Clarence, and raised his Speed Graphic. "Back a little, and hold it," he ordered, speaking to the whirlwind.

Kitten hesitated and seemed about to skitter away. "Bring it around slow and easy, Kitten," Pappy supplemented, "and turn it over—no, no! Not that way—the other edge up." The paper flattened out and sailed slowly past them, the headline showing.

"Did you get it?" Perkins demanded.

"Natch," said Clarence. "Is that all?" he asked the editor.

"Natc—I mean, 'that's all.' "

"Okay," said Clarence, picked up his case, and left.

The editor sighed. "Gentlemen," he said, "let's have a drink."

Four drinks later Perkins and his boss were still arguing. Pappy had left. "Be reasonable, Boss," Pete was saying, "you can't print an item about a live whirlwind. They'd laugh you out of town."

Managing Editor Gaines straightened himself.

"It's the policy of the *Forum* to print all the news, and print it straight. This is news—we print it." He relaxed. "Hey! Waiter! More of the same—and not so much soda."

"But it's scientifically impossible."

"You saw it, didn't you?"

"Yes, but—"

Gaines stopped him. "We'll ask the Smithsonian Institution to investigate it."

"They'll laugh at you," Perkins insisted. "Ever hear of mass hypnotism?"

"Huh? No, that's no explanation—Clarence saw it, too."

"What does that prove?"

"Obvious—to be hypnotized you have to have a mind. *Ipso facto.*"

"You mean *Ipse dixit.*"

"Quit hiccuping. Perkins, you shouldn't drink in the daytime. Now start over and say it slowly."

"How do you know Clarence doesn't have a mind?"

"Prove it."

"Well, he's alive—he must have some sort of a mind, then."

"That's just what I was saying, the whirlwind is alive; therefore it has a mind. Perkins, if those long-beards from the Smithsonian are going to persist in their unscientific attitude, I for one will not stand for it. The *Forum* will not stand for it. You will not stand for it."

"Won't I?"

"Not for one minute. I want you to know the *Forum* is behind you, Pete. You go back to the parking lot and get an interview with that whirlwind."

"But I've got one. You wouldn't let me print it."

"Who wouldn't let you print it? I'll fire him! Come on, Pete. We're going to blow this town sky high. Stop the run. Hold the front page. Get busy!" He put on Pete's hat and strode rapidly into the men's room.

Pete settled himself at his desk with a container of coffee, a can of tomato juice, and the Midnight Final (late afternoon) edition. Under a 4-col. cut of Kitten's toy was his column, boxed and moved to the front page. 18-point boldface ordered SEE EDITORIAL PAGE 12. On page 12 another black line enjoined him to SEE "OUR FAIR CITY" PAGE ONE. He ignored this and read: MR. MAYOR—RESIGN!!!!

Pete read it and chuckled. "An ill wind—" "—symbolic of the spiritual filth lurking in the dark corners of the city hall." "—will grow to cyclonic proportions and sweep a corrupt and shameless administration from office." The editorial pointed out that the contract for street cleaning and trash removal was held by the

Mayor's brother-in-law, and then suggested that the
whirlwind could give better service cheaper.

"Pete—is that you?" Pappy's voice demanded. "They
got me down at the station house."

"What for?"

"They claim Kitten is a public nuisance."

"I'll be right over." He stopped by the Art Department, snagged Clarence, and left. Pappy was seated in
the station lieutenant's office, looking stubborn. Perkins shoved his way in. "What's he here for?" he demanded, jerking a thumb at Pappy.

The lieutenant looked sour. "What are you butting
in for, Perkins? You're not his lawyer."

"Not yet, Clarence. For news, Dumbrosky—I work
for a newspaper, remember? I repeat—what's he in
for?"

"Obstructing an officer in the performance of his
duty."

"That right, Pappy?"

The old man looked disgusted. "This character—"
He indicated one of the policemen "—comes up to my
lot and tries to snatch the Manila-Bay paper away
from Kitten. I tell her to keep it up out of his way.
Then he waves his stick at me and orders me to take it
away from her. I tell him what he can do with his
stick." He shrugged. "So here we are."

"I get it," Perkins told him, and turned to Dumbrosky. "You got a call from the city hall, didn't you?
So you sent Dugan down to do the dirty work. What I
don't get is why you sent Dugan. I hear he's so dumb
you don't even let him collect the pay-off on his own
beat."

"That's a lie!" put in Dugan. "I do so—"

"Shut up, Dugan!" his boss thundered. "Now, see
here, Perkins—you clear out. There ain't no story
here."

"'No story'?" Perkins said softly. "The police force
tries to arrest a whirlwind and you say there's no
story?"

"Now?" said Clarence.

"Nobody tried to arrest no whirlwind! Now scram."

"Then how come you're charging Pappy with obstructing an officer? What was Dugan doing—flying a kite?"

"He's not charged with obstructing an officer."

"He's not, eh? Just what have you booked him for?"

"He's not booked. We're holding him for questioning."

"So? Not booked, no warrant, no crime alleged, just pick up a citizen and roust him around, Gestapo style." Perkins turned to Pappy. "You're not under arrest. My advice is to get up and walk out that door."

Pappy started to get up. "Hey!" Lieutenant Dumbrosky bounded out of his chair, grabbed Pappy by the shoulder and pushed him down. "I'm giving the orders around here. You stay—"

"Now!" yelled Perkins. Clarence's flashbulb froze them. Then Dumbrosky started up again.

"Who let him in here? Dugan—get that camera."

"Nyannh!" said Clarence and held it away from the cop. They started doing a little Maypole dance, with Clarence as the Maypole.

"Hold it!" yelled Perkins. "Go ahead and grab the camera, Dugan—I'm just aching to write the story. 'Police Lieutenant Destroys Evidence of Police Brutality.' "

"What do you want I should do, Lieutenant?" pleaded Dugan.

Dumbrosky looked disgusted. "Siddown and close your face. Don't use that picture, Perkins—I'm warning you."

"Of what? Going to make me dance with Dugan? Come on, Pappy. Come on, Clarence." They left.

"OUR FAIR CITY" read the next day. "City Hall Starts Clean Up. While the city street cleaners were enjoying their usual siesta, Lieutenant Dumbrosky, acting on orders of Hizzoner's office, raided our Third Avenue whirlwind. It went sour, as Patrolman Dugan could not entice the whirlwind into the paddy wagon. Dauntless Dugan was undeterred; he took a citizen standing nearby, one James Metcalfe, parking lot attendant, into custody as an accomplice of the whirlwind. An accomplice in what, Dugan didn't say—everybody knows that an accomplice is something pretty awful. Lieu-

tenant Dumbrosky questioned the accomplice. See cut.
Lieutenant Dumbrosky weighs 215 pounds, without his
shoes. The accomplice weighs 119.

"Moral: Don't get underfoot when the police department is playing games with the wind.

"P. S. As we go to press, the whirlwind is still holding the 1898 museum piece. Stop by Third and Main
and take a look. Better hurry—Dumbrosky is expected
to make an arrest momentarily."

Pete's column continued needling the administration
the following day: "Those Missing Files. It is annoying
to know that any document needed by the Grand Jury
is sure to be mislaid before it can be introduced in
evidence. We suggest that Kitten, our Third Avenue
Whirlwind, be hired by the city as file clerk extraor-
dinary and entrusted with any item which is likely to
be needed later. She could take the special civil exam
used to reward the faithful—the one nobody ever flunks.

"Indeed, why limit Kitten to a lowly clerical job?
She is persistent—and she hangs on to what she gets.
No one will argue that she is less qualified than some
city officials we have had.

"Let's run Kitten for Mayor! She's an ideal candi-
date—she has the common touch, she doesn't mind
hurly-burly, she runs around in circles, she knows how
to throw dirt, and the opposition can't pin anything on
her.

"As to the sort of Mayor she would make, there is
an old story—Aesop told it—about King Log and King
Stork. We're fed up with King Stork; King Log would
be welcome relief.

"Memo to Hizzoner—what *did* become of those
Grand Avenue paving bids?

"P. S. Kitten still has the 1898 newspaper on exhibit.
Stop by and see it before our police department figures
out some way to intimidate a whirlwind."

Pete snagged Clarence and drifted down to the parking lot. The lot was fenced now; a man at a gate
handed them two tickets but waved away their money.
Inside he found a large circle chained off for Kitten and
Pappy inside it. They pushed their way through the

crowd to the old man. "Looks like you're coining money, Pappy."

"Should be, but I'm not. They tried to close me up this morning, Pete. Wanted me to pay the $50-a-day circus-and-carnival fee and post a bond besides. So I quit charging for the tickets—but I'm keeping track of them. I'll sue 'em, by gee."

"You won't collect, not in this town. Never mind, we'll make 'em squirm till they let up."

"That's not all. They tried to capture Kitten this morning."

"Huh? Who? How?"

"The cops. They showed up with one of those blower machines used to ventilate manholes, rigged to run backwards and take a suction. The idea was to suck Kitten down into it, or anyhow to grab what she was carrying."

Pete whistled. "You should have called me."

"Wasn't necessary. I warned Kitten and she stashed the Spanish-War paper someplace, then came back. She loved it. She went through that machine about six times, like a merry-go-round. She'd zip through and come out more full of pep than ever. Last time through she took Sergeant Yancel's cap with her and it clogged the machine and ruined his cap. They got disgusted and left."

Pete chortled. "You still should have called me. Clarence should have gotten a picture of that."

"Got it," said Clarence.

"Huh? I didn't know you were here this morning, Clarence."

"You didn't ask me."

Pete looked at him. "Clarence, darling—the idea of a news picture is to print it, not to hide it in the art department."

"On your desk," said Clarence.

"Oh. Well, let's move on to a less confusing subject. Pappy, I'd like to put up a big sign here."

"Why not? What do you want to say?"

"Kitten-for-Mayor—Whirlwind Campaign Head-quarters. Stick a 24-sheet across the corner of the lot, where they can see it both ways. It fits in with—oh, oh! Company, girls!" He jerked his head toward the entrance.

Sergeant Yancel was back. "All right, all right!" he was saying. "Move on! Clear out of here." He and three cohorts were urging the spectators out of the lot. Pete went to him.

"What goes on, Yancel?"

Yancel looked around. "Oh, it's you, huh? Well, you, too—we got to clear this place out. Emergency."

Pete looked back over his shoulder. "Better get Kitten out of the way, Pappy!" he called out. *"Now,* Clarence."

"Got it," said Clarence.

"Okay," Pete answered. "Now, Yancel, you might tell me what it is we just took a picture of, so we can title it properly."

"Smart guy. You and your stooge had better scram if you don't want your heads blown off. We're setting up a bazooka."

"You're setting up a *what?*" Pete looked toward the squad car, unbelievingly. Sure enough, two of the cops were unloading a bazooka. "Keep shooting, kid," he said to Clarence.

"Natch," said Clarence.

"And quit popping your bubble gum. Now, look, Yancel—I'm just a newsboy. What in the world is the idea?"

"Stick around and find out, wise guy." Yancel turned away. "Okay there! Start doing it—commence firing!"

One of the cops looked up. "At what, Sergeant?"

"I thought you used to be a marine—at the whirl-wind, of course."

Pappy leaned over Pete's shoulder. "What are they doing?"

"I'm beginning to get a glimmering. Pappy, keep Kitten out of range—I think they mean to put a rocket shell through her gizzard. It might bust up her dynamic stability or something."

"Kitten's safe. I told her to hide. But this is crazy, Pete. They must be absolute, complete and teetotal nuts."

"Any law says a cop has to be sane to be on the force?"

"What whirlwind, Sergeant?" the bazooka man was asking. Yancel started to tell him, forcefully, then deflated when he realized that no whirlwind was available.

"You wait," he told him, and turned to Pappy. "You!" he yelled. "You chased away that whirlwind. Get it back here."

Pete took out his notebook. "This is interesting, Yancel. Is it your professional opinion that a whirlwind can be ordered around like a trained dog? Is that the official position of the police department?"

"I— No comment! You button up, or I'll run you in."

"By all means. But you have that Buck-Rogers cannon pointed so that, after the shell passes through the whirlwind, if any, it should end up just about at the city hall. Is this a plot to assassinate Hizzoner?"

Yancel looked around suddenly, then let his gaze travel an imaginary trajectory.

"Hey, you lugs!" he shouted. "Point that thing the other way. You want to knock off the Mayor?"

"That's better," Pete told the Sergeant. "Now they have it trained on the First National Bank. I can't wait."

Yancel looked over the situation again. "Point it where it won't hurt anybody," he ordered. "Do I have to do all your thinking?"

"But, Sergeant—"

"Well?"

"You *point* it. We'll fire it."

Pete watched them. "Clarence," he sighed, "you stick around and get a pic of them loading it back into the car. That will be in about five minutes. Pappy and I will be in the Happy Hour Bar-Grill. Get a nice picture, with Yancel's features."

"Natch," said Clarence.

The next installment of OUR FAIR CITY featured three cuts and was headed "Police Declare War on Whirlwind." Pete took a copy and set out for the parking lot, intending to show it to Pappy.

Pappy wasn't there. Nor was Kitten. He looked

around the neighborhood, poking his nose in lunchrooms and bars. No luck.

He headed back toward the *Forum* building, telling himself that Pappy might be shopping, or at a movie. He returned to his desk, made a couple of false starts on a column for the morrow, crumpled them up and went to the art department. "Hey! Clarence! Have you been down to the parking lot today?"

"Nah."

"Pappy's missing."

"So what?"

"Well, come along. We got to find him."

"Why?" But he came, lugging his camera.

The lot was still deserted, no Pappy, no Kitten—not even a stray breeze. Pete turned away. "Come on, Clarence—say, what are you shooting now?"

Clarence had his camera turned up toward the sky. "Not shooting," said Clarence. "Light is no good."

"What was it?"

"Whirlwind."

"Huh? Kitten?"

"Maybe."

"Here, Kitten—come, Kitten." The whirlwind came back near him, spun faster, and picked up a piece of cardboard it had dropped. It whipped it around, then let him have it in the face.

"That's not funny, Kitten," Pete complained. "Where's Pappy?"

The whirlwind sidled back toward him. He saw it reach again for the cardboard. "No, you don't!" he yelped and reached for it, too.

The whirlwind beat him to it. It carried it up some hundred feet and sailed it back. The card caught him edgewise on the bridge of the nose. "Kitten!" Pete yelled. "Quit the horsing around."

It was a printed notice, about six by eight inches. Evidently it had been tacked up; there were small tears at all four corners. It read: "THE RITZ-CLASSIC" and under that, "Room 2013, Single Occupancy $6.00, Double Occupancy $8.00." There followed a printed list of the house rules.

Pete stared at it and frowned. Suddenly he chucked

it back at the whirlwind. Kitten immediately tossed it back in his face.

"Come on, Clarence," he said briskly. "We're going to the Ritz-Classic—room 2013."

"Natch," said Clarence.

The Ritz-Classic was a colossal fleabag, favored by the bookie-and-madame set, three blocks away. Pete avoided the desk by using the basement entrance. The elevator boy looked at Clarence's camera and said, "No, you don't, Doc. No divorce cases in this hotel."

"Relax," Pete told him. "That's not a real camera. We peddle marijuana—that's the hay mow."

"Whyn't you say so? You hadn't ought to carry it in a camera. You make people nervous. What floor?"

"Twenty-one."

The elevator operator took them up non-stop, ignoring other calls. "That'll be two bucks. Special service."

"What do you pay for the concession?" inquired Pete.

"You gotta nerve to beef—with your racket."

They went back down a floor by stair and looked up room 2013. Pete tried the knob cautiously; the door was locked. He knocked on it—no answer. He pressed an ear to it and thought he could hear movement inside. He stepped back, frowning.

Clarence said, "I just remembered something," and trotted away. He returned quickly, with a red fire ax. "Now?" he asked Pete.

"A lovely thought, Clarence! Not yet." Pete pounded and yelled, "Pappy! Oh, Pappy!"

A large woman in a pink coolie coat opened the door behind them. "How do you expect a party to sleep?" she demanded.

Pete said, "Quiet, madame! We're on the air." He listened. This time there were sounds of struggling and then, "Pete! Pe—"

"Now!" said Pete. Clarence started swinging.

The lock gave up on the third swing. Pete poured in, with Clarence after him. He collided with someone coming out and sat down abruptly. When he got up he saw Pappy on a bed. The old man was busily trying to get rid of a towel tied around his mouth.

Pete snatched it away. "Get 'em!" yelled Pappy.

"Soon as I get you untied."

"I ain't tied. They took my pants. Boy, I thought you'd never come!"

"Took Kitten a while to make me understand."

"I got 'em," announced Clarence. "Both of 'em."

"Where?" demanded Pete.

"Here," said Clarence proudly, and patted his camera.

Pete restrained his answer and ran to the door. "They went thata-way," said the large woman, pointing. He took off, skidded around the corner and saw an elevator door just closing.

Pete stopped, bewildered by the crowd just outside the hotel. He was looking uncertainly around when Pappy grabbed him. "There! That car!" The car Pappy pointed out was even then swinging out from the curb just beyond the rank of cabs in front of the hotel; with a deep growl it picked up speed, and headed away. Pete yanked open the door of the nearest cab.

"Follow that car!" he yelled .They all piled in.

"Why?" asked the hackie.

Clarence lifted the fire ax. "Now?" he asked.

The driver ducked. "Forget it," he said. "It was just a yak." He started after the car.

The hack driver's skill helped them in the downtown streets, but the driver of the other car swung right on Third and headed for the river. They streamed across it, fifty yards apart, with traffic snarled behind them, and then were on the no-speed-limit freeway. The cabbie turned his head. "Is the camera truck keeping up?"

"What camera truck?"

"Ain't this a movie?"

"Good grief, no! That car is filled with kidnappers. Faster!"

"A snatch? I don't want no part of it." He braked suddenly.

Pete took the ax and prodded the driver. "You catch 'em!"

The hack speeded up again but the driver protested, "Not in this wreck. They got more power than me."

Pappy grabbed Pete's arm. "There's Kitten!"

"Where? Oh, never mind that now!"

"Slow down!" yelled Pappy. "Kitten, oh, Kitten—over here!"

The whirlwind swooped down and kept pace with them. Pappy called to it. "Here, baby! Go get that car! Up ahead—*get it!*"

Kitten seemed confused, uncertain. Pappy repeated it and she took off—like a whirlwind. She dipped and gathered a load of paper and trash as she flew.

They saw her dip and strike the car ahead, throwing paper in the face of the driver. The car wobbled. She struck again. The car veered, climbed the curb, ricocheted against the crash rail, and fetched up against a lamp post.

Five minutes later Pete, having left Kitten, Clarence, and the fire ax to hold the fort over two hoodlums suffering from abrasion, multiple contusions and shock, was feeding a dime into a pay phone at the nearest filling station. He dialed long distance. "Gimme the FBI's kidnap number," he demanded. "You know—the Washington, D.C., snatch number."

"My goodness," said the operator, "do you mind if I listen in?"

"Get me that number!"

"Right away!"

Presently a voice answered, "Federal Bureau of Investigation."

"Lemme talk to Hoover! Huh? Okay, okay—I'll talk to you. Listen, this is a snatch case. I've got 'em on ice, for the moment, but unless you get one of your boys from your local office here pronto there won't be any snatch case—not if the city cops get here first. What?" Pete quieted down and explained who he was, where he was, and the more believable aspects of the events that had led up to the present situation. The government man cut in on him as he was urging speed and more speed and assured him that the local office was already being notified.

Pete got back to the wreck just as Lieutenant Dumbrosky climbed out of a squad car. Pete hurried up. "Don't do it, Dumbrosky," he yelled.

The big cop hesitated. "Don't do what?"

"Don't do anything. The FBI are on their way now —and you're already implicated. Don't make it any worse."

Pete pointed to the two hoodlums; Clarence was sitting on one and resting the spike of the ax against the back of the other. "Those birds have already sung. This town is about to fall apart. If you hurry, you might be able to get a plane for Mexico."

Dumbrosky looked at him. "Wise guy," he said doubtfully.

"Ask them. They confessed."

One of the hoods raised his head. "We was threatened," he announced. "Take 'em in, lieutenant. They assaulted us."

"Go ahead," Pete said cheerfully. "Take us all in— together. Then you won't be able to lose that pair before the FBI can question them. Maybe you can cop a plea."

"Now?" asked Clarence.

Dumbrosky swung around. "Put that ax down!"

"Do as he says, Clarence. Get your camera ready to get a picture as the G-men arrive."

"You didn't send for no G-men."

"Look behind you!"

A dark blue sedan slid quietly to a stop and four lean, brisk men got out. The first of them said, "Is there someone here named Peter Perkins?"

"Me," said Pete. "Do you mind if I kiss you?"

It was after dark but the parking lot was crowded and noisy. A stand for the new Mayor and distinguished visitors had been erected on one side, opposite it was a bandstand; across the front was a large illuminated sign: HOME OF KITTEN—HONORARY CITIZEN OF OUR FAIR CITY.

In the fenced-off circle in the middle Kitten herself bounced and spun and swayed and danced. Pete stood on one side of the circle with Pappy opposite him; at four-foot intervals around it children were posted. "All set?" called out Pete.

"All set," answered Pappy. Together, Pete, Pappy and the kids started throwing serpentine into the ring.

Kitten swooped, gathered the ribbons up and wrapped them around herself.

"Confetti!" yelled Pete. Each of the kids dumped a sackful toward the whirlwind—little of it reached the ground.

"Balloons!" yelled Pete. "Lights!" Each of the children started blowing up toy balloons; each had a dozen different colors. As fast as they were inflated they fed them to Kitten. Floodlights and searchlights came on; Kitten was transformed into a fountain of boiling, bubbling color, several stories high.

"Now?" said Clarence.

"Now!"

"—AND HE BUILT A CROOKED HOUSE—"

AMERICANS ARE CONSIDERED CRAZY ANYWHERE in the world.

They will usually concede a basis for the accusation but point to California as the focus of the infection. Californians stoutly maintain that their bad reputation is derived solely from the acts of the inhabitants of Los Angeles County. Angelenos will, when pressed, admit the charge but explain hastily, "It's Hollywood. It's not our fault—we didn't ask for it; Hollywood just grew."

The people in Hollywood don't care; they glory in it. If you are interested, they will drive you up Laurel Canyon "—where we keep the violent cases." The Canyonites—the brown-legged women, the trunks-clad men constantly busy building and rebuilding their slap-happy unfinished houses—regard with faint contempt the dull creatures who live down in the flats, and treasure in their hearts the secret knowledge that they, and only they, know how to live.

Lookout Mountain Avenue is the name of a side canyon which twists up from Laurel Canyon. The other Canyonites don't like to have it mentioned; after all, one must draw the line somewhere!

High up on Lookout Mountain at number 8775, across the street from the Hermit—the original Hermit of Hollywood—lived Quintus Teal, graduate architect.

Even the architecture of southern California is different. Hot dogs are sold from a structure built like and designated "The Pup." Ice cream cones come from a giant stucco ice cream cone, and neon proclaims "Get the Chili Bowl Habit!" from the roofs of buildings which are indisputably chili bowls. Gasoline, oil, and

free road maps are dispensed beneath the wings of tri-
motored transport planes, while the certified rest
rooms, inspected hourly for your comfort, are located
in the cabin of the plane itself. These things may surprise, or amuse, the tourist, but the local residents,
who walk bareheaded in the famous California noon-
day sun, take them as a matter of course.

Quintus Teal regarded the efforts of his colleagues
in architecture as faint-hearted, fumbling, and timid.

"What is a house?" Teal demanded of his friend,
Homer Bailey.

"Well—" Bailey admitted cautiously, "speaking in
broad terms, I've always regarded a house as a gadget
to keep off the rain."

"Nuts! You're as bad as the rest of them."

"I didn't say the definition was complete—"

"Complete! It isn't even in the right direction. From
that point of view we might just as well be squatting in
caves. But I don't blame you," Teal went on magnan-
imously, "you're no worse than the lugs you find prac-
ticing architecture. Even the Moderns—all they've done
is to abandon the Wedding Cake School in favor of the
Service Station School, chucked away the gingerbread
and slapped on some chromium, but at heart they are
as conservative and traditional as a county courthouse.
Neutra! Schindler! What have those bums got? What's
Frank Lloyd Wright got that I haven't got?"

"Commissions," his friend answered succinctly.

"Huh? Wha' d'ju say?" Teal stumbled slightly in his
flow of words, did a slight double take, and recovered
himself. "Commissions. Correct. And why? Because I
don't think of a house as an upholstered cave; I think
of it as a machine for living, a vital process, a live
dynamic thing, changing with the mood of the dweller
—not a dead, static, oversized coffin. Why should we
be held down by the frozen concepts of our ancestors?
Any fool with a little smattering of descriptive geometry can design a house in the ordinary way. Is the
static geometry of Euclid the only mathematics? Are
we to completely disregard the Picard-Vessiot theory?
How about modular systems?—to say nothing of the

rich suggestions of stereochemistry. Isn't there a place in architecture for transformation, for homomorphology, for actional structures?"

"Blessed if I know," answered Bailey. "You might just as well be talking about the fourth dimension for all it means to me."

"And why not? Why should we limit ourselves to the —Say!" He interrupted himself and stared into distances. "Homer, I think you've really got something. After all, why not? Think of the infinite richness of articulation and relationship in four dimensions. What a house, what a house—" He stood quite still, his pale bulging eyes blinking thoughtfully.

Bailey reached up and shook his arm. "Snap out of it. What the hell are you talking about, four dimensions? Time is the fourth dimension; you can't drive nails into *that*."

Teal shrugged him off. "Sure. Sure. Time is *a* fourth dimension, but I'm thinking about a fourth spatial dimension, like length, breadth and thickness. For economy of materials and convenience of arrangement you couldn't beat it. To say nothing of the saving of ground space—you could put an eight-room house on the land now occupied by a one-room house. Like a tesseract—"

"What's a tesseract?"

"Didn't you go to school? A tesseract is a hypercube, a square figure with four dimensions to it, like a cube has three, and a square has two. Here, I'll show you." Teal dashed out into the kitchen of his apartment and returned with a box of toothpicks which he spilled on the table between them, brushing glasses and a nearly empty Holland gin bottle carelessly aside. "I'll need some plasticine. I had some around here last week." He burrowed into a drawer of the littered desk which crowded one corner of his dining room and emerged with a lump of oily sculptor's clay. "Here's some."

"What are you going to do?"

"I'll show you." Teal rapidly pinched off small masses of the clay and rolled them into pea-sized balls.

He stuck toothpicks into four of these and hooked them together into a square. "There! That's a square."

"Obviously."

"Another one like it, four more toothpicks, and we make a cube." The toothpicks were now arranged in the framework of a square box, a cube, with the pellets of clay holding the corners together. "Now we make another cube just like the first one, and the two of them will be two sides of the tesseract."

Bailey started to help him roll the little balls of clay for the second cube, but became diverted by the sensuous feel of the docile clay and started working and shaping it with his fingers.

"Look," he said, holding up his effort, a tiny figurine, "Gypsy Rose Lee."

"Looks more like Gargantua; she ought to sue you. Now pay attention. You open up one corner of the first cube, interlock the second cube at the corner, and then close the corner. Then take eight more toothpicks and join the bottom of the first cube to the bottom of the second, on a slant, and the top of the first to the top of the second, the same way." This he did rapidly, while he talked.

"What's that supposed to be?" Bailey demanded suspiciously.

"That's a tesseract, eight cubes forming the sides of a hypercube in four dimensions."

"It looks more like a cat's cradle to me. You've only got two cubes there anyhow. Where are the other six?"

"Use your imagination, man. Consider the top of the first cube in relation to the top of the second; that's cube number three. Then the two bottom squares, then the front faces of each cube, the back faces, the right hand, the left hand—eight cubes." He pointed them out.

"Yeah, I see 'em. But they still aren't cubes; they're whatchamucallems—prisms. They are not square, they slant."

"That's just the way you look at it, in perspective. If you drew a picture of a cube on a piece of paper, the side squares would be slaunchwise, wouldn't they? That's perspective. When you look at a four-dimensional figure in three dimensions, naturally it looks crooked. But those are all cubes just the same."

"Maybe they are to you, brother, but they still look crooked to me."

Teal ignored the objections and went on. "Now consider this as the framework of an eight-room house; there's one room on the ground floor—that's for service, utilities, and garage. There are six rooms opening off it on the next floor, living room, dining room, bath, bedrooms, and so forth. And up at the top, completely enclosed and with windows on four sides, is your study. There! How do you like it?"

"Seems to me you have the bathtub hanging out of the living room ceiling. Those rooms are interlaced like an octopus."

"Only in perspective, only in perspective. Here, I'll do it another way so you can see it." This time Teal made a cube of toothpicks, then made a second of halves of toothpicks, and set it exactly in the center of the first by attaching the corners of the small cube to the large cube by short lengths of toothpick. "Now— the big cube is your ground floor, the little cube inside is your study on the top floor. The six cubes joining them are the living rooms. See?"

Bailey studied the figure, then shook his head. "I still don't see but two cubes, a big one and a little one. Those other six things, they look like pyramids this time instead of prisms, but they still aren't cubes."

"Certainly, certainly, you are seeing them in different perspective. Can't you see that?"

"Well, maybe. But that room on the inside, there. It's completely surrounded by the thingamujigs. I thought you said it had windows on four sides."

"It has—it just looks like it was surrounded. That's the grand feature about a tesseract house, complete outside exposure for every room, yet every wall serves two rooms and an eight-room house requires only a one-room foundation. It's revolutionary."

"That's putting it mildly. You're crazy, bud; you can't build a house like that. That inside room is on the inside, and there she stays."

Teal looked at his friend in controlled exasperation.

"It's guys like you that keep architecture in its infancy. How many square sides has a cube?"

"Six."

"How many of them are inside?"

"Why, none of 'em. They're all on the outside."

"All right. Now listen—a tesseract has eight cubical sides, *all on the outside*. Now watch me. I'm going to open up this tesseract like you can open up a cubical pasteboard box, until it's flat. That way you'll be able to see all eight of the cubes." Working very rapidly he constructed four cubes, piling one on top of the other in an unsteady tower. He then built out four more cubes from the four exposed faces of the second cube in the pile. The structure swayed a little under the loose coupling of the clay pellets, but it stood, eight cubes in an inverted cross, a double cross, as the four additional cubes stuck out in four directions. "Do you see it now? It rests on the ground floor room, the next six cubes are the living rooms, and there is your study, up at the top."

Bailey regarded it with more approval than he had the other figures. "At least I can understand it. You say that is a tesseract, too?"

"That is a tesseract unfolded in three dimensions. To put it back together you tuck the top cube onto the bottom cube, fold those side cubes in till they meet the top cube and there you are. You do all this folding through a fourth dimension of course; you don't distort any of the cubes, or fold them into each other."

Bailey studied the wobbly framework further. "Look here," he said at last, "why don't you forget about folding this thing up through a fourth dimension—you can't anyway—and build a house like this?"

"What do you mean, I can't? It's a simple mathematical problem—"

"Take it easy, son. It may be simple in mathematics, but you could never get your plans approved for construction. There isn't any fourth dimension; forget it. But this kind of a house—it might have some advantages."

Checked, Teal studied the model. "Hm-m-m—Maybe you got something. We could have the same number of rooms, and we'd save the same amount of ground space. Yes, and we would set that middle cross-shaped floor northeast, southwest, and so forth, so that every room would get sunlight all day long. That central axis lends itself nicely to central heating. We'll put the dining room on the northeast and the kitchen on the southeast, with big view windows in every room. O.K., Homer, I'll do it! Where do you want it built?"

"Wait a minute! Wait a minute! I didn't say you were going to build it for me—"

"Of course I am. Who else? Your wife wants a new house; this is it."

"But Mrs. Bailey wants a Georgian house—"

"Just an idea she has. Women don't know what they want—"

"Mrs. Bailey does."

"Just some idea an out-of-date architect has put in her head. She drives a new car, doesn't she? She wears the very latest styles—why should she live in an eighteenth century house? This house will be even later than this year's model; it's years in the future. She'll be the talk of the town."

"Well—I'll have to talk to her."

"Nothing of the sort. We'll surprise her with it. Have another drink."

"Anyhow, we can't do anything about it now. Mrs. Bailey and I are driving up to Bakersfield tomorrow. The company's bringing in a couple of wells tomorrow."

"Nonsense. That's just the opportunity we want. It will be a surprise for her when you get back. You can just write me a check right now, and your worries are over."

"I oughtn't to do anything like this without consulting her. She won't like it."

"Say, who wears the pants in your family anyhow?"

The check was signed about halfway down the second bottle.

Things are done fast in southern California. Ordinary houses there are usually built in a month's time. Under Teal's impassioned heckling the tesseract house climbed dizzily skyward in days rather than weeks,

and its cross-shaped second story came jutting out at
the four corners of the world. He had some trouble at
first with tho inspectors over those four projecting
rooms but by using strong girders and folding money
he had been able to convince them of the soundness of
his engineering.

By arrangement, Teal drove up in front of the
Bailey residence the morning after their return to town.
He improvised on his two-tone horn. Bailey stuck his
head out the front door. "Why don't you use the bell?"

"Too slow," answered Teal cheerfully. "I'm a man
of action. Is Mrs. Bailey ready? Ah, there you are, Mrs.
Bailey! Welcome home, welcome home. Jump in, we've
got a surprise for you!'

"You know Teal, my dear," Bailey put in uncomfort-
ably.

Mrs. Bailey sniffed. "I know him. We'll go in our
own car, Homer."

"Certainly, my dear."

"Good idea," Teal agreed; " 'sgot more power than
mine; we'll get there faster. I'll drive, I know the way."
He took the keys from Bailey, slid into the driver's
seat, and had the engine started before Mrs. Bailey
could rally her forces.

"Never have to worry about my driving," he assured
Mrs. Bailey, turning his head as he did so, while he
shot the powerful car down the avenue and swung onto
Sunset Boulevard, "it's a matter of power and control,
a dynamic process, just my meat—I've never had a
serious accident."

"You won't have but one," she said bitingly. "Will
you *please* keep your eyes on the traffic?"

He attempted to explain to her that a traffic situation
was a matter, not of eyesight, but intuitive integration
of courses, speeds, and probabilities, but Bailey cut him
short. "Where is the house, Quintus?"

"House?" asked Mrs. Bailey suspiciously. "What's
this about a house, Homer? Have you been up to
something without telling me?"

Teal cut in with his best diplomatic manner. "It
certainly is a house, Mrs. Bailey. And what a house!

It's a surprise for you from a devoted husband. Just wait till you see it—"

"I shall," she agreed grimly. "What style is it?"

"This house sets a new style. It's later than television, newer than next week. It must be seen to be appreciated. By the way," he went on rapidly, heading off any retort, "did you folks feel the earthquake last night?"

"Earthquake? What earthquake? Homer, was there an earthquake?"

"Just a little one," Teal continued, "about two A.M. If I hadn't been awake, I wouldn't have noticed it."

Mrs. Bailey shuddered. "Oh, this awful country! Do you hear that, Homer? We might have been killed in our beds and never have known it. Why did I ever let you persuade me to leave Iowa?"

"But my dear," he protested hopelessly, "you wanted to come out to California; you didn't like Des Moines."

"We needn't go into that," she said firmly. "You are a man; you should anticipate such things. Earthquakes!"

"That's one thing you needn't fear in your new home, Mrs. Bailey," Teal told her. "It's absolutely earthquake-proof; every part is in perfect dynamic balance with every other part."

"Well, I hope so. Where is this house?"

"Just around this bend. There's the sign now." A large arrow sign of the sort favored by real estate promoters proclaimed in letters that were large and bright even for southern California: -

THE HOUSE OF THE FUTURE!!!

COLOSSAL—AMAZING—

REVOLUTIONARY

*See How Your Grandchildren
Will Live!*

Q. Teal, Architect

"Of course that will be taken down," he added hastily, noting her expression, "as soon as you take possession." He slued around the corner and brought the car to a squealing halt in front of the House of the Future. *"Voilà!"* He watched their faces for response.

Bailey stared unbelievingly, Mrs. Bailey in open dislike. They saw a simple cubical mass, possessing doors and windows, but no other architectural features, save that it was decorated in intricate mathematical designs. "Teal," Bailey asked slowly, "what have you been up to?"

Teal turned from their faces to the house. Gone was the crazy tower with its jutting second-story rooms. No trace remained of the seven rooms above ground floor level. Nothing remained but the single room that rested on the foundations. "Great jumping cats!" he yelled, "I've been robbed!"

He broke into a run.

But it did him no good. Front or back, the story was the same: the other seven rooms had disappeared, vanished completely. Bailey caught up with him, and took his arm. "Explain yourself. What is this about being robbed? How come you built anything like this—it's not according to agreement."

"But I didn't. I built just what we had planned to build, an eight-room house in the form of a developed tesseract. I've been sabotaged, that's what it is! Jealousy! The other architects in town didn't dare let me finish this job; they knew they'd be washed up if I did."

"When were you last here?"

"Yesterday afternoon."

"Everything all right then?"

"Yes. The gardeners were just finishing up."

Bailey glanced around at the faultlessly manicured landscaping. "I don't see how seven rooms could have been dismantled and carted away from here in a single night without wrecking this garden."

Teal looked around, too. "It doesn't look it. I don't understand it."

Mrs. Bailey joined them. "Well? Well? Am I to be left to amuse myself? We might as well look it over as long as we are here, though I'm warning you, Homer, I'm not going to like it."

"We might as well," agreed Teal, and drew a key from his pocket with which he let them in the front door. "We may pick up some clues."

The entrance hall was in perfect order, the sliding screens that separated it from the garage space were back, permitting them to see the entire compartment. "This looks all right," observed Bailey. "Let's go up on the roof and try to figure out what happened. Where's the staircase? Have they stolen that, too?"

"Oh, no," Teal denied, "look—" He pressed a button below the light switch; a panel in the ceiling fell away and a light, graceful flight of stairs swung noiselessly down. Its strength members were the frosty silver of duralumin, its treads and risers transparent plastic. Teal wriggled like a boy who has successfully performed a card trick, while Mrs. Bailey thawed perceptibly.

It was beautiful.

"Pretty slick," Bailey admitted. "Howsomever it doesn't seem to go any place—"

"Oh, that—" Teal followed his gaze. "The cover lifts up as you approach the top. Open stair wells are anachronisms. Come on." As predicted, the lid of the staircase got out of their way as they climbed the flight and permitted them to debouch at the top, but not, as they had expected, on the roof of the single room. They found themselves standing in the middle one of the five rooms which constituted the second floor of the original structure.

For the first time on record Teal had nothing to say. Bailey echoed him, chewing on his cigar. Everything was in perfect order. Before them, through open doorway and translucent partition lay the kitchen, a chef's dream of up-to-the-minute domestic engineering, monel metal, continuous counter space, concealed lighting, functional arrangement. On the left the formal, yet gracious and hospitable dining room awaited guests, its furniture in parade-ground alignment.

Teal knew before he turned his head that the drawing room and lounge would be found in equally substantial and impossible existence.

"Well, I must admit this *is* charming," Mrs. Bailey approved, "and the kitchen is just *too* quaint for words

—though I would never have guessed from the exterior that this house had so much room upstairs. Of course *some* changes will have to be made. That secretary now—if we moved it over *here* and put the settle over *there*—"

"Stow it, Matilda," Bailey cut in brusquely. "Wha'd' yuh make of it, Teal?"

"Why, Homer Bailey! The very id—"

"Stow it, I said. Well, Teal?"

The architect shuffled his rambling body. "I'm afraid to say. Let's go on up."

"How?"

"Like this." He touched another button; a mate, in deeper colors, to the fairy bridge that had let them up from below offered them access to the next floor. They climbed it, Mrs. Bailey expostulating in the rear, and found themselves in the master bedroom. Its shades were drawn, as had been those on the level below, but the mellow lighting came on automatically. Teal at once activated the switch which controlled still another flight of stairs, and they hurried up into the top floor study.

"Look, Teal," suggested Bailey when he had caught his breath, "can we get to the roof above this room? Then we could look around."

"Sure, it's an observatory platform." They climbed a fourth flight of stairs, but when the cover at the top lifted to let them reach the level above, they found themselves, not on the roof, but *standing in the ground floor room where they had entered the house.*

Mr. Bailey turned a sickly gray. "Angels in heaven," he cried, "this place is haunted. We're getting out of here." Grabbing his wife he threw open the front door and plunged out.

Teal was too much preoccupied to bother with their departure. There was an answer to all this, an answer that he did not believe. But he was forced to break off considering it because of hoarse shouts from somewhere above him. He lowered the staircase and rushed upstairs. Bailey was in the central room leaning over Mrs. Bailey, who had fainted. Teal took in the situation, went to the bar built into the lounge, and poured three fingers of brandy, which he returned with and handed to Bailey. "Here—this'll fix her up."

Bailey drank it.

"That was for Mrs. Bailey," said Teal.

"Don't quibble," snapped Bailey. "Get her another." Teal took the precaution of taking one himself before returning with a dose earmarked for his client's wife. He found her just opening her eyes.

"Here, Mrs. Bailey," he soothed, "this will make you feel better."

"I never touch spirits," she protested, and gulped it.

"Now tell me what happened," suggested Teal. "I thought you two had left."

"But we did—we walked out the front door and found ourselves up here, in the lounge."

"The hell you say! Hm-m-m—wait a minute." Teal went into the lounge. There he found that the big view window at the end of the room was open. He peered cautiously through it. He stared, not out at the California countryside, but into the ground floor room— or a reasonable facsimile thereof. He said nothing, but went back to the stair well which he had left open and looked down it. The ground floor room was still in place. Somehow, it managed to be in two different places at once, on different levels.

He came back into the central room and seated himself opposite Bailey in a deep, low chair, and sighted him past his upthrust bony knees. "Homer," he said impressively, "do you know what has happened?"

"No, I don't—but if I don't find out pretty soon, something is going to happen and pretty drastic, too!"

"Homer, this is a vindication of my theories. This house is a real tesseract."

"What's he talking about, Homer?"

"Wait, Matilda—now Teal, that's ridiculous. You've pulled some hanky-panky here and I won't have it— scaring Mrs. Bailey half to death, and making me nervous. All I want is to get out of here, with no more of your trapdoors and silly practical jokes."

"Speak for yourself, Homer," Mrs. Bailey interrupted, "I was not frightened; I was just took all over queer for a moment. It's my heart; all of my people are delicate and high-strung. Now about this tessy thing— explain yourself, Mr. Teal. Speak up."

He told her as well as he could in the face of numerous interruptions the theory back of the house. "Now as I see it, Mrs. Bailey," he concluded, "this house, while perfectly stable in three dimensions, was not stable in four dimensions. I had built a house in the shape of an unfolded tesseract; something happened to it, some jar or side thrust, and it collapsed into its normal shape—it folded up." He snapped his fingers suddenly. "I've got it! The earthquake!"

"Earthquake?"

"Yes, yes, the little shake we had last night. From a four-dimensional standpoint this house was like a plane balanced on edge. One little push and it fell over, collapsed along its natural joints into a stable four-dimensional figure."

"I thought you boasted about how safe this house was."

"It *is* safe—three-dimensionally."

"I don't call a house safe," commented Bailey edgily, "that collapses at the first little temblor."

"But look around you, man!" Teal protested. "Nothing has been disturbed, not a piece of glassware cracked. Rotation through a fourth dimension can't affect a three-dimensional figure any more than you can shake letters off a printed page. If you had been sleeping in here last night, you would never have awakened."

"That's just what I'm afraid of. Incidentally, has your great genius figured out any way for us to get out of this booby trap?"

"Huh? Oh, yes, you and Mrs. Bailey started to leave and landed back up here, didn't you? But I'm sure there is no real difficulty—we came in, we can go out. I'll try it." He was up and hurrying downstairs before he had finished talking. He flung open the front door, stepped through, and found himself staring at his companions, down the length of the second floor lounge. "Well, there does seem to be some slight problem," he admitted blandly. "A mere technicality, though—we can always go out a window." He jerked aside the long drapes that covered the deep French windows set in one side wall of the lounge. He stopped suddenly.

"Hm-m-m," he said, "this is interesting—very."

"What is?" asked Bailey, joining him.

"This." The window stared directly into the dining room, instead of looking outdoors. Bailey stepped back to the corner where the lounge and the dining room joined the central room at ninety degrees.

"But that can't be," he protested, "that window is maybe fifteen, twenty feet from the dining room."

"Not in a tesseract," corrected Teal. "Watch." He opened the window and stepped through, talking back over his shoulder as he did so.

From the point of view of the Baileys he simply disappeared.

But not from his own viewpoint. It took him some seconds to catch his breath. Then he cautiously disentangled himself from the rosebush to which he had become almost irrevocably wedded, making a mental note the while never again to order landscaping which involved plants with thorns, and looked around him.

He was outside the house. The massive bulk of the ground floor room thrust up beside him. Apparently he had fallen off the roof.

He dashed around the corner of the house, flung open the front door and hurried up the stairs. "Homer!" he called out. "Mrs. Bailey! I've found a way out!"

Bailey looked annoyed rather than pleased to see him. "What happened to you?"

"I fell out. I've been outside the house. You can do it just as easily—just step through those French windows. Mind the rosebush, though—we may have to build another stairway."

"How did you get back in?"

"Through the front door."

"Then we shall leave the same way. Come, my dear." Bailey set his hat firmly on his head and marched down the stairs, his wife on his arm.

Teal met them in the lounge. "I could have told you that wouldn't work," he announced. "Now here's what we have to do: As I see it, in a four-dimensional

figure a three-dimensional man has two choices every
time he crosses a line of juncture, like a wall or a
threshold. Ordinarily he will make a ninety-degree turn
through the fourth dimension, only he doesn't feel it
with his three dimensions. Look." He stepped through
the very window that he had fallen out of a moment
before. Stepped through and arrived in the dining
room, where he stood, still talking.

"I watched where I was going and arrived where I
intended to." He stepped back into the lounge. "The
time before I didn't watch and I moved on through
normal space and fell out of the house. It must be a
matter of subconscious orientation."

"I'd hate to depend on subconscious orientation when
I step out for the morning paper."

"You won't have to; it'll become automatic. Now
to get out of the house this time—Mrs. Bailey, if you
will stand here with your back to the window, and
jump backward, I'm pretty sure you will land in the
garden."

Mrs. Bailey's face expressed her opinion of Teal and
his ideas. "Homer Bailey," she said shrilly, "are you
going to stand there and let him suggest such—"

"But Mrs. Bailey," Teal attempted to explain, "we
can tie a rope on you and lower you down eas—"

"Forget it, Teal," Bailey cut him off brusquely. "We'll
have to find a better way than that. Neither Mrs.
Bailey nor I are fitted for jumping."

Teal was temporarily nonplused; there ensued a
short silence. Bailey broke it with, "Did you hear that,
Teal?"

"Hear what?"

"Someone talking off in the distance. D'you s'pose
there could be someone else in the house, playing
tricks on us, maybe?"

"Oh, not a chance. I've got the only key."

"But I'm sure of it," Mrs. Bailey confirmed. "I've
heard them ever since we came in. Voices. Homer, I
can't stand much more of this. Do something."

"Now, now, Mrs. Bailey," Teal soothed, "don't get
upset. There can't be anyone else in the house, but
I'll explore and make sure. Homer, you stay here with

Mrs. Bailey and keep an eye on the rooms on this floor." He passed from the lounge into the ground floor room and from there to the kitchen and on into the bedroom. This led him back to the lounge by a straight-line route, that is to say, by going straight ahead on the entire trip he returned to the place from which he started.

"Nobody around," he reported. "I opened all of the doors and windows as I went—all except this one." He stepped to the window opposite the one through which he had recently fallen and thrust back the drapes.

He saw a man with his back toward him, four rooms away. Teal snatched open the French window and dived through it, shouting, "There he goes now! Stop thief!"

The figure evidently heard him; it fled precipitately. Teal pursued, his gangling limbs stirred to unanimous activity, through drawing room, kitchen, dining room, lounge—room after room, yet in spite of Teal's best efforts he could not seem to cut down the four-room lead that the interloper had started with.

He saw the pursued jump awkwardly but actively over the low sill of a French window and in so doing knock off his hat. When he came up to the point where his quarry had lost his headgear, he stopped and picked it up, glad of an excuse to stop and catch his breath. He was back in the lounge.

"I guess he got away from me," he admitted. "Anyhow, here's his hat. Maybe we can identify him."

Bailey took the hat, looked at it, then snorted, and slapped it on Teal's head. It fitted perfectly. Teal looked puzzled, took the hat off, and examined it. On the sweat band were the initials "Q.T." It was his own.

Slowly comprehension filtered through Teal's features. He went back to the French window and gazed down the series of rooms through which he had pursued the mysterious stranger. They saw him wave his arms semaphore fashion. "What are you doing?" asked Bailey.

"Come see." The two joined him and followed his stare with their own. Four rooms away they saw the backs of three figures, two male and one female. The taller, thinner of the men was waving his arms in a silly fashion.

Mrs. Bailey screamed and fainted again.

Some minutes later, when Mrs. Bailey had been resuscitated and somewhat composed, Bailey and Teal took stock. "Teal," said Bailey, "I won't waste any time blaming you; recriminations are useless and I'm sure you didn't plan for this to happen, but I suppose you realize we are in a pretty serious predicament. How are we going to get out of here? It looks now as if we would stay until we starve; every room leads into another room."

"Oh, it's not that bad. I got out once, you know."

"Yes, but you can't repeat it—you tried."

"Anyhow we haven't tried all the rooms. There's still the study."

"Oh, yes, the study. We went through there when we first came in, and didn't stop. Is it your idea that we might get out through its windows?"

"Don't get your hopes up. Mathematically, it ought to look into the four side rooms on this floor. Still we never opened the blinds; maybe we ought to look."

" 'Twon't do any harm anyhow. Dear, I think you had best just stay here and rest—"

"Be left alone in this horrible place? I should say not!" Mrs. Bailey was up off the couch where she had been recuperating even as she spoke.

They went upstairs. "This is the inside room, isn't it, Teal?" Bailey inquired as they passed through the master bedroom and climbed on up toward the study. "I mean it was the little cube in your diagram that was in the middle of the big cube, and completely surrounded."

"That's right," agreed Teal. "Well, let's have a look. I figure this window ought to give into the kitchen." He grasped the cords of Venetian blinds and pulled them.

It did not. Waves of vertigo shook them. Involuntarily they fell to the floor and grasped helplessly at the pattern on the rug to keep from falling. "Close it! Close it!" moaned Bailey.

Mastering in part a primitive atavistic fear, Teal worked his way back to the window and managed to release the screen. The window had looked *down* instead of *out*, down from a terrifying height.

Mrs. Bailey had fainted again.

Teal went back after more brandy while Bailey chafed her wrists. When she had recovered, Teal went cautiously to the window and raised the screen a crack. Bracing his knees, he studied the scene. He turned to Bailey. "Come look at this, Homer. See if you recognize it."

"You stay away from there, Homer Bailey!"

"Now, Matilda, I'll be careful." Bailey joined him and peered out.

"See up there? That's the Chrysler Building, sure as shooting. And there's the East River, and Brooklyn." They gazed straight down the sheer face of an enormously tall building. More than a thousand feet away a toy city, very much alive, was spread out before them. "As near as I can figure it out, we are looking down the side of the Empire State Building from a point just above its tower."

"What is it? A mirage?"

"I don't think so—it's too perfect. I think space is folded over through the fourth dimension here and we are looking past the fold."

"You mean we aren't really seeing it?"

"No, we're seeing it all right. I don't know what would happen if we climbed out this window, but I for one don't want to try. But what a view! Oh, boy, what a view! Let's try the other windows."

They approached the next window more cautiously, and it was well that they did, for it was even more disconcerting, more reason-shaking, than the one looking down the gasping height of the skyscraper. It was a simple seascape, open ocean and blue sky—but the ocean was where the sky should have been, and contrariwise. This time they were somewhat braced for it, but they both felt seasickness about to overcome them at the sight of waves rolling overhead; they lowered the blind quickly without giving Mrs. Bailey a chance to be disturbed by it.

Teal looked at the third window. "Game to try it, Homer?"

"Hrrumph—well, we won't be satisfied if we don't. Take it easy." Teal lifted the blind a few inches. He saw nothing, and raised it a little more—still nothing. Slowly he raised it until the window was fully exposed. They gazed out at—nothing.

Nothing, nothing at all. What color is nothing? Don't be silly! What shape is it? Shape is an attribute of *something*. It had neither depth nor form. It had not even blackness. It was *nothing*.

Bailey chewed at his cigar. "Teal, what do you make of that?"

Teal's insouciance was shaken for the first time. "I don't know, Homer, I don't rightly know—but I think that window ought to be walled up." He stared at the lowered blind for a moment. "I think maybe we looked at a place where space *isn't*. We looked around a fourth-dimensional corner and there wasn't anything there." He rubbed his eyes. "I've got a headache."

They waited for a while before tackling the fourth window. Like an unopened letter, it might *not* contain bad news. The doubt left hope. Finally the suspense stretched too thin and Bailey pulled the cord himself, in the face of his wife's protests.

It was not so bad. A landscape stretched away from them, right side up, and on such a level that the study appeared to be a ground floor room. But it was distinctly unfriendly.

A hot, hot sun beat down from a lemon-colored sky. The flat ground seemed burned a sterile, bleached brown and incapable of supporting life. Life there was, strange stunted trees that lifted knotted, twisted arms to the sky. Little clumps of spiky leaves grew on the outer extremities of these misshapen growths.

"Heavenly day," breathed Bailey, "where is that?"

Teal shook his head, his eyes troubled. "It beats me."

"It doesn't look like anything on Earth. It looks more like another planet—Mars, maybe."

"I wouldn't know. But, do you know, Homer, it

might be worse than that, worse than another planet, I mean."

"Huh? What's that you say?"

"It might be clear out of our space entirely. I'm not sure that that is our sun at all. It seems too bright."

Mrs. Bailey had somewhat timidly joined them and now gazed out at the outré scene. "Homer," she said in a subdued voice, "those hideous trees—they frighten me."

He patted her hand.

Teal fumbled with the window catch.

"What are you doing?" Bailey demanded.

"I thought if I stuck my head out the window I might be able to look around and tell a bit more."

"Well—all right," Bailey grudged, "but be careful."

"I will." He opened the window a crack and sniffed. "The air is all right, at least." He threw it open wide.

His attention was diverted before he could carry out his plan. An uneasy tremor, like the first intimation of nausea, shivered the entire building for a long second, and was gone.

"Earthquake!" They all said it at once. Mrs. Bailey flung her arms around her husband's neck.

Teal gulped and recovered himself, saying:

"It's all right, Mrs. Bailey. This house is perfectly safe. You know you can expect settling tremors after a shock like last night." He had just settled his features into an expression of reassurance when the second shock came. This one was no mild shimmy but the real seasick roll.

In every Californian, native born or grafted, there is a deep-rooted primitive reflex. An earthquake fills him with soul-shaking claustrophobia which impels him blindly to *get outdoors!* Model Boy Scouts will push aged grandmothers aside to obey it. It is a matter of record that Teal and Bailey landed on top of Mrs. Bailey. Therefore, she must have jumped through the window first. The order of precedence cannot be attributed to chivalry; it must be assumed that she was in readier position to spring.

They pulled themselves together, collected their wits a little, and rubbed sand from their eyes. Their first

sensations were relief at feeling the solid sand of the
desert land under them. Then Bailey noticed something that brought them to their feet and checked Mrs.
Bailey from bursting into the speech that she had
ready.

"Where's the house?"

It was gone. There was no sign of it at all. They
stood in the center of flat desolation, the landscape they
had seen from the window. But, aside from the tor-
tured, twisted trees, there was nothing to be seen but
the yellow sky and the luminary overhead, whose
furnacelike glare was already almost insufferable.

Bailey looked slowly around, then turned to the
architect. "Well, Teal?" His voice was ominous.

Teal shrugged helplessly. "I wish I knew. I wish I
could even be sure that we were on Earth."

"Well, we can't stand here. It's sure death if we
do. Which direction?"

"Any, I guess. Let's keep a bearing on the sun."

They had trudged on for an undetermined distance
when Mrs. Bailey demanded a rest. They stopped.
Teal said in an aside to Bailey, "Any ideas?"

"No . . . no, none. Say, do you hear anything?"

Teal listened. "Maybe—unless it's my imagination."

"Sounds like an automobile. Say, it *is* an automobile!"

They came to the highway in less than another
hundred yards. The automobile, when it arrived, proved
to be an elderly, puffing light truck, driven by a rancher.
He crunched to a stop at their hail. "We're stranded.
Can you help us out?"

"Sure. Pile in."

"Where are you headed?"

"Los Angeles."

"Los Angeles? Say, where is this place?"

"Well, you're right in the middle of the Joshua-Tree
National Forest."

The return was as dispiriting as the Retreat from
Moscow. Mr. and Mrs. Bailey sat up in front with the
driver while Teal bumped along in the body of the

truck, and tried to protect his head from the sun. Bailey subsidized the friendly rancher to detour to the tesseract house, not because they wanted to see it again, but in order to pick up their car.

At last the rancher turned the corner that brought them back to where they had started. But the house was no longer there.

There was not even the ground floor room. It had vanished. The Baileys, interested in spite of themselves, poked around the foundations with Teal.

"Got any answers for this one, Teal?" asked Bailey.

"It must be that on that last shock it simply fell through into another section of space. I can see now that I should have anchored it at the foundations."

"That's not all you should have done."

"Well, I don't see that there is anything to get downhearted about. The house was insured, and we've learned an amazing lot. There are possibilities, man, possibilities! Why, right now I've got a great new revolutionary idea for a house—"

Teal ducked in time. He was always a man of action.

Excitement Reading

are you missing out on some great Pyramid books?

You can have any title in print at Pyramid delivered right to your door! To receive your Pyramid Paperback Catalog, fill in the label below (use a ball point pen please) and mail to Pyramid . . .

PYRAMID PUBLICATIONS
Mail Order Department
9 Garden Street
Moonachie, New Jersey 07074

NAME_____

ADDRESS_____

CITY_____STATE_____

P-5   ZIP_____

Self help & reference